THE

PLAYA'S

HANDBOOK

Also by Brenda Jackson

A Family Reunion
Ties That Bind
The Midnight Hour
The Savvy Sistahs

Anthologies:
The Best Man
Welcome to Leo's
Let's Get It On

And Coming Soon:
An All-Night Man

THE
PLAYA'S
HANDBOOK

Brenda Jackson

 St. Martin's Griffin ✺ New York

www.stmartins.com

Library of Congress Cataloging-in-Publication Data

Jackson, Brenda (Brenda Streater)
    The playa's handbook / Brenda Jackson.—1st ed.
      p. cm.
    ISBN 0-312-33178-9
    EAN 978-0312-33178-8
    1. Man-woman relationships—Fiction. 2. Dating (Social customs)—Fiction. 3. African American men——Fiction. 4. Male friendship—Fiction. 5. Divorced men—Fiction. 6. Gary (Ind.)—Fiction. 7. Widowers—Fiction. I. Title.

PS3560.A21165P56 2004
813'.54—dc22

                                        2004048696

First Edition: November 2004

10 9 8 7 6 5 4 3 2 1

ACKNOWLEDGMENTS

To the love of my life, Gerald Jackson, Sr.

To my nephews and male coworkers, who let me interview them for this book to get a male perspective. This one is for you.

To my family in Gary, Indiana—the Randolphs and the Sparks—thanks for hosting such a wonderful family reunion in 2003. I can't wait for another visit.

To my Heavenly Father. I'm everything I am because you love me.

BOOK ONE

The end of a thing is better than its beginning;
the patient in spirit is better than the proud in spirit.

Ecclesiastes 7:8

THE PLAYA'S HANDBOOK
TOP TEN RULES

- Never give a woman the key to your apartment.
- Playas "have sex," they don't "make love."
- Avoid crotch-grabbers, unless you like feeling assaulted.
- Before you get carried away with a woman, make sure everything she's packing is the real thing.
- Stay away from women who have reputations for "faking it."
- Beware of women who prefer the "on-top" position all the time.
- Avoid the "First Come, Last Served Syndrome" by making sure she's willing to go down on you if you're willing to go down on her.
- Don't be afraid *not* to commit, no matter how hot the sex is.
- Beware of women who ask what sort of work you do too soon in the conversation. Usually that's an indication they are trying to find out how much money you make.
- A woman can't use you if you use her first.

1

Lance

"This is Rachel Cason, and you're listening to V-103 and Chicago's most titillating late-night talk show, *Hot Throb,* that's exclusively for mature minds," the woman said as her opening.

"It seems our guest last night had a lot of men waking up this morning getting the evil eye from their women. Even *I* have to admit that Dr. Asia Fowler might have plucked hairs off a few brothers' chests when she got into the real nitty-gritty of her latest book, *Sistahs Beware*."

Rachel chuckled. "Our phones have been ringing off the hook with calls from guys who feel they deserve equal time, and you'll definitely get that with tonight's guest. But before I introduce that individual, I want to go to the phone lines to hear what some of our callers have to say about last night's show."

She leaned back in her chair. "Thanks for holding, Paul. What do you think about last night's show?"

"I think the women got their panties in a twist over nothing. Men are men and they can't expect us to be perfect. Not all men who have been unfaithful to their wives or girlfriends are players, but once in a while we screw up. Good men can stray, so get over it. Straying doesn't make us dogs."

"Hmm, but what *does* it make you, Paul?" Rachel asked jokingly.

"A man who takes advantage of a sexual opportunity that's too good to pass up."

"I guess that's one way of putting it, but I doubt most women would look at it that way, including me. Thanks for your call," Rachel said, disconnecting and going to the next caller without missing a beat. "And, Dennis, what is your take on last night's show?"

"Last night's show gave me a lot to think about, Rachel, and I think Dr. Fowler hit on some important points."

"Such as?"

"It's all about what you want out of a relationship. I wouldn't want my woman seeing other men, and I'm sure she wouldn't want me seeing other women. What's important for us is exclusivity. I'm hers and she's mine. It seems these days no one wants to belong to anybody. No one wants to commit."

"No one wants to commit . . ." Rachel repeated as if mulling over Dennis's last statement. "And I agree. So where do the playas fall within all of this? Do we go out and burn them at the stake, or just accept that this world is full of them and move on? That question is a wonderful intro for tonight's guest who is causing quite a stir around the country with his latest book, *The Playa's Handbook*. A book that's supposed to perfect the brotha's art of being single."

Rachel disconnected the line, and instead of picking up another, she turned to the man who, moments ago, had come to take the chair opposite hers: someone she was extremely aware of as a man. He was so good-looking that she was fighting the urge to start twitching in her chair.

She'd heard that he was as arrogant as he was handsome. He was a divorcé two times over, and had a reputation for changing women as often as he changed his socks. He was a true playa, so his books were based not only on his scholastic opinions but also on deeply ingrained experience.

She breathed in deeply before speaking to the listening audience. "I have with me Dr. Lance Montgomery, whose previous book, *How a Brotha Can Avoid Getting to the Altar,* also caused quite a ruckus a couple of years ago. Dr. Montgomery is a renowned divorce and relationship expert who gives advice to men on how to stay single and remain happy. Drawing on his own experiences, as well as those of men he has counseled in his acclaimed workshops and on his popular syndicated radio talk show, his books supposedly help men understand and accept that there is nothing wrong with being a playa and show them how to avoid the big C-word, commitment." Her voice grew soft and seductive. "Welcome to our show, Dr. Montgomery."

Lance smiled. "Thanks for the invitation, Rachel."

"Well, now, Dr. Montgomery, you have really stirred up a hornets' nest this time with your rules that playas should live by. I understand there are several marriage and family groups that are asking for a recall of your book."

He chuckled. "Yes, so I hear."

"And that doesn't bother you?"

Lance chuckled again. "Not at all. Unfortunately, the truth hurts at times, and some women refuse to own up to the fact that they are the main reason men are avoiding commitments, becoming bona fide playas, and preferring to remain as such."

Rachel leaned back in her chair. "Would you like to explain that, Doctor?"

He smiled. "Certainly. The majority of women fail to know what a man wants and needs, and those who have a clue don't give a damn. So what you have is an abundance of high-maintenance women who expect all and want to give nothing. What man wants a woman who could leave him in financial ruins? What some women don't like to admit is that in a way they are playas, too. Instead of playing around with other men, they resort to playing around with a man's mind, often being manipulative in the process, and they enjoy using sex as a power play instead of keeping it real."

Rachel glanced over at the computer monitor and noticed how it was flashing. The calls were coming in fast and furious already. It was apparent that the good doctor had hit a nerve with a majority of the radio audience and they had a lot to say. Some of her female callers could be ruthless, and she was anxious to hear how Dr. Montgomery would respond.

She pressed the button for caller number four and saw the name Erin pop up on the monitor. She smiled. Erin Drayton was a regular caller and a playa hater of the worst kind. "Hello, Erin, you're on."

Later that night . . . or rather very early the next morning, Lance lay in his Jacuzzi bathtub, leisurely soaking his body and absently watching the play of the lathered bubbles that covered his chest, torso and thighs.

Sexual fulfillment had him so relaxed, he could drift off to sleep at any moment. Somewhere in the back of his subconscious, he could still hear Rachel Cason scream his name when an orgasm ripped through her. She had almost burst his damn eardrums. The woman had been easy. After the show, he had suggested a night-cap at her place and could all but inhale the scent of her wet panties.

He shook his head as he began sponging the bubbles off his body. As far as he was concerned, hindsight was twenty-twenty. If he had to do it all over again, he wouldn't marry the first time and would certainly not have been stupid enough to do it twice before realizing there was no special woman out there for him. One of the most important aspects of being a man was knowing what was good for you, and what was not. Commitment was not for everyone, and for those who thought it was, they had his blessings. And for those who thought it wasn't, they had him to reinforce that ideology.

He smiled as he stepped out of the bathtub to dry himself off and glanced across the bathroom at the book that was lying on the floor next to the commode, *Sistahs Beware*.

It was the damnedest thing, but he was actually obsessed with a woman he had never met . . . at least not officially. Of course, since they were technically in the same line of work, he knew of Dr. Asia Fowler and was well aware of her books. He had purchased her current release out of curiosity, and although he didn't agree with her take on things, he had found her thoughts and ideas rather entertaining.

He had listened to Rachel Cason's show the other night when Asia Fowler had been a featured guest. He hadn't had anything better to do and figured her subject matter would be stimulating. But what he hadn't known or figured on was the sound of her voice seducing him across the airwaves, firing his libido and arousing him to the point where he'd had to go into the kitchen and get a cold drink of water. It wasn't anything she said in particular. Some men were leg, breast and booty men, but a sexy voice could get him hard each and every time. Even when she had referred to some members of his gender as "those damn no-good brothers," his erection had been throbbing.

Desire had purred through him, momentarily taking his mind off the disagreement he'd had with his agent about his refusal to participate in a panel discussion at the Harlem Book Fair next month. Asia Fowler's voice had had him thinking about hot summer nights, a bed with satin sheets and scented candles strategically placed around the bedroom to provide the ultimate romantic effect.

Too keyed up for bed just yet, he decided to indulge in a glass of wine. Tossing the towel aside, he strode butt-naked from his bathroom, through his bedroom and to his living room where he had a stocked bar for his enjoyment. After pouring a glass of wine, he decided to at least put on a bathrobe since it was the day for his housekeeper to pay a visit. He definitely didn't want to give Mrs. Jones heart failure.

Moments later he was sitting in a wingback chair that had a gorgeous view of Lake Michigan. It was a beautiful August night. With a classical piece by Mozart playing in the background, he stared out of the floor-to-ceiling window that dominated an entire wall. Living on the twentieth floor of one of the most luxurious apartment buildings in Chicago, he had certainly come a long way from his humble beginnings. He had been the third child of a single father whose wife ran off with another man within months of giving birth to the fourth child, taking the baby with her and leaving everyone to speculate that his father hadn't been the baby's daddy anyway.

Lance had been born thirty-three years ago in Gary, Indiana. One thing he and his brothers knew was that their hard-working father would not tolerate them getting into any kind of trouble. Jeremiah Montgomery would not have hesitated to beat the crap out of them if they had. Lance was proud of his two older brothers who had eventually graduated from medical school and were now specialists in their chosen fields. Instead of remaining in the Midwest, Logan and Lyle had moved as far away as their professions could take them. Lance had been content to make Chicago his home and at least once a week made the forty-five-minute drive to Gary, to check on his father. He had offered to move his pop to Chicago, but the old man preferred to remain in Gary.

They didn't hear from his "mother" again until he had reached adulthood and she had hit rock bottom. She had heard that he and his brothers were successful and had come looking for a handout. That had been almost ten years ago. After not giving her a damn thing and practically telling her she could go back to wherever she'd come from, neither he nor his brothers had heard from her since. But before taking off, she had tried using information she had about the whereabouts of their babysister—who she had placed years earlier in a foster home—as bargaining power. They weren't about to be manipulated and told her that she could very well keep the information to herself. Instead they hired a private detective to locate the babysister they had never seen, and within a year's time, at the age of eighteen, the streetwise, wild, reckless Carrie Montgomery had entered their lives.

It had taken his oldest brother, the easygoing Logan, to take charge of their she-cat of a babysister and domesticate her. Now, at the age of twenty-four with college behind her, Carrie was devoted to her job as a social worker, enjoyed the single life and had purchased a nice place near Logan's in Tampa.

Lance's thoughts shifted back to Asia Fowler. Her bio in the back of the book didn't tell much but her picture sure did. The face in the photograph projected the same sexiness that he had heard in her voice.

As he took a sip of his wine, he decided that he wanted to find out everything there was to know about Dr. Fowler. Reaching across the table he picked up the phone. Seconds later he could hear the gruff sound of his agent on the other end.

"Carl, this is Lance. I'll participate in that panel discussion in Harlem, but only on one condition." A smile curved his lips when he said, "Dr. Asia Fowler has to agree to be a participant as well."

2

Sam

Samuel Gunn glanced at his watch. It was almost lunchtime but he needed to finish the report he was working on. He enjoyed his job as an urban and regional planner for the city of Gary, something he'd been doing since graduating from Howard University.

He lifted his head from the paper he'd been reading when the telephone on his desk rang. He picked it up. "Yes, Alice, what is it?"

"Sir, you have a call from the former Mrs. Samuel Gunn," his secretary said in her ever-efficient and proficient voice.

He frowned, wondering why Kim would be calling. "Thanks, and please put her through."

He braced himself again while waiting for the connection. Unwanted images flashed through his mind of the woman who had stood with him before a minister and a packed church and promised to love him, and then, less than two years later, had betrayed him in the worst possible way.

"Sam?"

He sighed, remembering how he used to love hearing the sound of her husky, feminine voice. "Yes, Kim, what is it?"

There was a slight pause, then she said, "I thought you should hear this from me first."

With another deep breath he leaned back in his chair. "Hear what?"

Another pause. Then she said, "I've remarried."

It felt like a stake had been driven straight through Sam's heart. Everything got deathly quiet. There were no sounds around him, which made him wonder if the shock of her words had destroyed his hearing.

"Sam, are you there?"

Kim's words came through loud and clear, which let him know his hearing was still intact. He pushed past the deep lump that formed in his throat to respond. "Yes, I'm here." Then, moments later, he asked quietly, "Did you marry *him*?"

The pause that was becoming a habit reared its head again before she replied. "Yes."

Sam closed his eyes as he felt the sting of tears there. How often while growing up, a rough and tough kid on the streets of Gary, Indiana, had he heard that real men didn't cry. Especially over a woman, since they were a dime a dozen. But at the time he hadn't been able to understand that when a man loved the way he had loved Kim, finding out she had been involved with another man was definitely something to cry about.

"Sam?"

The sound of her voice reeled him back to the present. He again forced back the lump in his throat. "Yes?"

There was another pause. "Please say something."

The anger he had been trying to hold in suddenly snapped. "What do you want me to say? That I hope you'll be more faithful to James Aarons than you were to me? How does that sound for laughs?"

"Sam, please don't."

"Don't what, Kim? Don't feel pretty pissed because you have literally destroyed my life?"

"I never meant to hurt you."

"Evidently your definition of hurt and my definition are totally different," he angrily responded. "If there's nothing else you have to say, Kim, I prefer ending this call."

"All right, and please take care of yourself."

13

Before she fully completed her sentence, he had hung up the phone.

A couple of hours later, Sam was at the gym giving his body a brutal workout amidst a deluge of heavy sweat that covered his upper body and trickled down his solid chest and broad shoulders. His muscles ached but that was nothing compared to the ache he was determined to work from his heart. Moving away from the bench press, he proceeded to do push-ups, deciding it was time to work the pity out of his body.

An hour or so later, he was at his apartment, naked and standing beneath a spray of hot water that flowed down his soapy body. After spending three hours at the gym, his head was finally back on straight, his body relaxed and his thoughts not on Kim but on what he would have for dinner. He had some pretty good choices. He could do Teriyaki Chicken, Beanie Weenies with Rice, Shrimp and Noodles or any of the other assorted microwave dinners he had to choose from.

Stepping out of the shower, he dried off with a huge fluffy blue towel. Pulling on a pair of sweats and a T-shirt, he headed for the kitchen. He was about to open the refrigerator when the phone rang. He picked it up. "Yeah?"

"I got your message on my cell phone. What's up?"

Sam recognized Phillip McKenna's voice immediately. He and Phillip had been college roommates at Howard, and during one of Phillip's visits home with him for Christmas, he had introduced him to Rhonda, a friend of Sam's sister, Carolyn. Phillip and Rhonda hit it off and began dating, and when Phillip graduated from pharmacy school, he had returned to Gary and asked Rhonda to marry him.

That had been almost eight years ago. Sadly, Phillip and Rhonda's marriage had ended in divorce almost two years ago, but they were trying to maintain a good relationship because of their seven-year-old daughter, Chandra.

Sam closed the refrigerator after grabbing a bottle of water. "I heard from Kim today, man."

"Hell, what did she want?"

Sam ignored the anger in Phillip's voice since he knew his friend had never really cared for Kim anyway, which was something he had never really understood. "It was a courtesy call," he said, then took a swallow of water.

"What the hell is a 'courtesy call'?"

Sam shook his head. He could hear Phillip slamming drawers. Evidently he was looking for something that he couldn't find. "It was a call to let me know that she and what's-his-name have gotten married."

First there was silence. Then, "You got to be kiddin', man."

"Trust me, I wouldn't kid about something like that."

There was more silence. "You need me to come over?"

Sam couldn't help but smile. Phillip knew how much he had loved Kim and evidently felt he needed company about now. "No, I'm fine, the shock has worn off."

"You sure?"

"Yeah, I'm sure."

He heard Phillip's long, exasperated sigh. "Women. Who needs them?"

Sam decided now was probably not a good time to mention to Phillip that he evidently did, since the last time they had been together, he had confided, after a few beers, that he had started bumping and grinding with Rhonda. Having ex-sex was something Sam just couldn't fathom.

"And you sure you don't need me to come over? I can go by and grab Marcus and—"

"Damn, Phillip, I'm not suicidal for heaven's sake. I'll get over it like I got over everything else."

"I know, but remember I'm here if you need me."

"Thanks, man, I appreciate that."

An hour later, Sam was trying to concentrate on something on television and couldn't. He and Kim had officially separated five months ago, but their divorce hadn't been final but for six weeks. He had wanted to wait until after the divorce before getting back into the dating scene, although he wasn't looking forward to it. Hell, he hadn't dated in over five years. He and Kim had been engaged two years before they had actually married. He wouldn't know how to start hitting on a woman. All of his lines were probably outdated by now.

Remembering the package he had received in the mail a few days ago, he got up off the sofa, crossed the room to the bookcase and pulled a book out.

The Playa's Handbook by Lance Montgomery.

When he received the autographed book in the mail, he had smiled after reading the note that had accompanied it. Sam and Lance's friendship had formed so long ago he couldn't remember exactly when they had first met—probably as early as kindergarten, since everyone who lived in their neighborhood had attended Mrs. Mary's Little Lambs Day Care at one time in their lives. All he knew was that they had remained friends forever.

Flipping through the pages of the book, he came to the first chapter and read what Lance had noted as the top ten rules. Moments later, he was holding his stomach and rolling in laughter. Only Lance could manage to find humor in rules that, from what Sam heard, had a lot of women around the country fuming.

Deciding to read the rest of the book, he carried it back to the sofa and sat down. Perhaps he could learn something since one thing was for certain—he would never give his heart to another woman again. But him, a player? Hell, he wouldn't know where to start. Even in high school, the idea of having more than one woman at a time hadn't interested him. He could barely afford to take care of one on the part-time salary he made working at Mr. Neil's grocery store. Then, in college, his studies had dominated the majority of his time. After finishing college and returning home, he had met Kim at a party in Chicago one night and had known immediately she was the woman he wanted to marry.

He had been so into the book that he frowned a half hour later when the phone rang. He reached across the table to pick it up. "Yeah?"

"Hey, man, it's Marcus."

Sam closed the book but was careful to keep his finger on the page he'd been reading. He and Marcus had been friends since their late teens when Marcus and his mother had become members of his church. "Hell, man, where have you been?"

Marcus chuckled. "You mean where am I now? Didn't you get my message? I called from the airport and left word with your secretary that I had to fly to D.C. unexpectedly. I also left a message on your cell phone."

Sam sighed. After Kim's call, he left work immediately. His secretary hadn't been at her desk when he'd gone. "Sorry, my mind has been so screwed up today, I didn't think to check my messages."

"So what's going on?" Before Sam could respond Marcus said, "Hey, hold up a minute. I'm sitting at the bar in this hotel and the most gorgeous woman I've ever seen just walked in. Boy, you ought to see the tits on her, never mind her ass. I should be walking across the room to talk to her instead of sitting here talking to you."

Sam raised his eyes to the ceiling. Marcus was all talk and no action. His wife, Dottie, had died in a train derailment a little more than a year ago, and instead of jumping back into dating, he had thrown himself into his work to avoid getting into another relationship. He claimed he had a lot of issues to resolve, namely getting over his deceased wife. Marcus had told him and Phillip a few weeks ago that he had finally resolved those issues and was now ready to put himself out on the "open market."

"Well, call me back after making your hit," Sam said, knowing no matter what Marcus said, he wasn't any more ready to hit on a woman than Sam was. As far as Sam and Phillip were concerned, their friend still had issues. Marcus's house looked the same way it had while Dottie was alive. Sam hadn't been able to part with any of her things. Sam and Phillip understood that the grieving period varied from person to person, but for Marcus to still keep his home as a monument to his deceased wife—to the point that he still had her toiletries next to his on the vanity as well as her robe still hanging on the bathroom door—wasn't healthy. He had refused to seek grief counseling like they'd suggested, but finally, a few months ago, Marcus had agreed to receive some short-term therapy that was designed to help him bring closure to his loss.

"Umm, that's okay, we can talk," Marcus said, breaking into Sam's thoughts. "It seems Miss Sexy Mama was here to meet some guy," he added disappointedly. "So, what's going on?"

Sam shrugged. "Nothing, but I heard from Kim today."

"And?"

"And she wanted to let me know that she and lover boy had gotten married."

There was silence and then Marcus said, "Hey, man, I'm sorry to hear that, but maybe that's the push you need to move on with your life without her."

Sam frowned. "Look who's talking." He could hear Marcus softly chuckle.

"Yeah, I know, you, Phillip and I are nothing but a bunch of brothers who need therapy of the most extreme kind."

Sam nodded. At least he could understand Marcus's situation, but he and Phillip were really two pitiful asses. "When will you get back in town?"

"Friday evening."

"How about if the three of us get together at your place Saturday night and watch the game and get stoned," Sam suggested.

"Sounds like a good idea to me, but you may want to check with Phillip to make sure he doesn't have baby-sitting duty that night."

"Okay, I will. And take care, man, be safe."

"You too . . . and about this thing with Kim. Let it go. I believe there's a sistah out there who has your name written all over her. In fact, I can see it clearly tattooed right beneath her navel, just inches above the hairline of her—"

"Thanks, Marcus, I get the picture."

"So do I, man, and it's making me horny. It's been over a year for me, you know."

Sam nodded. How could he forget when Marcus reminded him and Phillip of how long it's been every time they got together? Hell, it had been almost eight months for him and he was almost at wits end, too. "Talk to you later."

After hanging up the phone, Sam knew what he had to do, although he didn't look forward to it. He inhaled deeply as he punched in his parents' phone number, hoping by chance they were out for the night since they stayed active in a lot of church activities.

His mother had always wanted to move to Ocala, Florida, to be near her only sister, and his father granted her that wish after he had retired from working at the mill. With Sam and his sister married, Henry Gunn felt there was no reason to tolerate the cold Indiana winters any longer. His parents had gladly moved to sunny Florida and loved every minute of it.

"Hello."

Sam felt the lump form in his throat. So much for hoping that his parents had gone to church tonight. "Hi, Dad, how are things going?"

"Can't complain, Son. How are things going with you?"

"They're okay. Is Mom around? There's something I need to tell the both of you." The reason he hadn't told them the truth about what had gone on in his marriage was he knew how hard it would be for his parents to accept that he and Kim wouldn't be getting back together. They considered Kim like another daughter. And because they didn't know everything, they still blamed him for the divorce, since he was the one who had filed for it.

"Well, I hope you're calling to tell us that you've come to your senses and that you and Kim are back together. Your mother has been praying real hard for that to happen."

Sam inhaled deeply again, hating to tell his father that no matter how much praying his mother did, a reconciliation between him and Kim was something that wouldn't be happening.

"Hold on, let me grab your mama."

It didn't take long for his mom to pick up the other extension so both of his parents could hear what he had to say. "Hi, Mom."

"Hi, Sammy. Daddy said you had some wonderful news to tell us."

Sam shook his head. That was *not* what he had told his father. He breathed in deeply and used the same intro that Kim had used on him earlier. "I thought you should hear this from me first."

"Yes?" his mother said in an anxious voice. "What's the wonderful news?"

"Kim has remarried."

He knew his statement had left his parents dumbfounded since it took a moment for either of them to respond. Then, quite naturally, it was his mother who did. "What do you mean *she* remarried? What you're saying is that the two of you remarried, right?"

Deciding there was no better way to break the news than right out, Sam took a deep breath and said, "No, she married someone else." He didn't have to be there to know the blood had probably drained from both of his parents' faces.

"W-w-what do you mean she married someone else?" his father stuttered.

Sam casually rested his right arm against the back of the sofa as he tried to retain control of his emotions, which threatened to crumble. "Just what I said, Dad. Kim met someone and got married."

"B-but the two of you have been divorced for less than two months."

"Yes, Mom, that's true." Time ticked off while he waited for his parents to put two and two together.

"What on earth did you do to that girl, Samuel Gunn, to make her run to another man so soon after divorcing you!"

Hearing his mother's accusing tone made him lose it. Anger so intense it had him shaking all the way to his toes flared through him. He stood up. "Why do I have to be the guilty party, Mom? Did it ever occur to you that it may have been Kim? Earlier this year, I found out my wife was having an affair with a guy at work, yet I loved her enough to forgive her and try and save my marriage. We even went to marriage counseling at church, but I later found out that even while we were doing those counseling sessions with our minister, Kim was still involved with the man. That's the reason I left her and filed for a divorce."

There was silence, then his father cleared his voice and said in a sad and regretful voice, "Son, we didn't know."

"No, you didn't know because I kept my personal business to myself."

"I'm sorry, Sammy, but I just can't imagine Kim doing such a thing," his mother said in a sorrowful voice.

"Yeah, but it was easy for you to imagine me mistreating her, wasn't it, Mom? For months I have listened to you and Dad accuse me of wrongdoing when I'm the one who's been suffering because of an unfaithful wife."

"Sam—"

"No, Dad. There's nothing else to say. I just thought the two of you needed to know Kim had remarried. I really didn't intend to air my dirty laundry. The only reason the two of you hadn't heard it from Carolyn was because I made sure Rhonda didn't know the reason Kim and I got a divorce. But I'm certain she'll get wind of the news that Kim has gotten married, and I wanted you and Mom to hear it from me."

"Sammy, are you okay? Is there anything we can do?"

He inhaled deeply. "I'm okay as much as I can be for a man who hates to admit that he's still in love with the woman who betrayed his love and trust. But I'm determined to get over her and move on with my life."

"That's the right attitude to take, Sam," his father said. "We're sorry. Your mother and I were wrong to think the worst of you."

"Yes, Dad, you were, but I accept your apology. What I need more than anything from you both right now is your prayers that God will see me through this."

"I've sent them up already and I know He will send a special woman to you."

Sam frowned. That's what his parents had thought Kim was when he had brought her home for the first time, a special woman that God had given him. If that was true and God didn't make mistakes then what the hell had happened? "Mom, Dad, I have to go. I need to be at work earlier than usual tomorrow, so I'm going to call it a night."

"All right, and always remember that we love you."

For some reason, that was exactly what he had needed to hear. And at that moment, he couldn't dismiss the deep love that he heard in his mother's voice. "And I love the two of you, too, Mom. Take it easy and I'll check with you as usual on Sunday."

"All right. Good night."

"Good night."

Sam hung up the phone and took a deep cleansing breath. In a way he was glad everything was out in the open. It had been hard knowing his parents had begun thinking of him as the scum of the earth. Not that he wanted them to think bad thoughts about Kim, but the truth was the truth, and this truth was about as naked as it could get.

He had always heard that the truth would set you free. Now he had plenty of time to kick back to see if it really did.

3

Phillip

There was nothing that relaxed a man more than indulging in invigorating, mind-blowing, off-the-chain sex. Phillip McKenna's lips curved into a smile as he pulled himself out of the luscious, hot body of his ex-wife and collapsed against her.

Ex-sex as Sam and Marcus called it.

When he and Rhonda had divorced nearly two years ago, the last thing he thought they'd eventually end up doing was get together occasionally for a little bumping and grinding. But their weekly ritual, which had begun six months ago, was like an illicit affair, sexually stimulating and physically satisfying. He didn't think sex had been this good between them while they had been married.

Well . . . maybe it had been in the beginning, for the first five years. But that was before Rhonda had gone back to college to get her degree and then landed the job she'd wanted. And let that job come to mean more to her than being a wife to her husband.

Phillip had been forced to settle for "once a month nooky," and at times was doing damn good if he got it at all. He had tried being the supportive and understanding husband but soon playing second fiddle got the best of him.

But what really took the icing off the cake was the time she no longer had for their child. Chandra, their beautiful little girl, had

gotten used to all the time she had spent with her mother while
Rhonda had been unemployed. She hadn't been able to adjust to
being replaced by a nine-to-five job.

Six months ago, Rhonda had shown up unexpectedly at his
house one night, upset that their six-year-old daughter's behavior
in school had been getting out of hand. It seemed that Chandra had
become every teacher's nightmare, and Rhonda had been at her
wits' end. Phillip had again asked for total custody of Chandra, and
again Rhonda had tearfully refused saying everyone would think
she was a terrible person if she didn't raise her own child.

In anger, he had been quick to point out that lately, with all her
out-of-town business trips and the hours she spent working late at
the office, he'd been the one spending more time with Chandra anyway. They had gotten into a heated argument and somehow in the
middle of all that heated anger, they had kissed and ended up in bed
together—a mixture of sexual and mental frustrations had finally
taken its toll. That night they had made love in a way they had
never made love before, and since neither of them had gotten seriously involved with anyone during the two years they'd been apart,
they had decided there was nothing wrong with getting together at
least once a week to fulfill their physical needs.

Somehow once a week quickly became several times a week, and
some people who saw them together naturally assumed they were
working out past problems and thinking about getting back
together. They weren't. Truthfully, they were as far apart as they
had been when they'd gotten divorced. The only thing that was har-
monious between them was the sex.

Since his divorce, he had been quite selective with his lovers and
had gotten kind of fed up with women wanting to exchange sex for
a marriage ring. They saw his good-paying job as a chemist with a
large pharmaceutical firm as attractive. But remarriage was not for
him. He had been there, done that and didn't plan to go that way
again.

Phillip turned his head and looked at his ex-wife. She had
changed a lot over the past ten years, and unfortunately for him, all

of those changes hadn't been good. But he could admit that she looked as beautiful now as she'd been the first time they had met, though he had found out the hard way that physical beauty wasn't everything.

The light that flowed in from beneath the closed bedroom door placed a golden glow on Rhonda's features. He was convinced that after they'd made love were the only peaceful moments she allowed herself. It seemed that come hail or high water, she intended to do whatever it took to get ahead. Her introduction into the corporate world had come later than most, and at the age of thirty, she felt she was at a disadvantage to most of the younger kids fresh out of college and was trying to make up time.

"Why didn't you tell me everything about Sam and Kim's divorce?"

He heard the question but refused to open his eyes and answer her. Evidently she had spoken to Sam's sister, Carolyn. Moments passed and when he didn't respond, she poked him in the side with her elbow. "Don't pretend to be asleep because I know you aren't. So answer my question."

He slowly opened his eyes, glanced over at her and then closed them again. "The reason I didn't tell you anything was because it wasn't any of your business."

He could tell by her snort that she didn't appreciate his statement. "I don't know why you wouldn't think it wasn't my business since they are friends of ours."

Now that statement made Phillip chuckle. He opened his eyes and stared at Rhonda who had sat up and was leaning over him. He glanced down, preferring to look at her breasts than at her face since she was glaring at him. "You never liked Kim so don't pretend otherwise, Rhonda."

Rhonda's frown deepened. "It's not that I didn't like her, we just never hit it off. It was obvious we didn't have anything in common."

Phillip rolled his eyes knowing that was an understatement. Rhonda never liked Kim because Kim always seemed to have it together while Rhonda had still been trying to find her way.

"You don't know how shocked I was tonight when I received a call from Carolyn telling me the real reason behind Sam and Kim's divorce," Rhonda said, breaking into his thoughts. "I got really pissed knowing you knew all along and didn't tell me."

Phillip stared up at her. "Like I said, it wasn't your business."

"Well, I think it was."

Phillip sighed deeply, knowing where their disagreement was headed and quickly decided he wasn't in the mood to go there. He turned and rolled out of the bed.

"And just where are you going?" Rhonda asked him as if exasperated.

He glanced up from putting on his pants. "Home. I'll see you again later this week."

"Don't bother."

He pulled his shirt over his head and then looked at her. "Don't bother what?"

"Don't bother stopping by again for sex. It's something I wanted to talk to you about."

Phillip crossed his arms over his chest and waited. When Rhonda didn't say anything, he said, "Well, what did you want to talk about?"

Seconds ticked by again and he knew Rhonda was gathering her thoughts. Then she said, "This thing between us isn't working. Somehow we've forgotten that we're supposed to be divorced."

He chuckled. "I haven't forgotten, Rhonda, trust me."

"Then why are you here and why have we been sleeping together as if we aren't divorced? We should have moved on with our lives but we haven't. I know we tried but I think the only reason we ended up back in each others' bed was because we're comfortable with each other and we're both too scared to see what else is out there."

He turned his back on her to pick his belt up off the floor. He knew that a part of what she said was true. It wasn't that he was scared to see what was out there. He had seen it and didn't like it worth a damn. The women were more aggressive, demanding and harder to please. Falling back in bed with Rhonda had made things easy for him. He knew where the two of them stood and didn't have to worry about there being any ulterior motive in their love-making beyond pleasure.

And still, although he *somewhat* agreed with Rhonda, he wouldn't admit it to her. "You've been watching too many episodes of *Dr. Phil*," he said, putting on his belt while glancing over at her. "The reason we have sex is because we enjoy it. And we're still friends. Besides, it's better now than it was when we were married."

Rhonda pulled herself up on her knees. Completely naked, she looked way too luscious glaring at him with her hands on her hips. "I think we need to end things tonight."

"We ended things a couple of years ago," he reminded her.

"I mean this; us sleeping together."

He shrugged. "If you want to stop what we're doing, then that's fine with me." He said the words but he really didn't mean them.

Rhonda nodded. "Good." A few moments later, while he was sitting down in the chair and putting on his shoes, she said, "Now, I have a huge favor to ask of you."

He looked at her. "What?"

"Can you take care of Chandra for two weeks?"

He stood and stared at her. "Of course I can, but why?"

She had settled back down in the bed. "I need a break and decided to go on a trip. A couple of the single women at work are taking this cruise to Alaska and I want to go. I haven't taken a real vacation in years and think it will be fun."

Phillip nodded. "When do you plan to leave?"

"Next month. And you're sure Chandra staying with you won't be a bother?"

"I'm positive," he said as he headed for the door. One day she would realize that parents who truly cared for their kids never would consider them a bother. No matter what.

"Phillip?"

He turned around before opening the door. "Yeah?"

"Thanks, and I meant what I said. I need to move on with my life and so do you. No more sex."

He stared at her for a long moment, then said, "Fine."

And without giving her a chance to say anything else, he walked out of the bedroom and closed the door behind him.

Later, as Phillip was entering his home, he heard the phone ringing and rushed over and picked it up. "Hello?"

"Hey, man, this is Marcus. Did you remember to go by the cleaners and pick up my jacket?"

Phillip shook his head. "Yes, I remembered," he grumbled. Rhonda had pissed him off. He was angry and ready to go off on somebody, and Marcus would make the perfect victim. "You need to get your shit together man and stop depending on me and Sam to run your errands. Every week it's something different. Last week you asked Sam to return those videos to Blockbuster, and the week before that you conveniently dropped your grocery list off at my place."

"Only because you mentioned you had to go to the grocery store anyway, and there were only a couple of items that I needed picked up."

Phillip rolled his eyes. "That's beside the point."

"And just what is the point?"

"Sam and I are doing things for you that Dottie used to do."

"No, you're not!"

"Yes, we are!"

A few moments later, Marcus said, "You never complained before."

Phillip snorted. "Well, I'm complaining now," he said, as he fished in the drawer of the table for the bottle of aspirins he kept there. He felt a damn headache coming on.

A few moments later, Marcus asked in a quiet voice, "What the hell is wrong with you tonight, Phillip?"

Phillip suddenly felt chills rack his body. He was having sex withdrawal already. Just knowing that Rhonda had cut him off was getting to him. "Rhonda and I broke up."

"Again?"

Phillip frowned, knowing just how crazy that must have sounded. "Yes, again," he said in an exasperated voice.

"Good night, Phillip."

Phillip frowned. "What do you mean good night? Don't you have anything to say?"

"Nothing that would do any good. You and Sam are having problems with your exes, and I prefer not to get involved in your issues."

"Like you don't have any?"

Marcus sighed deeply. "Look, Phillip, I only called to let you know I was back in town, and to make sure you remembered to go by the cleaners for me. I also needed to know if you're free tomorrow night."

"Why?"

"Sam wants us to get together at my place for the game."

Phillip rubbed a hand over his face, still frustrated and angry. "That's fine. You need me to bring anything?"

"Yeah, a better attitude."

And the next thing Phillip heard was the dial tone when Marcus hung up the phone.

4

Marcus

"I can do this. I can do this," Marcus mumbled repeatedly as he packed up his wife's belongings.

He had been doing this off and on for the past two months, a little at a time, and the process was taking him a lot longer than he had expected. He hadn't thought that with each article he picked up he would be ambushed by the memories it held.

He glanced around his bedroom. With traces of Dottie removed, the place felt lonely. It looked empty and was a startling reminder that she really was gone, taken away from him unexpectedly by a bunch of kids who thought it would be fun to place huge rocks on the tracks, a joke that led to the train derailment that claimed his wife's life.

Marcus would never forget that call he'd received at work a little over a year ago and the tormented and anguish-filled hours he endured after that. His family and friends had been there to give him support, but it was in the late wee hours of the night—while alone in bed with no one to curl up with or to share those innermost conversations he and Dottie always had after making love, that the depth and extent of his loss would hit him the hardest.

He and Dottie had been married for four wonderful years and had bought into the ideology *get to know the two of you before there becomes three of you.* They had wanted to build a solid, loving and close relationship before having any children. From the time they met, they had done almost everything together, and it hadn't surprised anyone when they'd decided to marry after dating less than six months.

He had dated in college but it was only after returning home to Gary and taking a job as an engineer in Chicago that he had turned his thoughts toward a future and a woman in it. Dottie, who had come to town to care for an aging aunt, had ended up liking the area and taking a job with the Gary school system as a high school teacher.

Marcus sighed deeply as he began taping up the box. He had appreciated Sam and Phillip, his two closest friends, for having a candid conversation with him one night while they had been visiting. They had told him that after nearly two years, continuing to grieve like this wasn't healthy.

At the time he hadn't understood their concern that Dottie's things were still around and that her voice was still on his answering machine. At first he hadn't been able to explain that he'd felt that to remove any of her possessions would seem to him like violating her memory; memories he wanted to keep forever.

And he certainly hadn't been able to think about getting involved with someone. Dottie had been the love of his life, and no one could ever replace her. So he had put all of his energy into his work.

He had even placed his sexual wants and needs on the back burner and channeled his efforts into projects that had been important to Dottie, like the work she did with the underprivileged kids at the high school where she taught. He had established a scholarship in her name to help a deserving student get a college education. He had found great comfort in doing that.

But recently he had joined a group called Grief Relief that consisted of individuals trying to heal after losing a loved one. It had been good to share his feelings with others who were going through the same thing. After a couple of months he had even made some progress. Enough to finally start packing up her things. Once he taped up the box, all traces of her would be gone from their home.

No, he mentally corrected. There was no way all traces of Dottie would ever be gone from their home or his life. He intended for the picture they had taken together the week before she'd died, at a surprise birthday party he'd given her, to continue to sit on the dresser in his bedroom as well as on his desk at work. And she would forever remain in his heart.

And now, although he wanted more than anything to finally take the plunge back into the world of the living and start checking out women and dating again, deep down inside he was scared shitless.

He hadn't gone out on a date in over six years. In fact, he found the mere thought of dating a woman nerve-racking. How would he make small talk? If he were to take her to a restaurant, what would he order off the menu to give her the impression that he was a really cool guy? How would he know if his date was having a good time? How would the woman expect the date to end? Were most women putting out on the first date? Would she expect *him* to put out on the first date?

He talked plenty of trash about wanting to get into some woman panties and about being the ultimate player, but so far he had been all talk and no action. Damn, maybe he was putting too much thought into something that wasn't that complicated. All he wanted to do was start living again, and have a good time doing it.

Standing, he stretched and inhaled deeply. Sam and Phillip would be coming over later to watch the game and drink beer. He enjoyed the time they spent together, and since Dottie's death, they had been his support. Although he had a mother and a bunch of cousins, there was nothing like your homeboys who had your back.

Speaking of family, he should call his mother to let her know he had returned to town, and hope and pray she didn't mention anything about some young woman from her church that he might be interested in. He had seen the young women from her church, and he wasn't interested. There hadn't been a single one who had sparked his interest, not even a teeny-tiny bit . . . other than Naomi Monroe. Hell, he bet she sparked even Reverend Wallace's interest.

The first time he had seen Naomi since high school had been

when he had visited his mother's church six years ago in observance of Family and Friends' Day. She had been sitting a couple of pews over. Their eyes had met, held, connected. Interest had sparked.

Although she'd been a few grades behind him in school, he remembered she had always been a cute, friendly girl who everyone liked. He had intended to speak to her directly after the service but before he could get to her, his aunt Mildred had brought another woman over for him to meet—Dottie. And he fell in love with her right then and there.

His thoughts slowly drifted back to Naomi. The woman had a way of looking like a sex goddess even while wearing church clothes. The last time he had been to his mother's church, Naomi had been wearing a shocking blue dress with the hat and shoes to match. She had looked damn good, and he would bet that none of the men at church that day had noticed her hat or shoes. Their eyes, like his, had probably been glued to that delectable backside of hers and how it moved with each and every step she took. She wasn't a bad catch . . . and she had a good job as a supervisor at the post office.

According to his mother, who he knew really liked Naomi, she was looking for a good Christian man. He wondered why his mother felt he would fall into that category since he still blamed God for giving him such a good woman and then taking her away from him.

As far as Marcus was concerned, that was cruel and unjust punishment. He had paid his tithes each Sunday and attended church regularly, so he couldn't accept the way things had turned out. To say he was bitter was an understatement.

He made his way into the kitchen and picked up the phone and began dialing his mother's number.

"Hello?"

"It's me, Mama. I got back late yesterday."

"It's good to hear your voice, son. How was your trip?"

"It was busy. How are things going with you?" His mother still lived in the house where he had been born and raised. His father had died when Marcus turned ten, making his mother a single parent and a darn good one. She liked to cook, and on Saturday evenings she usually spent a lot of time in the kitchen preparing her Sunday dinner.

"Things are going fine, son. Are you coming to church tomorrow?"

Marcus cringed. He hated when she asked because she knew good and well that he wasn't. He hadn't stepped foot inside a church since Dottie's death. While Dottie was alive, they had been members of a church in Chicago.

Occasionally, he would get a call from his former minister saying the congregation missed him. He had to admit that he missed them as well, but there was no way he could go back without Dottie by his side. She had been the one who had gotten him back in the church after college, and he had enjoyed attending all the married couples' activities the church offered. Now, without Dottie, there was no point.

He decided to stick with the same line he used whenever his mother asked him about church. "I don't know if I can make it tomorrow, Mama, I'll have to see."

He heard her sigh. Then she said, "Naomi was at prayer meeting Wednesday night and asked about you."

Marcus frowned. "What did she want to know?"

"How you were doing."

Marcus sighed deeply. He hadn't told his mother about the time Naomi had shown up at his house, unexpected and uninvited, barely six months after Dottie's death, claiming she wanted to pray with him since his mother had mentioned that he had stopped going to church.

At the time, he'd inwardly admitted he probably needed all the prayers he could get and had let her inside. She had whipped out her Bible and they had sat next to each other on the sofa. When she began praying, they closed their eyes and it was only during her "And Lord, please send Marcus just what he needs . . ." that he felt a hand on his thigh.

He cracked opened an eye in time to see that she had boldly placed her hand on his thigh, and he watched from beneath lowered lashes as that hand slowly began inching toward the crotch of his pants. In a quick instant, his shaft had gotten hard and had been ready to play right into her hand. In disgust, he had jumped up and sent Naomi packing, real quick like and in a hurry. But every time he saw her, he remembered. And whenever they would run into each other at the grocery store, gas station or post office, the thought that he had dishonored Dottie's memory by getting aroused by another woman so quickly would flood him with both guilt and anger.

"Marcus?"

His mother's voice reclaimed his attention. "Yes, Mom?"

"Naomi is a nice-looking girl and what she needs is a good man."

Marcus released a long sigh. He would be the first to admit that she was a nice-looking girl, but he definitely wasn't the good man she needed. He decided to quickly change the subject. "So did Mr. Collins do a good job painting your kitchen?"

For the next ten minutes, he listened while his mother told him how pleased she was with the way her kitchen had turned out and thanked him for paying to have it done. He wished she would agree to let him put her in another home, but she was content to live in the same neighborhood she'd lived in for over forty years.

"Okay, Mama, I got to go. Sam and Phil are coming over later and we're going to watch the game."

"And drink."

Yeah, that, too, he thought, already tasting the Budweiser on his lips. Although he had heard the disapproval in his mother's voice, he chose to ignore it. Hell, he was thirty-two years old and there was no reason for him not to have a few beers if he wanted them.

"You know what the Bible says about drinking?"

Marcus smiled. "Yes, I remember distinctly when Jesus turned grapes into wine for them to drink at a wedding. They had wine, Mama, not lemonade." He knew she didn't like that comment. There was a pause before she answered. He figured she was trying to get a rebutting verse together.

"You're trying to take things out of context, Marcus Reynard Lowery."

"No, ma'am, I'm just stating the facts, and I personally don't see anything wrong with a person drinking as long as they know their limitations."

Not to get her dander up any more, he said, "If you don't see me tomorrow at church," *which I'm one-hundred percent certain that you won't,* "then I'll drop by for dinner later."

"All right, son, and I love you."

"And I love you, too, Mama."

"And God also loves you, Marcus."

Marcus hung up the phone without replying to her last statement, not totally convinced of that, considering his present situation. He glanced around the room. He had time to deliver the boxes to the Salvation Army before Sam and Phillip arrived. They would be surprised to see the changes he'd made to the place.

He had taken a huge step today in getting his life back. Now, he just hoped that he would have the strength to go the rest of the way.

5

The Gang

Later that evening, Sam and Phillip entered Marcus's home and stopped dead in their tracks.

"I can't believe the changes you've made to this place," Sam said as he glanced around, surveying the living room where so much of Dottie's things used to be. The walls were no longer white but were now a bright blue, and the flowered sofa and loveseat had been replaced by a sectional leather set.

Sam met his friend's gaze. "I know it had to have been hard, man."

Marcus nodded. "But it's okay. Like I told you guys, I'm ready to move on with my life because I know that's what Dottie would want. It will be a long time before I entertain thoughts of a long-term relationship, but I am sick and tired of being lonely."

"Tell me about it. Loneliness can be a real bitch," Phillip said, heading straight for the cooler that was sitting on one of the tables. He reached in and pulled out a cold beer. "Now that Rhonda has officially cut me off, it looks as if I'm back to hitting the streets again, which is another bitch. You won't believe the women out there. They're greedy as hell, and their expectations are downright ridiculous. Their idea of chivalry is a rent payment."

Sam smiled. "I think I know just we need," he said, pulling a book out of the bag he was carrying. "Lance sent me this autographed copy of his latest book, and I enjoyed it so much that I thought I'd tell you guys about it."

Phillip frowned and took the book from Sam's hand and read the title. *The Playa's Handbook.* "It just so happens that I picked up a copy of this same book at Wal-Mart last week; not that I intended to read it. I only bought it because Montgomery is a close friend of yours, and I wanted to support the brotha," he told Sam. "Do we look like men who need a damn book to tell us how to get some nooky?"

"Yeah, that fits our description, all right," Marcus said, chuckling as he took the book from Phillip and opened it up. "I picked up a copy last week myself while in Barnes and Noble, but hadn't gotten around to reading it yet. I haven't been out in the dating world for years and, shit man, I need all the help I can get."

He thought of Naomi. "Women these days are bold as all outdoors. If you're not careful, you'll be walking down the aisle before you know it—thinking with that head between your legs and not the head connected to your neck."

"The hell I will," Phillip said, after taking a huge swig of beer. "Rhonda has ruined me for life. Marriage is the last thing on my mind."

"Mine, too," Sam said, reaching into the cooler to grab his own beer. "But I read the book and really enjoyed it. That Lance is freakin' crazy. I heard this book is causing a damn uproar with the sistahs, and after reading it I can see why. Just look at the page that lists his top ten rules."

Marcus quickly flipped to the page and did a quick scan. His face lit into a huge smile and then he began rolling in laughter.

"Hell, what does it say?" Phillip asked, grabbing the book from Marcus. He was curious to know what had Marcus in stitches since he could certainly use a good laugh himself.

A few moments later he was rolling, too. "Hey, I like this one about the crotch-grabbers. I'm probably one of the few men who wouldn't mind feeling assaulted if some woman grabbed my crotch; especially if she planned to take things further."

"Yeah," Marcus said, "and how can we tell if a woman's boobs are the real thing or not?"

Sam smiled. With the popularity of plastic surgery these days, he'd think most men would know, but he knew there were some who would still be clueless. "There's a chapter that gives you a few hints about what to look for."

Marcus lifted a brow, grinning. "You're kidding, right?"

Sam chuckled as he shook his head. "No, I'm not, and I don't want to think about how he did his research. All ten rules have their own chapters and they go into explicit details. Like I said, Lance really jumped into the fire with this one."

He looked at his two friends. "All I'm suggesting is that the two of you read the book, and if you think there's nothing in there that will help, then fine. But I read it and now I feel better knowing how to deal with being on the dating scene again. I know what I want, which is a good time with a woman; what I don't want is any of them getting the idea that I'm ready to get serious. Kim left my head screwed up and I can't get serious with a woman until I get it unscrewed."

Phillip and Marcus nodded, understanding completely. Phillip glanced down at the page of rules again. "Hey, I'm dying to read the chapter on why men should beware of women who prefer to be on top."

Sam chuckled. "You'll be surprised by what you learn." He glanced at his two friends. "I suggest we use the book as a guide to help us deal as single men looking for love."

Phillip held up his hand. "Hold it. First of all, I'm not looking for love," he said, remembering all the stuff he'd been through in the name of love. It was stuff he didn't plan to repeat. "What I'm looking for is sex and plenty of it," he decided to clarify.

"Same here," Sam and Marcus said simultaneously.

"Then we need to stay focused on the rule about not committing, no matter how hot the sex is," Phillip pointed out.

Sam and Marcus nodded. The men then clicked their beer bottles in a toast as the three of them agreed. They weren't looking for love. They were looking for sex; hot sex . . . and plenty of it.

6

Lance

A woman can't use you if you use her first.

Hands on his hips, Lance Montgomery stood in his agent's office frowning, not pleased with what he was being told. "What do you mean you couldn't get Asia Fowler to do the panel discussion for the Harlem Book Fair?" he asked, watching as his agent rumbled through his desk drawer for the bottle of antacids he kept there.

Lance knew he should feel bad for giving Carl an upset stomach, but he didn't. Carl would tolerate him no matter what because from the first book to the last, he had made the man a lot of money.

Hell, he would even be honest enough to say that they made each other a lot of money. When it came to business, Carl was as suave as they came. He didn't just go after good contracts, he went after the best and wouldn't hesitate to walk away from the table if he felt Lance was getting screwed or wasn't getting the most a publisher had to offer.

After watching Carl swallow a handful of the pills then wash them down with a huge glass of water, Lance decided to sit down. There was no need to stand any longer since it appeared he wouldn't be getting any good news.

"Don't take it personal, Lance," Carl finally said, leaning back in his chair. "I talked to her agent, Melissa James, and she explained that Ms. Fowler is scheduled to be somewhere else that day, which is why she hadn't planned to participate in the book fair. But I could tell that Ms. James kind of liked the idea of you and her client squaring off in some sort of heated debate. It would have been great publicity for book sales. However, prior commitments are prior commitments, and evidently Ms. Fowler doesn't want to change her schedule."

Lance sighed deeply, deciding not to tell Carl that squaring off in a heated *debate* was not what he had in mind for him and Asia Fowler. He wanted them to square off in a different way entirely . . . still heated, of course. For some strange reason, he couldn't get her out of his mind. Sight unseen, she had gotten under his skin and he knew of only one way to get her out. "I want to know her touring schedule," he said.

Carl lifted a dark bushy brow. "Pardon me?"

Lance sighed again. He hated repeating himself. "I said I want Asia Fowler's touring schedule. Since her book is still fairly new, I'd think she's doing a number of signings and interviews."

Carl frowned. "And what if she is?" He stared at Lance hard before asking, "For Pete's sake, Lance, you aren't turning into some kind of freakin' stalker or something are you?"

Lance smiled that particular smile that made women love him as well as hate him. He knew he was a challenge to some women and a pain in the ass to others. He got tired of counting the number of women who thought they could change him. He knew better than anyone it was damn impossible. He wasn't looking to be reformed anyway. He loved his life just the way it was. "I play women, Carl, I don't stalk them."

Carl continued staring at him, disapproval lining his gaze. "And that's something you like boasting about?"

Lance chose his words carefully. "A woman can't use you if you use her first."

Seeing the dark frown on Carl's face, he smiled charmingly. "But I do have a conscious, believe it or not. I don't play every woman that comes my way."

He decided not to tell Carl that his hot-to-trot daughter Danielle was one of them. The college-age young woman had shown up at his place one night with another woman inviting him to partake in a threesome. He had sent Danielle and her friend packing.

"I'm glad to hear that," Carl said, interrupting Lance's thoughts and standing to stretch his legs. Lance studied the older man and knew that although he was presently just one of Carl's successful clients, he was the one Carl had never been completely sure about. And Lance liked it that way. He picked his friends carefully, and when it came to his associates he didn't mind keeping them guessing. The only people he knew he could count on were his brothers and his childhood friend Samuel Gunn.

"So, how soon can you get me Ms. Fowler's touring schedule?"

Carl narrowed his gaze as he sat back down. "You're actually serious, aren't you?"

Lance chuckled as he gave the man a leveled stare. His blood stirred at the thought of just how serious he was. "Yes, Carl, I'm serious and would really appreciate any information you can provide."

Remembering the photo of her in the back of her book, he had a sudden, vivid image of making love to Asia Fowler in his bed while the jazzy sound of Miles Davis bathed the room through the speakers he had installed in his bedroom. The images were as sinful as they were sensuous.

Asia Fowler had definitely gotten into his system, and he planned to enjoy each and every moment getting her out of it.

With a cup of steaming hot coffee in her hand, Asia Fowler stepped out onto the balcony and breathed in the rich scent of bagels. Their smell floated through the predawn air from a deli shop not far away. One of the things she loved most about living in New York was the sights, sounds and smells; especially the smell of bagels, not to mention pizzas, steamed hot dogs and coffee.

Carefully taking a sip of her coffee, she inhaled deeply as she glanced out over the parts of New York that she could see from where she stood in her home in the West Village. She had lived here long enough to know that this was the only time the city was quiet, during the predawn hours.

As she leaned against the rail and glanced down at the deserted sidewalk below, she knew soon it would change. In a couple of hours, the place would be alive and awake. Yellow cabs and walking bodies would be everywhere, and the peaceful solitude would be gone.

This was the time she liked best, when she could stand on her balcony and think . . . plan . . . appreciate. Her thoughts immediately went to Sean Crews. Last night he had asked her to marry him.

More than anything she appreciated Sean's friendship—always had, but what he was asking for was something she needed to carefully think about, and thankfully, he had agreed to give her time to think. In her own way, she did love him but not with a deep, dying passion the way a woman was supposed to love a man. She loved him for the good person that he was. He knew her history and she was grateful for the part he played in her life, especially in her emotional healing.

She closed her eyes as she remembered what it had taken, the painful yet much-needed process, to get her from where her life had been to where it was now. She was still working hard to put her past behind her, and whether or not Sean had agreed with the things David had done, it couldn't change the fact that Sean was David's brother.

Opening her eyes, she allowed herself a private smile when she thought of the first time she had seen David Crews. It was probably the only time in their relationship that she could vividly recall with fondness and a complete lack of bitterness. She had been twenty-two, still a virgin and only a few months away from graduating with a MBA from the University of Miami. She had been at a social event, a party given by several corporations wanting to recruit potential employees—the brightest and the best.

She had been talking to one of the HR representatives from Microsoft when someone laughed out loud at some joke a CEO told, and she had glanced across the room and caught his eyes.

Whammo!!

She'd thought the floor beneath her feet had crumbled out from under her. That had been her first experience with sexual chemistry and it had literally taken her breath away. David Crews had been the most gorgeous man she had ever seen. And as she had studied him, she felt that he represented everything she'd worked so hard to achieve. He was as polished as he was handsome.

A few moments later, he had excused himself from the group he'd been with to cross the room and introduce himself. She'd known within five minutes of their conversation that he was the man she wanted. All she knew was that he was a good-looking brother, a corporate attorney working in the legal department of CNN who pulled in a six-figure salary. He was going places and she was just the woman to go there with him. Without much thought, that night she had accepted his invitation to visit him for a week in Atlanta after graduation.

She would never forget the first time they had slept together. She could recall lying awake in the middle of the night, listening to his breathing while he slept and gazing at the lines of his handsome face, thinking about how much she loved him. She saw a big house, nice furniture, a Mercedes parked in the driveway and a little girl who looked just like her daddy. But most importantly, she could not imagine having that dream without him. In her mind, he had suddenly become the half that made her whole: her perfect partner.

Evidently, he hadn't felt the same way because a year into enduring a long-distance romance—she had landed a good job in Texas although she had applied for several in Atlanta to be close to him— he still hadn't even mentioned marriage. She had convinced herself that he was waiting for the right time.

After almost two years of him flying to see her in Dallas and her visiting him in Atlanta, she decided to broach the subject with him. That night in his apartment he had told her in no uncertain terms that he wasn't ready for marriage and wasn't sure if he ever would be. He claimed he had issues to resolve before he took a big step like committing his life to someone. She had listened and decided that it was okay if he had issues. They could work through them, and in the end she would change his mind. She would change him.

It took another two years to discover that David could not be changed. She had also come to the painful realization that he could not be trusted. All the time she had been planning their wedding, he had been playing her big time . . . her and a couple of other women. When she confronted him about it, he made her realize that at no time during their relationship had he promised that she would be the *only* one.

Assuming had broken her heart and after leaving David and trying to heal, she fell into a series of affairs that led nowhere. But the exposure introduced her to men who, like David, could easily lure her with smooth talk, a hefty bank account, debonair ways, a handsome face and a well-built body. She had even taken up with a man old enough to be her father.

He brought her gifts every time he came over and she had eagerly accepted each one until she woke up one morning, glanced around her apartment, and saw that almost everything in it had been bought with *his* money—her kitchen appliances, her living room furniture, the expensive lingerie she wore and even the bed she slept in. It had been pretty damn depressing to realize she was truly a "kept" woman.

It was then that she had made the decision to do something about her situation and not depend on a man for her happiness. Wanting to further her education, she began taking night classes at college to work toward her doctorate. Just when she thought she had her stuff together, David reappeared in her life and within months he had it screwed up again. It was then that she realized she had never truly gotten over him, and the only reason she had become involved in meaningless relationships after their breakup was to prove there was nothing wrong with her. And that the reason things didn't work out between her and David wasn't because of any deficiencies she had.

It didn't take long for David to have her dangling on a string again. It had only been with Sean's help that she had opened her eyes. He had come to tell her that David and another woman were honeymooning somewhere in Jamaica. It had been a slap in her face to learn that when he left her bed it had been to catch a plane to attend his rehearsal dinner.

That had really done it for her. The shock of David's betrayal had almost destroyed her. Sean had seen her through those rough times and convinced her to get on with her life.

And she had.

She had completed her doctorate in psychology, and based on her experiences, she wrote her first book, *You Can't Change Him.*

Now, three years and two books later, she could keep her focus and remember the lessons she had learned. Sadly, David had eventually left his wife and was once again out there playing other women the same way he had played her. The books she wrote while going through her healing process had been books for women who'd been damaged, hurt and emotionally abused.

She took another sip of her coffee and glanced down at her watch. She would be speaking today at the Betty Shabazz Center, and it was time to get moving. The women who were attending were between the ages of twenty-one and forty, and they wanted her to speak candidly about sexual issues. Another smile touched her lips. After being celibate for over a year, she hoped she was ready for that topic.

"So, Ms. Fowler, are you saying that women should never sleep around?"

Asia smiled at the young woman in the audience who had stood up to ask the question. She was in her early twenties, and she had an expression on her face that said she felt her question was a very important one.

"No, that's not what I'm saying. There's nothing wrong with a man and woman sharing a wonderful and healthy sexual relationship. But I've discovered that when a woman feels the need to sleep with different men, it's because she is running away from something instead of running toward something."

"And what is she running away from?" another woman in the audience asked.

Asia looked to her left to respond. "Usually, it's a relationship that went bad and the woman never got over it. Often we're too filled with emotional debris to do anything but hop from bed to bed, thinking an orgasm will cure the hurt. Although a good night of sex might make us feel good, our problems will still be there in the morning."

"So what do you suggest that we do?"

Asia smiled again. "Stop thinking that whenever a man walks away there has to be something wrong with you. That belief leaves you wanting to go out and prove otherwise, which can make you lose focus on the things you should have learned from the last relationship."

She sighed deeply then added, "I can look back at some of the men I used to be involved with and ask myself why? What on earth was I thinking? Why was I wasting my time? How could I have been that stupid? Then it hit me, that some men actually thrive on weak women. They don't know the meaning of love and commitment. They are experts on detecting what they see as wounded souls, women who haven't recovered from past hurts, who have messed up minds and are filled with insecurities. These men try to convince us they are what we need, the answer to our prayers, the way to happiness and that we should be grateful to them for giving us the time of day. They want us to believe that we should overlook any issues they might have and disregard their blatant lack of respect and mistreatment of us."

She paused, remembering David so well. "They want us to think it's okay to accept sex for love and put up with all the head trips they want to take us on. All I'm saying is that as women, it's okay to want more from a relationship—a man who is kind, respectful and trustworthy—and if you're not getting what you really need, then there's nothing wrong with pulling back and saying, time out, get the hell out my face. I need to regroup and get my act together before going one step further. It may take a few weeks, months or maybe even a year, but you'll never put that failed relationship behind you and find a man that's totally right for you until you make up your mind to do so. A relationship isn't like riding a bike. You don't get right back on and try it again after falling off. You have to give yourself time to recover."

"And have you recovered, Ms. Fowler?"

"Not fully," she answered smoothly, yet honestly. "But I'm still working on it. I'm proud to say that I've been celibate for over a year, and it's important to me to get myself together before becoming seriously involved with a man again. I still have issues, and the only man a woman with issues can attract is a man with issues and frankly I don't need or want that. I can have a pity party all by myself. I want a man who's got it together, but then he deserves a woman who's got it together as well."

After the session ended and Asia was getting her things together to leave, she couldn't help but hope that she had said something that would make a difference in someone's life. She had once been where she knew some of them were now, thinking that they needed a man—just about any man—in their life to really be a woman. That was so far from the truth.

"You're good."

Asia paused in putting the items in her briefcase to cast a side-long glance at the man who was standing a few feet away from her. Then she looked up and gave the person her complete attention.

It may have been the smooth yet husky sound of his voice that first captured her attention, but now it was definitely his looks that had her silently enthralled. Okay, there was more to a man than good looks. She of all people knew that since she preached it constantly in her books. Yet the one standing a few feet away from her was one who could be appreciated, and since she was definitely a woman, she could at least give him his due.

With an inward sigh, she turned up one corner of her mouth in a smile and said, "Thank you. I was glad to see there were a few men in the audience. It's always good to have a mixed group."

He nodded and moved a step closer, coming fully into the light and Asia inhaled sharply. This man, whoever he was, was the epitome of everything she had tried to avoid over the past year. Besides being handsome, he was dressed to the nines in a well-tailored designer suit, expensive shirt, tie and shoes and had a Rolex on his wrist. It wasn't that he was overly flashy, in fact he really wasn't. His looks and his clothes were well balanced, but everything about him exuded power, confidence and success, the very things David had had.

Sexual chemistry.

It was there too, whether she wanted it to be or not. It was strong. The current was almost overbearing and they had only spoken a few words. He was man. She was woman. At the moment just making eye contact with him had blood pumping fast and furiously through her veins.

And she didn't like it.

Hadn't she just told the audience that she hadn't fully recovered from damaging affairs? The last thing she needed was this guy coming on to her in a weak moment. Had he latched on to her bold statement that she was celibate as a challenge? Hell, she recognized the look in his eyes. She hadn't been born yesterday. He was a man on the make. Standing there, the only two people left in the huge auditorium, made the place suddenly seem small. She felt the temperature rise. This connection that was sizzling between them was just the beginning.

Neither of them said anything for the longest time as they continued to study each other, which she found amusing . . . if she had been inclined to find humor in the situation, which she wasn't. This was a man who could knock her off the wagon and right onto her back—spread-eagle.

Something about him pricked her mind. It was as if she knew him or had at some point in time seen him before. But she was fairly certain that if they had met she would have remembered him. He wasn't a man a woman was likely to forget.

Inhaling deeply and deciding that enough was enough and that her mind and senses could only handle so much, Asia leaned against the table and said, "I hope you enjoyed the lecture."

He smiled and leaned against the podium. His smile made her breath catch. It also did crazy things to her insides. Unfortunately, she was one of those women who enjoyed the slow buildup of hot seduction, and there was no doubt in her mind that the man standing before her had the technique down to an art form.

"I did enjoy it," he said.

To Asia's way of thinking, his voice, a low rumble of sound, rubbed her in all the right places . . . or should she say the wrong ones.

"I particularly liked listening to your voice," he added, reclaiming her attention. "It's very sexy; a total turn-on."

Vibrations curled through her belly, and she tried to downplay the stir when she realized once again that they were alone. She didn't know him and she didn't know if she should feel threatened by such a blatant sexual comment. He evidently picked up on her sudden tenseness and immediately said, "I'm completely harmless, I assure you, but maybe I should introduce myself."

Her guard up, Asia responded by saying, "Yes, maybe you should."

He straightened away from the podium and took a step closer. His features were flawless against a backdrop of the creamiest chocolate brown skin she had ever seen. His eyes were deep brown and were highlighted with golden flecks that seemed to radiate heat, and she could immediately smell the warm robust scent emanating from him. Coming to stand directly in front of her, he extended his hand. "I'm Lance Montgomery."

Her hand, which had automatically extended when he had held out his, suddenly froze; her chest tightened and her brows raised. "*The* Dr. Lance Montgomery?" she asked, barely able to get the name out.

His dark eyes took in her surprise and he said, "Yes."

Asia couldn't help but stare. So this was Dr. Lance Montgomery, the widely acclaimed relationship expert. The man who was on a mission to perfect the art of being single. From what she'd heard, he was a master at sex and seduction. So the stories went, he had a game out of this world and was reputed to be able to get any woman he went after. He was an expert at pushing any relationship right to the bedroom and not letting it go any further. His sexy escapades often gave various newspapers something hot to talk about. He wrote what he lived and lived what he wrote, and no one doubted that he enjoyed being footloose and fancy-free, a prowler and definitely a playa.

She knew that when it came to the concept of playa-ism, no one questioned his knowledge on the subject. There were some who claimed he could be rude and arrogant when it suited him, and there were countless others who would attest that when it came to those he considered friends, he could be true and loyal to a fault. She was seeing a professional playa at work and without a doubt he was displaying a very inhibited skill.

She was jerked out of her thoughts when he took her hand to complete the handshake they had started. The moment the warmth of his fingers gripped hers, engulfing her hand in a startling sensation, an ache she hadn't felt in a long time suddenly clenched her middle. To maintain control as well as keep her sanity, she slowly pulled her hand from his.

She cleared her throat and said, "If you thought I was good, Dr. Montgomery, then I'm definitely flattered." Her voice, she noted, had lowered to a husky pitch.

He smiled again; this one just as devastating and seductive as the first and showing perfect pearly white teeth. "Like I said, you're good. And also like I said, I like the sound of your voice. It's sexy."

Catching a movement in the distance, Asia glanced behind him to see a maintenance man who had entered to remove the extra chairs that had been brought in. Feeling more relaxed now that they weren't alone, she turned her attention back to Lance. "So, you have a thing for the sound of a woman's voice?"

He nodded. "Yes, and I definitely have a thing for yours," he said smoothly, honestly, without missing a beat.

Asia couldn't help but chuckle at the blatant come-on. Now that she knew his identity, her senses were sharpened and her mind was alert. She was ready to face a formidable foe. "I'm sure it was more than my sexy voice that brought you here today, Dr. Montgomery," she found herself saying.

The look in his eyes was light and teasing. "Yes, you're right, Dr. Fowler," he murmured, the sound making the pulse at the base of her throat erratic. "I had to see the entire package."

Asia breathed in deeply, thinking the man was definitely good. Real good. And he was a whiz at slow seduction, her downfall. If she wasn't careful, she could become hypnotized by his words. He had a way of making a woman feel feminine and sexy without much effort on his part. But she intended to stay on her toes, one step ahead of him, no matter what. However, curiosity got the best of her and she asked, "And what do you think about the total package?"

He gave her that sexy smile again and said, "Hmmm, I think it was well worth the trip."

She lifted a brow. "The trip?"

"Yes, I flew in this morning from Chicago. That publicity photo in the back of your book doesn't do you justice. You are a very beautiful woman."

Asia shook her head. Lance Montgomery was laying it on thick and she was barely strong enough to resist. Deciding she could no longer stand on both legs, she perched her hip on the table beside her. "And you want me to believe that you flew in from Chicago this morning just to see and hear me?"

"Yes."

Asia didn't miss the way his eyes had moved to glance down at her legs when she shifted one leg over the other. She tugged down her skirt and watched as the corner of his lips lifted into a grin. "So, can I assume you're finally acknowledging my theories on relationships, Dr. Montgomery?"

He chuckled. "No. I don't buy into your belief that there is a soul mate for everyone. And the very idea that love alone is enough is too cushy and sweet for me to swallow. And let's not forget the myth you promote that true love conquers all, and to put the icing on the cake, the information you gave out today was totally out of my range of acceptance. There is absolutely nothing wrong with a woman engaging in sexual relationships with men—as many as she likes, just as long as protection is used—and as long as they both know what they want, and usually the key word is pleasure. Why muddy the waters by throwing in words like love and commitment?"

Asia frowned. His assessment of things shouldn't bother her. After all, he was a bona fide playa. There was no hope for him. He was one of those men a woman couldn't change. Shaking her head she glanced down at the floor. After a brief moment to recollect her thoughts, her gaze was drawn back to his face.

She felt it again—that automatic sexual pull, that slow sizzle that started to fuse her nerve endings. "Boy, aren't you the skeptic. I thought you said I'm good," she said, barely able to get the words out.

He held her gaze. "You are. But like a lot of women, you're also confused about a lot of things when it comes to men. You, Dr. Fowler, have a lot to learn."

Asia stood and narrowed her eyes. David had taught her all she needed to know and she didn't intend to take another course. "If you came all the way from Chicago to insult me, please don't waste your time," she said, turning her back to him to finish packing her stuff.

He moved around in front of the table. He would be in her line of vision if she was to look up, but she refused to do so until she closed her her briefcase with a snap.

"I didn't mean to insult you," he said huskily, apologetically. "And to prove just what a nice guy I am, I'd like to take you out to dinner tonight."

She glared at him. "Sorry, I have to decline your offer."

Humor deepened his voice when he said, "If not tonight, then another time, perhaps?"

"I don't think so. We're evidently like oil and water. We don't mix."

He chuckled, the tone amusing, teasing and filled with a private challenge. Oh, they mixed all right and he couldn't wait to demonstrate to her just how well. He had to acknowledge that her haughty attitude met his approval. Maybe it was a good thing that she had turned down his invitation to dinner. He had to plan, strategize and conquer. He was an expert at all those things. The only thing he needed to decide was what approach would work best for a woman like Asia Fowler.

"I think you misunderstood me," he said, lowering his voice to a husky, seductive pitch as he leaned over the table. "I don't want to be your enemy. I intend to be your lover."

Asia's eyebrows shot up. "My lover? You're kind of sure of yourself, aren't you, Dr. Montgomery?"

His smile extended to the corners of his eyes when he said, "Yes, I guess I am. And you know they say confidence is a good thing." He then took a step closer. "I'll leave you now but I'm looking forward to the day we'll see each other again. And rest assured that there *will* be a next time, Asia."

The sound of her name, rolling from his lips, traveled like a soft caress, a sultry breeze, over intimate parts of her body. "Until then," he leaned over the table and whispered, his lips mere inches from hers.

Transfixed, her gaze followed him as he slowly pulled back, turned and exited the stage. Her eyes stayed glued to him as he walked down the aisle then closed the heavy metal door behind him, without looking back.

It was only then that she released a long, slow breath.

7

Sam

*Don't be afraid **not** to commit, no matter how hot the sex is.*

Sam hummed a classic Luther Vandross tune as he carried the bag of groceries from the elevator toward his apartment. Shifting the bag onto his hip, he unlocked the door, went inside and closed the door behind him with the heel of his shoe. He quickly crossed the living room to the kitchen and set the bag on the countertop of the dividing bar.

Now that the truth was out and he wasn't the bad person everyone had thought he was, his family had been either calling him every day or, in the case of his sister, Carolyn, periodically sending him cheerful Hallmark cards in the mail. No matter how many times he told them that he was fine, the calls and the cards kept coming.

As he began unloading the bag and placing the items on the countertop, he couldn't help but think of how peaceful his life had been over the past few weeks. After being in a long-term relationship, a person forgot what it was like to be on their own and think about themselves. Although he regretted the demise of his marriage, each day he was getting stronger and facing life's challenges head-on. The pity party had ended and he woke up each morning feeling great. He'd had time to analyze the situation with Kim and had decided she had been his biggest mistake in life and he didn't intend to make another one. He wholeheartedly embraced Phillip and Marcus's decision to stay clear of any lasting relationships until they were ready, and for him that could very well be never.

It had been a month since they had made that pact over at Marcus's house, and he found it wasn't as hard as he'd thought it would be to get back into dating. Within a few days after that night he had met Kathie Wilkins while out shopping for T-shirts at Wal-Mart.

She had been shopping for a gift for her younger brother and had asked his opinion about what type of underwear most men preferred, boxers or briefs. That question had led to conversation and he had found himself asking her to join him for a drink at a bar not far away. To his surprise, as well as his delight, she had accepted.

By the time he had gotten home that night, there was no doubt in his mind that Kathie liked him and he'd definitely liked her. She was the first woman he'd been sexually attracted to since Kim, and over drinks she had told him she was also a divorcée. She and her husband had married young, right out of high school, mainly because she had gotten pregnant at seventeen. Now at thirty-one she had a fourteen-year-old daughter. Kathie had gone to one of those career schools to get a dental hygienist degree and worked at a dentist's office in Chicago.

She had invited him to dinner at her place the following weekend and he had accepted. Although the outside of her home needed painting and other repairs, the inside was clean and comfortable looking. He had gotten a chance to meet Kathie's daughter Maury, who he thought seemed a bit on the wild side because of her hairstyle and the way she was dressed. And he could easily tell that mother and daughter didn't get along by the snippy conversations they shared. It had turned out to be a rather nice dinner after Maury had left to meet some friends. And she planned to spend the night with a girlfriend.

After dinner he and Kathie had sat on the sofa and talked some more about their respective jobs, the economy and terrorism. When things began getting cozy—after she turned down the lights and lit a couple of candles, not to mention kicking off her shoes and undoing the first few buttons on her blouse—Sam had done just as *The Playa's Handbook* had suggested. He was up front with her, making sure she understood that for the time being he wasn't looking for a lasting relationship, just an intimate connection. Kathie had seemed perfectly fine with that, and he got the impression she had appreciated his honesty.

Sex that night with Kathie hadn't been as hot as he knew that it could have been for him, mainly because a part of him felt he was being unfaithful to Kim . . . if that wasn't a bunch of crap, considering everything she had done to him. But still, it had been the first time he had slept with another woman in over four years, and it felt awkward to the point where he couldn't really enjoy it the way he wished.

Kathie was indeed a sexy woman and had done everything to make him feel comfortable. Even their discussion of protection had been up front and open, and he'd been surprised just how knowledgeable she was about condoms. Although he had brought his own, she had been quick to tell him she had her own stash in case he ran out.

Before he'd left that night, he had told her that he would be calling her but so far he hadn't and he doubted that he would. He couldn't dismiss the fact that she was a woman who'd constantly asked during their lovemaking . . . no, he corrected, their sex-making . . . for him to tell her that she was attractive. Like she needed to hear it often to believe it. That had really bothered him.

As he began unloading the grocery bag, he couldn't help but smile when he thought about Tina Arnold, another woman he had met a couple of weeks ago while attending a business meeting in Chicago. She was one good-looking sistah, all professional with not one strand of hair out of place.

Instantly, he had imagined her in bed with her hair messed up and making love to him. Their eyes kind of met across the room and they both smiled. After the meeting was over, he had approached her and after a couple of minutes of small talk, he had asked for her home phone number. She hadn't hesitated in giving it to him and he had given her his.

Later that night he had called her and they'd had a nice friendly conversation. He'd discovered she was twenty-nine, only three years younger than himself, and that she was a woman on the move with plans of succeeding in her career as a financial planner. They had gone out for drinks that week and had made plans to do dinner next week.

He had discovered during their conversations that Tina liked Italian food so he had purchased an Italian cookbook and planned to try his hand at a couple of the dishes before inviting her over to his place for an Italian feast night. He had felt real savvy going to the grocery store and shopping for the ingredients listed in the recipe. He had decided that since neither he nor Tina were interested in a serious relationship, she was someone he wanted to spend time with.

After putting things away either in the cabinet or refrigerator, Sam was about to grab a beer out of the mini cooler that sat on the kitchen table when he heard the sound of his doorbell. Wondering who it could be, he left the kitchen and crossed the living room to the door.

He opened it to find a beautiful woman standing there. He was surprised but definitely not disappointed with his discovery. "Yes?"

"I'm sorry to bother you," she said, her eyes filled with apology. And he thought they were the most gorgeous pair of honey-brown eyes he had ever seen on a woman. And if that wasn't enough, silky waves of honey-blond hair flowed down her shoulders and deeply accentuated her cocoa-colored skin, not to mention the cut-off jeans and midriff top she wore that showcased an incredibly nice-looking body. Gold loop earrings hung from her ears and a matching bracelet adorned her right wrist. And the way she was holding a soda can in her hand, she could have been a Beyoncé double for a Pepsi commercial. It didn't matter one bit that she probably got that breathtakingly radiant hair from a bottle. All that mattered was that the coloring went well with her complexion and eyes. The total package was enough to make any man take notice.

And he was definitely a man.

"I'm Falon Taylor and I just moved into the apartment down the hall," she was saying, interrupting his thoughts. "And unfortunately my phone isn't hooked up yet, and I seem to have a problem with my alarm system and need to call the company about it."

His gaze immediately dropped to her hand and he noticed she wasn't wearing a ring. "I'm Sam Gunn and sure you can use my phone, but I'm surprised that you don't have a cell phone," he said, stepping aside. In this day and time, it was a smart idea for a single woman to have a mobile phone as a backup.

"I do, but my roommate's cell phone battery was low and so borrowed mine and then had to leave unexpectedly."

Roommate? He wondered if her roommate was male or female. Deciding he could find that information out later, he asked, "What seems to be the problem with your security system?"

"It hasn't been activated yet, and I was assured by this company I'm using that it would be working first thing this morning. I refuse to spend the night in an apartment that is not secured."

Sam nodded, he couldn't blame her there. Although their apartment complex was in a nice area of town, he'd always believed in taking extra precautions. Besides, with an alarm system your rental insurance rates were cheaper, and he was discovering as a single man that every little bit of savings helped.

He then remembered what she'd told him about her phone. "And when is your phone getting hooked up?"

"The phone company is supposed to get here within the next hour," she said glancing around. "Your girlfriend won't mind me using your phone, will she?"

Sam smiled. He didn't know if she was genuinely concerned or if she was being outright nosey. He'd give her credit and believe it was the first. "I live alone and I decide who can or can't use my phone," he said handing it to her. "And on that same note, I hope your roommate won't have an issue with you being alone here with me."

She grinned, knowing they were clearing up a few things. "Marcy is my cousin and she won't have an issue with it," she said, accepting the phone. "Thanks."

He went into the kitchen to give her some privacy to make the call. Except for the few dishes he'd left in the sink before leaving for the grocery store, he was glad his apartment was clean. One thing he couldn't tolerate was sloppiness, which was one of the reasons he doubted he would ever consider getting a roommate. He had gotten used to Kim's once a week cleaning and was one of those men who didn't think twice of doing housework, which meant he had spent more time cleaning than she did.

Wondering why he was even thinking about Kim, he proceeded to wash the dishes in the sink. He had just rinsed the last dish and placed it in the drainer when he heard the sound of Falon's voice behind him.

"Thanks, Sam, for letting me use your phone."

He turned around as he dried his hands on a kitchen towel. "Hey, no problem. That's what neighbors are for."

He couldn't help but notice where she was standing—right in front of the bar separating his kitchen from his living room—and the sun that was shining through the window hit her at an angle that seemed to radiate her beauty even more. His breath caught and for a moment he felt transfixed.

"Are you okay?" she asked as he continued to stare at her.

Her words broke the daze and he nodded. "Yeah, I'm fine, and if you need to use the phone again, just come back. I plan to be here for the rest of the day."

"Thanks for the offer but the security company assured me they will have my system activated in less than an hour, and I'm holding them to that. I put down a huge deposit."

He nodded, understanding about deposits. "Can I offer you something to drink?"

"No thanks, I'm fine," she said holding up her soda can. She then noticed the cookbook on his counter. "You're into Italian food?" she asked.

"No, not really," he replied casually. "But I've decided to try a few things out of there. It will be a change from the microwave dinners I've been eating a lot of lately." He watched as she flipped through the book. "What about you? Are you into Italian food?"

She glanced up at him and he watched as a smile curved her glossy lips. "I'm into all types of food. That's my profession."

He lifted a brow. "What?"

She chuckled, and the husky, feminine sound floated across the dividing bar to him. "Foods. I'm a chef," she said.

"Wow," he said sincerely, since that bit of news surprised the hell out of him. He couldn't imagine all of that glorious hair pinned up and tucked under a chef's hat. Nor could he imagine her dressed in all white. That was definitely not the image he had of her. Although there was nothing wrong with her being a chef, he'd had her pegged as a businesswoman, someone holding some high-powered job. Just listening to the sound of her voice as she'd spoken on the phone let him know that she was articulate and very professional.

"There are a lot of good recipes in here," she said, once again breaking into his thoughts. "And the majority of them are very tasty."

"And where do you work?"

"Blakes."

Sam lifted a brow, clearly impressed. Everyone in the Midwest and beyond was familiar with Blakes, one of the most elite restaurants in Chicago. It had a reputation for serving the best food anywhere. He'd heard that people—the rich and famous—flew in from almost everywhere in the world just to eat there. It was definitely a place where important people made it their business to dine. He'd heard the cost of a meal there would run you well over a couple of hundred but that you got your money's worth. It was not a place you took a woman unless you really wanted to impress.

"How long have you worked there?" he asked.

"For almost a year. Before that I worked for the Valencia hotel chain, and when I got the chance to work at Blakes I went for it and I'm glad that I did. I love working there."

Sam watched as she glanced at her watch. "I need to get back to my apartment and I'm sure I've taken up enough of your time," she said apologetically.

He smiled as he came out of the kitchen to walk her to the door. "Like I said, it was no problem. I know how things were on moving day for me. They were hectic as hell."

She glanced up at him. "You haven't lived here long?"

"Only six months. You'll like it here. It's pretty quiet most of the time, and the tenants that do have children make sure they follow the rules. The management firm that runs this complex wants to uphold its reputation of being a nice place to live, and so far I haven't been disappointed."

Falon smiled. "Thanks for letting me know that."

They had reached the door and she turned to him. "Thanks again, Sam, for letting me use your phone."

"You're welcome and like I said if you need to use it again just let me know."

He opened the door and watched as she walked down the hall to her apartment. Her shorts clung to every curve and he could only stand there and stare, appreciating every inch of her backside. An ass like hers was a rarity and he wanted to take it all in.

When she reached her apartment she glanced back at him and waved her hand, and he waved back before closing his door.

She was gone but her scent still lingered in his apartment. And it was a rather nice scent, alluring and seductive, a difficult combination to resist. He would even go so far as to say it had been sexual, which muddied the waters even more.

There were a number of things he wondered about Falon Taylor, one of which was whether or not she had a boyfriend. Women with her looks and her figure usually did. He couldn't imagine her not being attached.

He smiled. She was his neighbor and hopefully he would have

plenty of time to get to know her since there was a lot about her that drew his interest. However, he immediately ruled out the possibility of them being more than friends even if she wasn't attached. She was definitely not the type of woman he wanted to get involved with now. For some reason, he saw her as a girl a guy would want to take home to Mama, and that was the last type of woman he wanted.

Besides, with her living down the hall, that was too close to home. Even while in college, he'd had a firm policy of not dating anyone who lived within a certain radius of him. Doing so could open a single man up to all kind of complications; complications that he didn't need.

Deciding he wanted to hear some music, something old and funky, he crossed the room and turned on the CD to the sound of Ike and Tina. Going back into the kitchen, he decided to dry the items he had placed in the drainer and put them away, and as he did so Ike and Tina blasted out "Proud Mary" through the speakers he had placed in the kitchen.

He tried forcing his mind away from Falon Taylor and back to Tina Arnold, the woman he was presently pursuing. But he couldn't help but mentally compare the two.

Like most men he appreciated beauty and both women definitely were lookers. And although he'd only had a brief conversation with Falon, he could even go so far as to say that both were undoubtedly intelligent. There was also no doubt in his mind that although their occupations were vastly different, both had a genuine professional air about them.

Now what about sensuality? Hmmm, he thought, leaning against the counter. Both could claim it hands down. Dressed in cut-offs and a top, there'd definitely been something sexy about Falon. But then on the same note, all of Tina's business attire had suited her, made her looked confident, elegant and sexy.

The first time he had seen Tina, heat had immediately flooded his stomach and his mouth had curved in appreciation to see a sistah so well put together, from the expensive powerhouse business suit and pumps she wore, to the immaculate way she wore her makeup and hair. But it had been her face that he hadn't been able to push from his mind for almost an entire week. With skin the color of coffee, eyes that were just as dark, and lips that were covered in an enticing shade of red, she had definitely made him aware that he was man. He had known within seconds that he wanted to get to know her up close and personal. His hit on her had been deliberate, and he'd needed to know if he had what it took to interest a woman of her caliber. Evidently he had.

And then Falon Taylor had definitely delivered him a stunning blow to certain parts of his body when he'd opened his door to find her standing there. She appeared to be the type of woman who could probably get right under a man's skin without even trying, and before he knew it, she was doing so. Caution lights had been going off in his head with her.

Both Tina and Falon were very impressive women, but one was definitely off-limits. Falon Taylor.

And Sam knew he had to remember that.

8

Phillip

Playas "have sex"; they don't "make love."

"Mr. McKenna, I can understand that you feel your daughter is still trying to adjust to you and your wife's divorce," the woman said in a cool, yet weary voice. "But this school cannot tolerate her behavior any longer. According to Ms. Waterston, Chandra's teacher, there's not a week that goes by when Chandra isn't disrupting the class. I have requests from parents asking that either she be removed from this school, or they will transfer their children elsewhere."

Phillip rubbed his hand down his face. They were talking about a six-year-old for heaven's sakes, and not a seventeen-year-old delinquent. "Really, Mrs. Jones, don't you think these parents are getting carried away with all of this? I'm sure Chandra's behavior can be disturbing for a teacher, but don't you think removing her from this school is a little extreme?"

He could immediately tell that he'd said the wrong thing when a dark frown planted itself firmly on the woman's face. "I would like to know how you would feel if your child came home with this type of mark on her body," she said, placing a photograph in front of him.

Mark on her body? Phillip wondered what the woman was getting at as he picked up the picture that had been placed in front of him of a nice-looking little boy who clearly had teeth prints on his cheek. The close-up shot also showed how the bite had broken the kid's skin.

A lump formed in Phillip's throat. He straightened up in his chair. "Jesus! Chandra did that?" he asked incredulously. All Rhonda had mentioned to him was that their daughter was misbehaving in school by having occasional outbursts and throwing temper tantrums. She'd told him nothing about Chandra biting other children.

The older woman glared at him. "Yes, she has quite a record. During the past month, that little boy was victim number three, her next to the last."

Phillip swallowed deeply, hoping he was misreading what the woman was insinuating. "Her next to the last?"

"Yes. The reason I called you here was because she bit another child today, a little girl. Your daughter seems to take great pleasure in going for the cheeks, and she caused even more damage this time."

Phillip glanced down at the picture he held in his hand and for the life of him didn't see how more damage was possible. Evidently, Mrs. Jones read his expression and said, "Today she bit a little girl on both cheeks."

"Oh, my God!" Phillip dropped the photograph, shaking his head in despair and disbelief. It's a wonder the parents of all those kids didn't want to skin his daughter alive. He was raising a little cannibal.

"I take it you didn't know just how serious things were, Mr. McKenna."

He lifted his head. "No, I didn't. The only thing my ex-wife mentioned was that Chandra was misbehaving and having outbursts and tantrums, which I assumed had gotten under control since she hadn't mentioned anything about them in a couple of weeks."

Mrs. Jones lifted a dark brow. "I find that strange when Ms.

McKenna and I discussed the biting of Anthony Franklin just days before Ms. McKenna mentioned she would be leaving to go out of town for two weeks, and that Chandra would be with you while she was away. She was told at that time that if an incident occurred again, we would be taking drastic means to remove Chandra not only from Ms. Waterston's class but from this school."

Phillip shook his head in disgust. A part of him was outraged that Rhonda hadn't told him how serious things were with Chandra. His daughter was only in the first grade and already she was facing expulsion. "Where is Chandra now, Mrs. Jones?"

"She's across the hall in the assistant principal's office with her teacher."

"And the little girl that she bit today, how is she?"

"Star Davenport's mother was called to take her to the doctor since the bites in both places were bleeding. You may not be aware of it, but whether a bite is minor or serious, it is suggested that the parents notify their doctor since the risk of infection is high."

Phillip swallowed again. "Infection?"

"Yes, infections such as hepatitis, but more common bacterial infections such as staph can spread easily through bites. That's why we have to take bites seriously. Luckily, with the first bite case, your ex-wife brought in proof that Chandra was in good health. But still, according to the mother of Star, when she got to the doctor's office today, they gave her daughter a tetanus shot."

Phillip's guts clenched painfully at the thought of what the little girl had endured because of his daughter. "Is there a way I can contact the parents of the child to make sure she's okay?"

Mrs. Jones nodded. "Yes, in fact Terri Davenport has requested that you call her later. She wants to talk to you about this incident."

Phillip nodded. She probably planned to make him pay for her daughter's medical bills and she'd be completely justified. "Thanks, and I will. I'd also like the names and phone numbers of the parents of the three other children," he said, standing after Mrs. Jones had shoved back from her desk and stood.

"Well, you're certainly taking this a lot further than Ms. McKenna did. I suggested that she take this approach, and she said that with her busy schedule she didn't have the time."

Phillip inhaled. Why wasn't he surprised? "Well, a parent has to make the time and this is one of those times. I'm asking that you don't expel Chandra. I'd like to keep her at home with me for a couple of days, and I'll do whatever I can to make sure the problem is resolved."

Camilla Jones nodded. "All right, but I will have to change teachers since most of the kids in Chandra's class are outright afraid of her and won't feel comfortable if she were to come back. Plus, I did promise their parents that Chandra wouldn't be returning."

"Thanks."

"You're welcome, but if there's another biting incident, Mr. McKenna, then there won't be any further discussion on the matter. You will be asked to enroll Chandra elsewhere."

Phillip nodded. "I understand," he said, taking the sheet of paper from Mrs. Jones that listed the names, addresses and phone numbers of the parents.

After bidding the woman a good day, which he figured would be a lot better than his, and definitely a lot better than Chandra's once he had a serious talk with her, he went to collect his daughter.

Ringing the doorbell, Phillip stood next to his daughter as they waited for Terri Davenport to answer the door. This was the fourth and final home they needed to visit, and just as she'd done with the others, Chandra was expected to apologize to each child she had bitten as well as to the parents.

He glanced down at his daughter. She was such a beautiful child with her copper skin tone and mass of braids on her head. She was slightly smaller than most six-year-olds and had always been pretty mild mannered. But lately, that had changed. With the divorce and Rhonda spending less and less time with Chandra, Phillip had begun noticing the difference in her behavior with other children.

She hadn't said much when he'd brought her home from school. When he had asked her why she had bitten those other children, she had merely shrugged her shoulders and said she didn't know. After leaving the school with Chandra, he had stopped by Chandra's pediatrician who was also a friend. While his nurse entertained Chandra in another room, Larry had explained that most kids stopped biting at age four, and for Chandra to be biting now meant she was probably frustrated and trying to get attention.

Phillip knew that Chandra had never adjusted to the divorce, and Rhonda's hectic work schedule didn't help matters. Now he realized they may have to take things a step further and get their daughter professional help. He was frustrated but determined to do everything that he could for his daughter.

Only one parent was still riled up. Jessica Hargrove wouldn't open the door and said she didn't want Chandra anywhere near her daughter ever again. The woman even claimed that her daughter had taken to imitating Chandra and was now biting her younger brother. She said she had been of the mind to have her daughter bite Chandra back.

"Yes, who is it?" a soft feminine voice asked through the thick wooden door.

Phillip held Chandra's hand tighter in his. "Mrs. Davenport, I'm Phillip McKenna, and I spoke with you earlier on the phone."

"Oh, yes," she said, opening the door.

Phillip's mouth couldn't help but curve to a smile and he thought that Mr. Davenport was a very lucky man. Terri Davenport's beauty was simply priceless. She appeared to stand at least five eight and the flowing top and slacks she was wearing showed a shapely and petite figure. Her hair was dark brown and cut short, worn in a very chic style that complimented her nutmeg-colored features. She had the softest-looking skin he had ever seen on a woman and her features could leave a man breathless. He immediately guessed her age to be late twenties.

"Mrs. Davenport?" he said, quickly recovering and extending his hand. "Thanks for agreeing to see me and Chandra this evening."

She smiled. "I appreciate your wanting to stop by and check on Star." She then glanced down at Chandra, and Phillip watched as she bent down to his daughter's level. "Hi, Chandra. How are you today?"

His daughter eyed the older woman nervously before saying in a soft voice, "Fine."

"That's good and I'm glad your daddy brought you by to see how Star is doing. Would you like to come in?"

Chandra quickly nodded her head. Straightening, Terri Davenport met Phillip's gaze and said, "Please come in. I'm sure Star will be happy to see you both."

He considered her words. It would surprise the heck out of him if Star was indeed happy to see Chandra. Most of the other children had hidden behind their parents.

"Thanks," he said as he and Chandra stepped into the warmth of her huge living room. The Davenports lived in a newly developed area of Gary where the houses were stylish and the yards were immaculate. He was curious as to why Terri Davenport was so calm after what Chandra had done to her daughter. A sudden thought hit him. Maybe she and her husband had already contacted their attorney and had decided to sue.

"Star and I finished dinner a while ago, but if either of you would like anything to eat or drink, I'll be happy to get you something."

"No, that's not necessary but thanks for the offer," he said, wondering where her husband was and when they would hit him with the news of the impending lawsuit.

He cleared his throat. "Like I told you over the phone, Mrs. Davenport, Chandra owes your family an apology and I want to make sure she delivers it."

"All right, just let me go and get Star."

"And Mr. Davenport?"

Some deep emotion of pain flitted across her face. She met his inquisitive gaze. "There isn't a Mr. Davenport any longer. My husband passed away a little over a year ago."

Compassion immediately pulled at him for her loss. Then, just

as quickly, something else was pulling at him. Lust. With the realization that there was no husband, it registered that the good-
looking Terri Davenport was single. He squashed the thought. The
woman was probably still grieving.

"I'm sorry," he said sincerely.

She nodded. "Thanks." She inhaled deeply. "Won't you and
Chandra please have a seat? I'll be back in a moment."

He watched as she gracefully walked out of the room, leaving a
subtle, sexy scent in her wake. She was wearing a sleeveless top and
he couldn't help noticing the tattoo of a star on her upper left
shoulder. He smiled thinking of her daughter's name. Then he felt a
pull at his hand and glanced down at his daughter.

"Daddy, aren't we going to sit down like Star's mommy
said?"

He smiled. "Sure, honey." He loved his little girl so much, more
than life, and he would do anything for her. He knew that apolo-
gizing to the children and their parents hadn't been easy for her, but
he wanted to teach her responsibility for her actions, and how if
you did something wrong you had to ask for forgiveness. And just
as her pediatrician had suggested, he would get Chandra professional help if the divorce was causing his daughter to feel like she
needed attention. He was also concerned with all the hours Rhonda
was working. When she returned, he would again bring up the subject of him getting full custody of Chandra though Rhonda had
been against the thought the last time he had suggested it.

Taking a seat, he set his daughter beside him and continued to
hold her hand. He glanced around thinking that he liked the inside
of Terri Davenport's home as much as he liked the outside. It was
beautiful and spacious. She had done a good job at decorating, and
he especially liked how she had combined hunter green with cream
tones to give the living room a somewhat soothing effect, one that
made you feel comfortable. Although it was evident from the pictures on the wall and the children's books that lined a bookcase
that a child was in residence, there wasn't the clutter one would
expect . . . like the way Rhonda usually kept things until Mrs.

Green, the housekeeper, was given the chore of straightening things up.

He looked up when Terri Davenport reentered the room holding the hand of a beautiful little girl who could have been the woman's clone. Standing and bringing Chandra to her feet also, his heart took a dive when he saw one of her cheeks was bandaged and the one exposed still clearly showed teeth prints. It's a wonder Terri Davenport had let him and Chandra inside her home.

"Star, Chandra and her father have come to pay a visit," Mrs. Davenport said to her daughter, reclaiming his attention.

Phillip smiled at the little girl. "Chandra came to apologize to you and your mother for what she did to you today, didn't you, Chandra?" he asked his daughter gently.

She looked up at him. "Yes, Daddy." She then looked at Star and said, "I'm sorry for biting you." Then seemingly as an afterthought she quickly added, "Two times."

Star nodded then glanced up at her mom before saying, "Okay."

He looked at Mrs. Davenport. "I really appreciate you letting us drop by, and I'm willing to reimburse you for any medical expenses that you incurred today."

Terri Davenport smiled. "How about if we let the girls play together in the backyard while we sit out on the patio and watch them and talk?"

Phillip nodded cautiously. "All right." Was this the part where she would tell him about the lawsuit?

They sat at a table while the two little girls scurried off toward a swing set. "And you're sure you don't want anything to drink?"

"Yes, I'm positive," he responded. Not one for beating around the bush, Phillip said, "This is going to cost me more than Star's medical expenses isn't it?"

He watched Terri Davenport's face get confused. Then with strained patience he waited for her to answer. "And just what do you think it will cost you?" she finally asked smoothly.

"I'm not certain but I take it you've seen an attorney?"

He watched as she lifted a brow and then watched as humor, of all things, crept into her eyes. "I am an attorney, Mr. McKenna," she said simply.

Damn! He was in bigger trouble than he thought. He cleared his throat and sat back. "You're an attorney?" he asked and saw humor still lurking around in her eyes.

"Yes."

He cleared his throat again. "So . . . considering that, I guess my question is still the same. This is going to cost me more than Star's medical expenses isn't it?"

With a laugh, Terri Davenport stood. "Mmm, I think I'll let you ponder that a moment while I go get you something to drink after all. I think a glass of iced tea might help that throat of yours. Please watch the girls until I come back."

Not knowing what else to say, Phillip said, "All right."

His pulse quickened as he watched Terri Davenport walk away, noting the graceful way her body moved. The woman might very well be getting ready to take him to the cleaners, and he couldn't help thinking about how she probably looked without a stitch of clothing. A sudden tightening in his groin caused him to gasp. He hadn't had sex since Rhonda had cut him off almost a month ago and it had started to wear on him.

He shook his head. He was just plain pathetic. You're still a man, he thought, coming to his own defense. He liked what he saw when it came to Terri Davenport, and there was nothing wrong with admiring a beautiful woman.

When he heard his daughter laugh, he snapped to attention. He was supposed to be watching the girls and not sitting there getting physically aroused.

Terri Davenport returned with two glasses of iced tea.

Phillip stood and accepted the glass thinking it would take the whole damn pitcher to cool him down. "Thanks." He waited until she was seated before he sat back down.

"How are the girls?" she asked, glancing to where they were still playing.

"They're doing fine."

"Good." She took a sip of her tea and shot him a grin over the rim of the glass. "I have no plans to sue you, Mr. McKenna. I understand how children are. Besides, a year ago I was where you are now."

Phillip lifted a brow. "In what way?"

"Star was the class pincher."

Phillip straightened up in his seat. "But, why?"

Terri Davenport smiled. "Probably for the same reason Chandra is the biter. I hope you don't mind but Mrs. Jones mentioned that you and your wife were recently divorced."

Phillip shrugged. "It's not all that recent. It's been nearly two years."

Terri nodded. "Sometimes it takes kids longer than that to adjust. Star had been a daddy's girl and losing her father was hard on her. He was here one day and gone the next."

Phillip nodded as he took another sip of his tea. "And how did your husband die? Was he ill?"

Terri shook her head and Phillip could feel the hurt and the pain. He had been around Marcus enough to know that adults had a hard time adjusting to a loss as well. "No, he was a police officer who was killed in the line of duty. He wasn't even supposed to be working that night but had gone in because they were short-handed. A couple of officers were out with the flu."

For a long moment, she didn't say anything then said, "I didn't know just how hard Star was taking his death until I was called by the school because she was being disruptive and pinching other children."

Phillip studied the contents of his glass before tilting his head to the left and saying, "I discussed Chandra's behavior with her pedi-atrician today, and he suggested that perhaps I need to take her to see a therapist. He said most kids grow out of biting at the age of four. He thinks it has to do with her wanting attention."

He sighed deeply and met Terri's gaze. "I appreciate your under-standing in all of this. I met some of the other parents today and

74

they weren't as gracious and understanding as you, and I meant what I said about being responsible for Star's medical expenses."

"That's not necessary. I have good medical insurance, Mr. McKenna. Besides, my main concern is Chandra and that she is all right."

Phillip smiled, actually believing that. In just a short span of time, he could tell that besides being good looking, Terri Davenport was also a caring person. "Considering the situation with our girls, can we skip the formality now? I'm Phillip."

She chuckled. "And I'm Terri." After taking a sip of her tea she asked, "What about your ex-wife? Have you discussed today's incident with her? How does she feel about Chandra being seen by a professional?"

At the moment, Phillip didn't give a royal damn how Rhonda felt since she had kept Chandra's behavior from him. "My ex-wife is out of town and won't be returning for another week. But I can tell you she won't like it. She'll see it as if we're saying our daughter isn't normal in some way."

Terri nodded. "Oh, I see."

Phillip wondered if she really did. He finished off the last of his tea and said, "Thanks for everything, but I don't want to take up any more of your time. Because of the biting incident, I'm keeping Chandra home for a few days. I'm taking time off from work to spend time with her."

Terri nodded as she stood. "That's a good idea." She glanced over at the two girls playing. "If I didn't know about that incident today, I would swear they were the best of friends."

Phillip agreed and stood also. "Yeah, crazy isn't it?"

"Maybe not as crazy as you might think. Kids bounce back pretty quickly. It's the adults who have a hard time letting go and moving on."

He drew in a deep breath, wondering if she was talking about her own inability to move on after her husband's death. He inhaled the tantalizing scent of her perfume and realized, as well as accepted, that he felt something vital. As strange as it was, he wanted to see Terri Davenport again. He needed to see her again. He quickly made a decision to take a chance and go for broke. "Do you think we can see each other again, Terri?"

He watched as she lifted an arched brow and a guarded look appeared in her eyes. It was as if a wall had gone up between them. "Why?" she asked.

Phillip inwardly sighed, thinking that asking her had been a bad idea. Clearly she wasn't ready to get back into dating. He latched onto the first thought that came into his mind. "To discuss the girls."

Her brow inched a little higher. "The girls?"

"Yes."

He stood almost transfixed as she wet her lips, the tip of her tongue darting out between her teeth as she gave his suggestion serious deliberation. He could sense her wavering and decided to give her a push. "I think your past experience with Star might help me understand how to deal with Chandra," he said. Phillip felt tense as she continued to consider his suggestion.

"I can't make any promises. I suggest you call me to see how my schedule is," she finally said.

Phillip nodded, knowing that was the best he would be able to hope for. But still, the thought of seeing her again, spending time with her alone sent a lustful quiver through his stomach. He definitely wanted to get to know Terri Davenport but a part of him wondered if she would give him that chance.

Later that night, as Terri Davenport slipped between the cool sheets of her bed alone, she couldn't help but think of Phillip McKenna, the man with the friendly and gentle eyes. He seemed like such a nice person and a wonderful father.

As she stared up at the ceiling, she remembered how Lewis had also been a wonderful father as well as a warm, loving and thoughtful husband. When they had first met and all through their courtship, he had treated her like a lady, a china doll. Unfortunately for her, the same thing continued through the eight years of their marriage, which provided little excitement in the bedroom.

It wasn't that their lovemaking had been awful but it hadn't been all that she had wanted it to be. Lewis strongly believed that the missionary position was the only position a man was supposed to use when making love to his wife. The one time she had suggested a different position, he had looked at her like she had completely lost her mind. So over the years, she'd had to suppress her desire for something "more and different." And after a while, she had begun questioning why she even wanted those things, why was there this wild, sensual being within her that wanted to experience and explore more? She had begun asking herself if such wants and desires were normal.

Her thoughts shifted back to Phillip McKenna. She wondered what type of woman he preferred in the bedroom. There was something about him that she couldn't let go of. Since Lewis's death, several men had asked her out but a part of her was closed up. She wouldn't mind the dating part but was afraid to get serious with anyone where the relationship would escalate to the bedroom. What if the wild and sensual being within her were unleashed? Would the man think she was some kind of freak? The same thing Lewis would have thought had he known her secret desires.

She knew she needed professional help to get beyond this particular hang-up and had decided to see a therapist. Her first appointment with one was in a couple days.

And as for Phillip McKenna, she knew that until she fully understood every aspect of her sexuality, she wasn't ready to move forward just yet.

9

Marcus

Before you get carried away with a woman, make sure
everything she's packing is the real thing.

Marcus sat in his favorite lounging chair, chuckling to himself as he
reread parts of *The Playa's Handbook*. He had already read it from
cover to cover; however, he liked going back and rereading certain
chapters.

Sam was right, Lance was freakin' crazy. "If you want to be a
playa, you've got to learn to live by the rules," the Introduction
said, and in Marcus's opinion, Lance had provided some damn
good rules.

So far Sam had been the only one who had scored. Phillip was
busy with his daughter and Marcus was still exploring his options.
He had heard about Internet dating from one of the guys at work
and decided to give it a try.

He had done his research and had gone with a reputable dating
service. Following the company's suggestion, he had carefully chosen a screen name to use. The first screen name he'd picked,
2Hot2Handle, turned out to be disastrous. Since he hadn't put up
his picture yet, most of the responses he'd received were from men
who thought he was a woman looking for a good time. He had
quickly chosen another screen name, one that didn't appear gender
specific. See-U-2 was his choice and he liked the sound of it,

thought it was rather catchy. His photograph was now posted on the site and already he had received a number of interested e-mails from women. So far he hadn't had a good feel about most of them and hadn't agreed to meet with anyone.

But a certain woman he had been corresponding with for the past two weeks seemed promising. Her screen name was Dimples22 and from the photograph posted on-line, he liked what he saw. Her picture was a body shot and she was one voluptuous sistah. He had nothing against full-figured women and the breasts on her were to die for. Chances were he wouldn't have to check to make sure they were real since they were in sync with the rest of her. Everything about her seemed all-natural.

They had been e-mailing each other back and forth now for a while and were going through that "getting to know you" stage.

Marcus looked up when he heard the phone ring, figuring it was his mama reminding him that tomorrow was Sunday, like he would forget. He picked up the phone. "Yeah, Mama."

"This is not your mother, Marcus."

Marcus sucked in a deep breath. "Oh, sorry. Hi, Naomi."

"Hi. Are you okay?"

"Yes, I'm doing fine and what about you?" He glanced across the room wondering what excuse he could use to get her off the phone.

"I'm fine. I was calling to invite you to dinner tomorrow."

He lifted a brow. "Dinner?"

"Yes. I talked to your mama and she told me what some of your favorite dishes are and I want to prepare one of them for you."

Marcus shook his head. Naomi sounded so excited and sincere. He hated his mama for putting ideas in the woman's head like there was a chance he would become interested in her. Naomi had turned him off when she had pulled that stunt after Dottie's death. He didn't think he could ever fall for a woman who hadn't shown respect to his deceased wife.

"Thanks for the invitation, Naomi, but I've made other plans," he said, glad he wasn't lying since he planned on getting together with Sam and Phillip tomorrow.

"Oh." Then after a few moments she said, "I really regret what I did, Marcus."

There was a long pause and he inhaled slowly, deeply, before saying, "I'll admit what you did bothers me a lot, Naomi. I haven't mentioned it to anyone, not even my mama. I've kept it between us. But I really didn't appreciate you coming into my wife's home and doing what you did while I was still in mourning."

She hesitated. "I just . . . wanted to remind you that you were still a man—a living, breathing man—something you seemed hell-bent on forgetting. Your wife had been dead for six months."

Her words suddenly angered him. Was there a rule written somewhere that dictated how long a husband was supposed to mourn for his wife? "I don't care if she had been dead for six years, you had no right to do what you did. You dishonored her memory by coming here and doing that."

"I said I was sorry. Is there anyway we can start over?"

"No."

"Marcus, please listen—"

"Look, I think we've said enough to each other, and I would appreciate it if you didn't call me again. Good-bye." He hung up the phone, fuming.

Slowly he counted to ten, hating that she had gotten him so upset. He had always been a man who prided himself on his self-control, but it didn't take much for Naomi to make him lose it.

He sat there and studied the phone for a moment, hoping that she had finally gotten his message. He intended to talk to his mother tomorrow, and he would make sure she understood there was no way he and Naomi were ever getting together, so she could get that thought out of her matchmaking mind.

Standing, he shook his head as he made his way toward the computer that sat on the desk in a corner of the room. After booting it up, he logged on to his private-message board to see if Dimples22 was logged on. She wasn't but he decided to leave her a message anyway.

Although the two of them hadn't shared a lot of personal information, he knew she was someone he wanted to get to know better. The e-mail and messages they had exchanged had been fun, and he felt she was an honest dater. That had been his biggest fear when he'd decided to venture into Internet dating.

He felt that he was ready to meet Dimples22 face-to-face and would throw out the suggestion tonight when they talked. If she didn't feel comfortable quite yet, he wouldn't push it. But he hoped she was ready.

He smiled when he heard his computer beep, letting him know that Dimples22 had entered his chat room. She was early. Eagerly, he punched in his greeting:

"D22, CU2 here. How was your day?"

He waited for her response.

"Work wasn't too bad, considering it was a Saturday."

Marcus nodded. He knew she was a divorcée, a nurse who worked at a hospital, but he didn't know where and which one. She knew he was an engineer and a widower who was trying to ease back into the dating scene.

He proceeded to type in another message.

"I was wondering if you felt comfortable with a meeting one night next week. In a public place, of course."

He waited and he could tell that at first she was hesitant.

"Are you sure you're ready to make that move?"

He smiled. *"Yes. I really want to meet you."*

He waited awhile then read her message.

"And I want to meet you, too."

He began typing again. *"Good. Then it's settled. What about us getting together this coming Wednesday night?"*

He paused, waiting for her to reply.

"That night is fine. Where do you want to meet?"

He typed a response. *"I'll let you pick out a place. Think about it and let me know tomorrow night."*

He waited for her to type a reply.

"OK."

Marcus leaned back in his chair, getting excited about the meeting that would take place. He typed out another message. *"I can't wait."*

He waited for her to send the closing response.

"Neither can I."

Tami Wallace smiled at Naomi after giving her a hug. "Sorry you had to wait so long but we had a large crowd today, and it took longer than expected to say hello to everyone."

Naomi nodded, understanding completely. Today was the second Sunday, and as usual the young adults had been in charge of the service and the church had been packed. Everyone enjoyed coming to hear their young adult mass choir, which was into a lot of urban-contemporary gospel music. Being the First Lady of Greater Jerusalem Baptist Church, it was Sister Wallace's place to stand beside her husband, Reverend Wallace, and greet everyone as they departed from church after the service.

Naomi inhaled deeply while she waited for Sis Wallace to unlock the door to her office. As the pastor's wife, Sister Wallace often counseled the women of the church. She also conducted a lot of single women's seminars around the country.

"Come on in and have a seat, Naomi, and tell me what I can do for you. Are you here to talk about the church carnival scheduled in two months?"

Naomi took the chair in front of Sister Wallace's desk and watched as the woman went behind her desk to sit down. She inhaled deeply. She had prayed about this last night, especially after having that conversation with Marcus. She needed guidance. She cleared her throat.

"No, everything is going fine with the carnival and we have a lot of good participation," she said about the event she was chairing this year. "What I wanted to talk to you about is personal."

Sister Wallace leaned forward on her desk and gave Naomi that particular smile that made the ladies feel like they could tell her just about anything. "All right, what do you want to talk about?"

Naomi inhaled deeply as she looked into Sister Wallace's eyes. They were soft eyes, filled with understanding, compassion. She was the type of wife every minister needed to help their congregation grow, prosper and reach their full potential as Christians.

"There's this man that I'm interested in," Naomi began, then suddenly stopped and glanced down at her manicured fingers. She decided she needed to be completely honest with Sister Wallace. She glanced up and met her gaze again. "I'm more than interested in him. I think I've loved him for a long time, even when we were in high school, although he never noticed me. Then he left for college and during that time I met my husband Carter. Although Carter was a good man I couldn't love him the way he should have been loved, and I know that deep down he knew that my heart belonged to another. I accept full responsibility for my failed marriage. I'm just glad that after our divorce Carter met someone else and is happy."

Naomi didn't say anything for a while, then she continued. "This other man who had my heart returned home around a year after my divorce. I heard he was back and wondered how I would react when I saw him again. I wondered if he'd been nothing more to me than just an adolescent crush. The day arrived when he came to the church to visit one Sunday. I knew my feelings for him were still the same. I made up my mind to take a chance and let him know I was interested in him, but before I could do that he met someone else and married her."

For a moment Naomi remained silent as she remembered that time. It had been hard on her, harder than anyone would ever know because only she and God had known how much she loved Marcus Lowery. "I saw that as something final and decided to get on with my life, not once thinking there was a possibility there would ever be a chance for us.

"Last year his wife died in a tragic accident. My heart went out to him because I knew he had loved her deeply. I had even met her a few times and have to say that she was a beautiful person, both inside and out, and I never resented that she was the woman who had gotten his heart. It was six months after his wife's death, and I'd heard how withdrawn he'd become, so convincing myself I was only thinking about him and what was best for him, I thought I would visit him, share God's words with him."

"And what happened then?" Sister Wallace asked quietly.

Naomi glanced away, then she met the older woman's gaze. "My intentions were good until I saw him, and then all I could think about was how much I've always wanted him. I held the Bible in my hand, and listened to the devil tell me that I had waited long enough, he was free and it was all right for me to make my move; I had been in the background long enough."

Naomi inhaled deeply. "I was praying, but I was so aware of him and actually placed my hand on him . . . on his thigh . . . close to his you know what. For some reason, I just had to touch him there, to remind him that although his wife was dead, he was still a man; a man with needs."

Sister Wallace asked calmly, "And what was his response to that?"

"His body responded to my touch although I'm sure he didn't want it to. He got angry with me and I know that he had every right to do so. He had just lost his wife and hadn't expected behavior like that from someone he thought was a godly woman." Naomi glanced away, not able to meet Sister Wallace's gaze any longer.

"And you *are* a godly woman, Naomi. None of us is perfect and God knows that." When Naomi remained silent and continued to study the wall, Sister Wallace said, "We fall down but we get up, pray about it and move on."

Naomi looked at Sister Wallace. "I've tried but Mar—he won't let me. He won't forgive me. He won't let us move beyond this. It's been almost a year and he still holds it against me. He tries to avoid me. Yesterday I invited him to Sunday dinner and he turned me down. He said that he didn't appreciate the way I came into his home and dishonored his wife's memory the way I did, and asked that I not call him again."

Sister Wallace raised her eyebrows. "And will you abide by his wishes and not call him again?"

Naomi swallowed. "Yes."

"And for the time being I think that's for the best. Losing someone you love, the person you believed was your soul mate, the love of your life, the person you had expected to get old with, retire with, spend the rest of your days with, is extremely hard, Naomi. I feel bad for you because you have secretly loved this man for so long, and I also feel bad for him because there's a woman who loves him but he's not willing to open himself up to accept that love."

She stood and came around to the front of her desk to stand in front of Naomi. "What both you and that young man need is prayer and I will pray for you. I pray one day his eyes will open to see the beautiful and caring person that you are, that one day he will come to know the love you have for him and accept it as another blessing from God. The Father gives, He takes away, but He gives again, and we have to be willing to accept all the gifts that He wants us to have, sometimes without question."

Sister Wallace then reached out and took Naomi's hand in hers. "And as women, we have to know and accept that some men don't appreciate aggressive women. They prefer to make the first move, and that's okay if that's how they want to handle things."

She sighed deeply then added, "I know your heart is hurting but that's okay, too. That's one of the beauties of being a woman. God made us strong. He gave us the ability to endure things a man couldn't cope with. Our beauty isn't just in the clothes we wear, our makeup or the way we fix our hair. It's in who we are, deep in our heart where love resides.

"The Lord's way may not be your way, Naomi. There's a chance at some point in your life you may have to realize that this man isn't for you and that you aren't for him. Are you willing to accept whatever happens? Whatever is God's will?"

Naomi nodded. "Yes."

A smile touched Sister Wallace's lips. "Okay then, stand up, let's bow our heads and pray."

"Hell, Marcus, are you really going to go out with this woman you met on the Internet?"

Marcus grinned at Sam after downing the last of his beer. He licked his lips. "Yeah, and I'm so excited I've been walking around with a hard-on all day. You saw her picture. Wouldn't she make you hard?"

Sam blew out a breath. "Yeah, if I hadn't had any in over a year, I guess she would."

Marcus's eyes narrowed at him. "What the hell is that supposed to mean?"

Sam shrugged. "It means that I saw her picture and she doesn't appear to be my type."

Marcus glared. "Meaning?"

Sam smiled. "Too much woman. Damn man, I wouldn't know what to do with that much woman. I might hurt myself being greedy. Everything on that sistah looks real."

Marcus grinned. "I definitely plan to find out."

"You plan to find out what?" Phillip asked, coming out of the bathroom.

Marcus explained.

Phillip laughed as he grabbed a beer out of the cooler. "I'd love to get my hands on a big woman."

He popped the tab of the beer can and lifted the can to his lips to take a huge sip. Then he added, "Shit, I'd love to get my hands on any woman. I haven't had one in over a month, and I'm desperate enough to stick it to a woman who's all bones. At this stage I can't afford to be picky."

Sam shook his head. "Damn, man, what are you waiting for?"

Phillip chuckled. "For you to give me the go-ahead to hit on your Beyoncé look-alike since you don't seem the least bit interested."

Sam raised his eyes to the ceiling. "Her name is Falon and I *am* interested, but I want to see how things with Tina Arnold pan out first. Tina and I are seeing each other again this week."

He hadn't told Phillip the truth. He wasn't interested in Falon, but just because he'd decided she was off-limits to him didn't necessarily mean he wanted her seeing one of his friends. He couldn't understand his reasoning, but at the moment he planned to go with it, deciding that he was doing the right thing and saving her a lot of grief since Phillip and Marcus had issues.

Sam had seen her only once since the time that she had used the phone in his apartment. Unfortunately, Phillip had been with him after coming from the gym. It had taken everything he had not to knock the hell out of Phillip for insisting on an introduction. Luckily for him, Falon had entered her apartment and closed the door before he could get her attention to make one.

"Why wait to see how things pan out with Tina Arnold when you can become involved with them both?" Marcus asked, interrupting Sam's thoughts. "That's the beauty of being a playa; you're not tied down to any one woman. Didn't you read chapter one?"

"Yeah, but this is the way I prefer doing things," he said. He didn't owe anyone an explanation.

"And I prefer just doing *it*," Phillip moaned.

Sam grinned as he took another sip of beer. "If you're that horny, I'll send Kathie Wilkins your way."

Phillip lifted a brow. "Isn't she the one who needs a compliment with every damn thrust?"

Ignoring Marcus's hoot of laughter, Sam tried keeping a straight face when he said, "Yeah, she's the one."

Phillip frowned. "Then forget it. I don't do compliments while I'm busy knocking boots."

"Beggars can't be choosy," Sam said laughing.

"Hey, man, what about that attorney you had the hots for weeks ago?" Marcus asked, emptying more chips into the bowl and grabbing another beer.

Beer and chips.

He didn't want to think about what he was probably missing out on when he'd turned down Naomi's offer. She had told him that she wanted to fix his favorite meal, and if she had talked to his mama that meant rice and gravy, a thick juicy pork chop, macaroni and cheese, green beans and corn bread. And for dessert, banana pudding.

"Shut up, Marcus," Phillip said, interrupting his thoughts.

Hearing the anger in Phillip's voice, Marcus glanced over at him and found Phillip was scowling at him.

"What in the hell's wrong with you?" Marcus asked, confused.

"It's not going to be like that between me and her, so knock it off. I don't want to talk about her." A part of him regretted that he'd mentioned anything about Terri Davenport to the guys. He saw her as more than just a body he wanted to get into. The woman was real classy. The way she had handled the situation involving his daughter had meant a lot to him.

Sam pinned him with a questioning look. "So are you saying you aren't going to try and see her again?"

Phillip frowned and his eyes darkened. His mouth tightened. "That's not what I'm saying. What I'm saying is that whatever goes on between us won't be up for discussion."

Marcus and Sam stared at him intrigued. Then a long moment later Sam said, "Hey, man, we understand if you want to start getting serious about someone."

"Dammit, don't put words into my mouth. All I'm saying is that Terri Davenport isn't the type of woman a man would want to play around with."

Sam held both hands up, palms out. "Hey, man, calm down. There's no need to get into a funk about this. We're all past the age where we're expected to kiss and tell. We're still gentlemen and that's not what this is about. It's about us getting over rough times in each of our lives. If we meet a really nice sistah along the way, that's great. How we handle things with her is our business. All we're doing right now is getting together to watch the game, drink beer and bullshit around."

Phillip nodded and his temper eased. "Thanks, I needed to hear that."

Marcus chuckled. "I think we all did."

Marcus glanced down at his watch. It was ten past seven and he and Dimples22 were supposed to meet at seven. He had been here since six-thirty, determined not to be late. They had decided not to exchange their real names until they officially met tonight.

The restaurant she had chosen was right in the busy section of downtown Chicago. This was just a get-together: first time for the two of them, no big deal. But still, he was extremely nervous.

"Would you like more water, sir?"

Marcus glanced up at the waiter. He had been served three glasses of water already and felt his bladder getting heavy. "No, I'm fine," he said. He glanced at his watch again. He hoped Dimples22 hadn't chickened out on him.

Deciding he needed to make a quick run to the rest room, he told the waiter, "I'm expecting someone and if she arrives while I'm in the rest room, please show her to this table."

The man nodded. "Yes, sir. And what is her name?"

Marcus glanced up at the man as he stood. "Dimples22."

The man lifted a brow. "Dimples22, sir?"

"Yes, and she'll be wearing a green dress." She had told him last night what color her outfit would be.

"All right, sir."

Marcus quickly walked away to the men's room. When he returned moments later, he discovered his date still hadn't arrived. He went back to the table and sat down, deciding to get another glass of water. He glanced toward the door and a woman wearing green entered.

He swallowed as he studied her. Boy was she fine and looked just like her picture, thank God. He hated to admit it but since they had decided to meet, he'd been having nightmares that she wouldn't look a thing like the picture posted on the dating site.

He continued to sit transfixed. Her face was the color of rich cocoa and her hair was fixed in twists. Her makeup was flawless and her legs—damn, they were thick and shapely. So were her breasts. Hell, forget about what *The Playa's Handbook* said. It wouldn't bother him one bit if she preferred to be on top all the time. He would love getting smothered by that delectable body. He smiled joyfully. Her body wasn't just fine, it was slamming—all doors.

"Is that the lady you were expecting, sir?"

Marcus glanced up, almost annoyed at the interruption. "Yes, that's her."

"Do you want me to escort her over to your table?"

Marcus smiled. *Hold your breath for that one,* he thought. He wouldn't let any other man do the honor. "Thanks, but that's okay. I'll let her know that I'm here."

He straightened his suit jacket and stood, glad he'd worn baggy pants because he had a hard-on that just wouldn't wait. But it had to. Tonight might not be the night but he definitely intended to make plans to get some of that. He'd be a fool to let Dimples22 get away.

Taking a deep breath, he rounded other tables as he crossed the room, noticing she was even more attractive the closer he got.

Have mercy.

His body continued to throb and he forced his stomach to stop quivering when he came to a stop in front of her. "Dimples22?" he asked smiling, silently drooling.

She returned his smile and his stomach began quivering again. She was an Amazon. Full-figured. Built like a brick house. The Statue of Liberty could be her mama . . . if she'd been black. And she had a scent that was arousing him even more. She extended her hand. "See-U-2?" she asked. She also had the throaty voice of Tina Turner. And he loved Tina.

He accepted her hand. Mesmerized. Energized. Harder than nails. "Yes, and I'm glad to meet you."

She blushed and he felt the heat of it in his groin. "I'm glad to meet you, too."

He smiled, liking the way things were going so far. "I have a table for us over this way," he said, still holding her hand, not wanting to let go. It had been years since he'd experienced sexual attraction like this and it was hitting him hard.

"Thanks, just lead the way. And I'm sorry I'm late. Traffic was awful."

His smile widened. "Hey, no problem. You were worth the wait." *No lie.*

She grinned, letting him know that she liked his comment. "Thanks."

He escorted her over to the table and pulled out her chair. Her dress wasn't mini, but it was short and it definitely revealed a nice set of thighs. Thighs he couldn't wait to ease between.

He cleared his throat and moved to take his own chair across from hers. "So, Dimples22, are you going to tell me your real name now, although I can see why you use Dimples."

She had a gorgeous set in both cheeks. He wondered if she had them anywhere else on her body and was dying to find out.

She smiled at him from across the table. "My real name is Francine Conyers."

He nodded. "And I'm—"

"Francine! What are you up to? It's a good thing I followed you after seeing you dressed like that."

Marcus jerked around and stared at the man standing next to their table. He was glaring at Francine and at him. "Wait until I tell Mama about this."

Marcus blinked. *Mama?*

He shook his head, convinced he hadn't heard the word "mama." He stood. "Excuse me, sir," he said to the young man standing beside their table causing a scene. "May I help you?"

The man, who he took to be in his early twenties, no more than twenty-three or twenty-four, turned furious eyes on him. "What is she doing here with you? My parents would kill her if they knew she was messing around with an old man."

Parents? An old man? Marcus quickly glanced at Francine. He could tell she was truly embarrassed. He studied her face and noticed something for the first time . . . something he would have picked up on immediately if he hadn't been so busy checking out her other body parts. Francine did look a bit young, though it was hard to tell underneath her makeup.

"Is anything wrong, sir?"

The waiter had returned, concerned about the scene.

"Yes, there's a lot wrong," the belligerent young man said. "He's out with my sister and she supposed to be at home. She has school tomorrow."

"School!" Marcus and the waiter, along with the couple at the table next to theirs who'd evidently been eavesdropping, all said at the same time.

Marcus stared at Francine in disbelief. "You said you were twenty-eight!"

The belligerent young man snorted, then chuckled. "If that's what she told you, then she lied. She's not twenty-eight. I'm twenty-three and she's seventeen."

"Seventeen! Jesus!" Marcus said, dropping down in his chair. Shocked. Devastated. His hard-on went down like a deflated balloon. He wondered what the age for statutory rape was in Illinois. He had to quickly remind himself that he hadn't touched the girl in any inappropriate way. All those lustful thoughts that had run through his mind didn't count. Or did they?

He met her gaze that was now tear-filled. "We communicated over the Internet for two solid weeks. You have your photo posted and everything. Why did you tell me you were twenty-eight?"

"Because the boys at my school are nothing but piss-pants jerks and I wanted to know how it felt to date a real man."

Marcus was speechless. Then he recovered his voice. He frowned. "Regardless, what you did was deceitful and wrong. We could have both gotten into trouble over this."

Dammit he was thirty-two, fifteen years older than she was. He had a policy of not dating women who were more than five years younger than him. Marcus stood up again and turned to the young man who was still standing beside the table. "And this is your sister?"

The guy nodded. "Yeah, she's my sister. I bet her friend Shari made her up like this. Shari works part-time as a makeup artist for Macy's."

Marcus shook his head, not believing how the night had turned out. He sighed deeply as he pulled a hundred dollar bill from his wallet. "Look, I want you to enjoy dinner with your sister and then make sure she gets home, okay?"

The young man quickly took the money and smiled. "Hey, sure thing. Thanks. I'm sorry Francine screwed you like this."

Marcus nodded. He decided not to tell the kid that Francine most definitely had *not* screwed him, but boy had he intended for her to. He sighed deeply and looked at Francine.

"You placed yourself in a risky situation tonight. You're lucky I'm a gentleman and not some sick pervert. I suggest you pull your photograph and bio off that Web site and start dating guys your own age, no matter what kind of jerks you think they are."

He then turned and walked out of the restaurant.

BOOK TWO

Ponder the path of thy feet,
and let all thy ways be established.
Proverbs 4:26

10

Lance and Asia

Lance was a man who didn't want for anything.

But he wanted Asia Fowler.

He glanced at his watch as the limo cruised down the interstate. He smiled. He couldn't wait to see the surprised look on her face when he showed up at the airport to pick her up. She was expecting the limo but she certainly wasn't expecting him.

He resisted the urge to pour a drink from the mini-bar, deciding he needed all his faculties when he saw her. He inhaled deeply, absorbing the scent of the bouquet of flowers he held in his hand. He was a smooth operator and he planned on using every skill he possessed on her.

Closing his eyes, he couldn't help but remember the moment he had first seen her that day in New York. Even from where he'd been sitting in the audience, he had been captivated by Asia's stunning beauty. Her attractiveness alone could make a man's blood stir. It didn't take much to figure out from the talk she'd given to the packed auditorium that she had been through hell with some man, which made her believe all the things she was preaching. Her past was dictating her present, just as it was for him. The only difference between them was Asia still wanted to believe in things he no longer deemed important.

Like love.

A laugh broke across his lips as he thought about just how wrong she was. Love hadn't stopped his mother from screwing around on his father, and it certainly hadn't held his own marriages together. He had learned the hard way that the three things that worked were charm, praise and money—with the latter being the most impressionable. Ply a woman with money and she would be yours for life . . . or until the next man came along who was willing to put out more. And even though she put up a tough front, Lance had no reason to assume that Asia Fowler was any different.

He shook his head as he remembered her admission that she'd been celibate for over a year. What a waste . . . and he intended to put an end to that. Their affair would be a mutually satisfying one and they would understand one another. Otherwise, he would be opening himself up for all sorts of complications; and complications were something Lance Montgomery didn't do.

Life was good but an affair with Asia Fowler would make things even better.

Following the instructions her publicist had given her, Asia stepped outside the glass doors of the Dallas/Fort Worth airport. She was in town to participate in a three-day sisterhood tour. She had lived in Dallas for five years and loved the city and always looked forward to coming back.

She watched as a limo came to a smooth stop beside the curb and the uniformed driver got out. "Ms. Fowler?"

She blinked, surprised. She wondered how the man had recognized her and thought further that he had timed his arrival perfectly. "Yes?"

"Welcome to Dallas," he said, coming around the car to take her luggage.

"Thank you. I'm looking forward to my visit." She waited while he opened the door for her then slid into the back of the limo. It was only once she was inside with the door closed shut that she saw she wasn't alone.

She inhaled sharply, surprised for the second time that day, and then gave the other passenger who was sitting cool, calm and collected in the back seat a distrustful look. "What are you doing here, Dr. Montgomery?"

He smiled and eased back against the leather upholstery. "I knew you would be coming here and decided to fly in to see you. And these are for you," he said, handing the flowers to her.

Asia took the flowers but glared at him anyway. She didn't want to admit it but her heart was pounding and heat was curling all through her. She also didn't want to admit that she had thought of him often since that day in New York. But thinking of him and tolerating him were two different things.

"You are beginning to become a nuisance, Dr. Montgomery," she said, when the vehicle began to move.

He smiled, as if he was fascinated with her opinion. "And I think you are more beautiful than before," he said and actually meant it. She was dressed in a pair of dark slacks and a crème-colored blouse. There was nothing great about her outfit other than that she looked good in it. He had to concur that it was the outward trimmings that captivated his interest.

Her hair was different. Today she had it flowing down her shoulders instead of having it pinned up on her head as she had the first time they'd met. He had wondered how she would look with her hair down. Now he knew and liked what he saw.

He watched as she leaned over to inhale the scent of the flowers. She lifted her head and met his gaze and his breath caught. "Flattery will get you nowhere," she said softly.

He let out a labored breath and said, "I was hoping it would get me a chance to take you to dinner tonight. I assumed after your flight that you would be hungry."

She tilted her head sideways, to study him. He was right that she was hungry, but she didn't intend to have dinner with him tonight or any night. "You assume too much."

"Do I?"

"Yes." Her stomach fluttered as she continued to look at him, but it wasn't from hunger. It was desire. She was woman enough to recognize it for what it was. He was dressed totally different than before. Today he was wearing jeans and a chambray shirt. She couldn't help but smile. Evidently he bought into the saying, When in Rome do as the Romans do. He was in Texas so he had decided to dress the part, and she had to admit he looked damn good doing it. A Texas-born native probably couldn't look any better.

Her gaze drifted to his mouth; the one feature she had thought of often over the past month. His lips had come just inches from hers, and even now she could recall the heat that he had generated within her. A man's mouth had never been a turn-on for her before, but his was. His lips were full and his mouth was beautifully shaped.

"Will you have dinner with me tonight, Asia?"

The sound of his voice reclaimed her attention, reminding her of who he was and just what he was doing here. She inhaled deeply. She knew for some reason he saw her as a challenge. Her belief that there was such a thing as a lasting relationship actually unnerved him, and it was driving him to seek her out and prove her wrong. In her opinion, he was going to a lot of trouble for nothing. Although she hadn't yet been blessed to engage in a lasting relationship, she believed it was possible and didn't want any woman to sell herself short and just settle for what was out there.

"At least let me know that you're thinking about it."

His voice claimed her attention yet again. She smiled. Lance Montgomery had all the skills needed to break any other woman's resistance down. But he would find out the hard way that he wasn't dealing with just any woman. He was dealing with Dr. Asia Fowler, David Crews's cast-off, his most ardent and well-learned student. Since David, she had raised her standards and quite frankly she doubted that a man like Lance could even meet them.

The last time she had seen him he told her that she had a lot to learn about men. Maybe it was time that a woman showed him that he had a hell of a lot to learn about women, too.

With a toss of her head she met his gaze, held it and locked it in. Ignoring the fierce surge of desire ripping through her, she pulled her confidence level up a notch and said, "Yes, I'm thinking about it."

Once the limo deposited them at the entrance to the Adams Mark Hotel, Asia looked upward at the shimmering skyscraper. She loved this hotel, which was reputed to be the largest in all of Texas. This chain of hotels was always her first choice whenever she traveled.

As expected the lobby was bustling with activity, and as Lance walked beside her toward the check-in desk, Asia couldn't help but wonder if he had really flown into Dallas to see her or if he had business to tend to.

Efficient as ever, it didn't take long for the clerk to check her in and give her a passkey. She turned and met Lance's gaze. He was still there, standing beside her. "I thought you were just being the gentleman by walking me inside. I really didn't expect you to stick around."

"Mmm," he said, grinning down at her. "While *I* might consider myself a gentleman, I've been told many times that my name and that word don't belong in the same sentence."

Asia's lips couldn't help but curve into a smile. She found his honesty refreshing but knew not to let her guard down. "I'm sure there must be a very good reason why."

He chuckled. "Remind me to tell you sometime," he said as they walked away from the desk toward the row of elevators.

"I think I already know." She smiled reluctantly, appreciating the camaraderie between them.

He pushed the button for the elevator and when one arrived, they stepped inside with a couple of other people. She leaned back against the wall, wondering if he actually thought she would let him in her room. He had mentioned in the limo that he was staying at the Adams Mark also, but he hadn't pushed a button for his own floor. With him standing beside her, she couldn't help but feel his control and again thought that this was nothing more than a game to him; a game she intended for him to lose.

As if reading her thoughts, his gaze met hers, and as much as she didn't want to, she read the hot, intense look of desire in his eyes. And her body responded in kind. Ripples, the likes she'd never experienced before, moved up her arms to her chest and down to her stomach. They traveled all over her body and finally settled smack between her thighs.

She inhaled deeply when the elevator came to a stop on the fifteenth floor. Without saying anything, she stepped out when the doors opened. He followed. They walked together toward her room saying nothing. Gripping the passkey in her hand, she turned to face him when they reached her room.

"Well, this is where I must insist that we part ways," she said, trying to keep her voice steady.

His gaze locked with hers. "What about dinner tonight? Like I said, I came to Dallas specifically to see you. I'm flying out in the morning."

Asia dipped her head and regarded him through the veil of her lashes. "Why?"

"Why?"

She lifted her head. "Yes, why are you doing this? Why are you so persistent when I'm not interested?"

He hesitated before answering, as if he was choosing his words carefully. "Because *I'm* interested, Asia. *You* interest me, even though we're worlds apart in our views and ideals. You're single and so am I. I think you are a beautiful woman, one I want to get to know personally as well as intimately," he said smoothly, placing all his cards on the table so there wouldn't be any misunderstanding.

"I heard everything you said that day in New York," he continued. "I know you aren't involved with anyone and at the moment, neither am I, although the last thing I'm looking for is a serious involvement. Life is too short to place restraints on something like pleasure, and as long as the two individuals agree, I don't see anything wrong with it."

It was a pity, Asia mused. When all a man and woman shared was pleasure in the bedroom, they were missing out on everything important outside of the bedroom. She shook her head sadly. "It won't work, Lance."

He lifted a brow. "And why won't it?"

"Because what you want, I'm not delivering."

His brows arched. "Oh, because of the celibacy thing?"

She frowned, then gave a short laugh and took two steps back, feeling the need to distance herself from him starting now. Lance Montgomery was dangerous . . . at least to a woman's heart if she were to let him get close enough. He could run circles around David, and that's what scared her the most.

She hadn't come this far to be taken in by a handsome face, a well-built body and sizzling heat. "Yes, if you want to call it that. I want to think of it as assurance that there's more sustaining my relationship with a man than sex."

He shook his head. "That's going to be a hard sell when that's all some men want from a relationship, Asia. Don't get me wrong, there's always a getting-to-know-you period, but basically men like me don't think of relationships as long term."

She nodded. "And women like me feel it would be unhealthy to become involved in a physical relationship where we have nothing in common with the individual other than our ability to give each other an orgasm."

Lance's chuckle was lighthearted, endearing and sensual. He took a couple of steps closer, recovering the distance, nearly placing her back firmly against the hotel room door. "Yes," he said huskily, sexily, "but orgasms are . . . so good."

Asia fought back the surge of pleasure, the hot, steamy kind that wanted to entrench itself in her bones, and shrugged. "So are carrots."

The sound of Lance's laugh echoed through the hallway and she was grateful it was deserted at the moment. "But I bet you would enjoy an orgasm more . . . especially the Lance Montgomery kind," he whispered, close to her ear. Too close.

She swallowed thickly. Yeah, she bet she would, too, but would never confess that to him. "It's getting late and I really do need to get in my room and rest up."

His lashes fluttered as he lowered them, and she wondered if it was another skill he had perfected when she felt her stomach clench at the gesture. He then slowly lifted his gaze and met hers. Then reaching out, he lifted her chin with his finger. His touch caused her breath to catch and when he lowered his face close to hers she thought she would stop breathing entirely.

"And dinner?"

His lips were so close she thought she could taste him. She was definitely breathing him in, and she couldn't help when something inside her pushed her over the brink and made her lean in closer.

And he took full advantage.

His lips captured hers and it was as if he had to acquaint himself with every taste of her, and his attempt to do so sent a sensuous quiver through every part of her body, coming to rest deep in her womb. It had been a long time since she had been kissed senseless by a man, but never to this degree. She had to admit, accept and acknowledge that Lance Montgomery was definitely a rare breed of man, a perfect combination of pure masculinity and genuine sensuality, and after a year of being celibate she would give anything for one of those orgasms—the Lance Montgomery kind—that he had mentioned moments earlier.

While he continued to plunder her mouth, taking it in a way it had never been taken before, as his tongue expertly mated with hers, her imagination kicked in and she had visions of him sliding his hands over her naked body, cupping her breasts, caressing her belly then methodically replacing his mouth with his hands and continuing the journey down her thighs to settle right in the middle, then slipping a greedy tongue into the wet, slick—

"Harrumph."

Asia jumped and was grateful when Lance pulled back and used his body to block her from the curious prying eyes of a couple who were passing by. She inhaled deeply, appreciating his attempt to protect her identity but figured it wouldn't do any good since she and Lance were standing smack in front of her room.

"That was close," he said, his voice low, his lips close. They were so close that it appeared as if he was getting ready to kiss her again. And dammit, she actually wanted him to. A part of her wanted to feel ashamed but she was too overwhelmed to feel anything but pleasure. She was certain embarrassment would come later. But now she needed to inhale deeply, get her bearings and put as much distance between herself and Lance Montgomery as she could. He had managed to make her lose control; a control it had taken her a struggle to build.

"Dinner?"

She inhaled again. If nothing else the man was persistent. He had all the moves down, from the slow build-up of seduction to the climax with an explosive kiss. "There's no way I can have dinner with you, Lance," she said, slowly drawing in breath and realizing she had spoken his given name for the first time. There was no need for them not to be on a first-name basis when their mouths knew each other so intimately.

She watched as he drew his head back. "So you want to continue to play hard to get?" he asked. He looked disappointed and for a brief moment she felt pretty damn pleased with herself. Evidently it showed and he lifted her chin up to meet his gaze. The disappointed look had been replaced by determination and there was nothing sheer about it. It was the "you haven't seen anything yet" kind.

She held his gaze, intent on not bending; not giving in; not allowing him to catch her at a weak moment ever again. "And what if I do?"

She watched as a slow smile formed on his lips. "Nothing, just as long as you know I won't give up until you're in my bed, Asia. I'm going to enjoy making up for all the time you've been holding out. After going without for a year, I want to see you go up in flames."

His words caused her to draw back, feeling the heat he was talking about. When she discovered she couldn't go any farther since she was backed into her hotel room door, she crossed her arms protectively across her chest as if doing so would stop the nipples on her breasts from aching. "It won't happen."

He smiled. "And I'm totally convinced that it will. I'm going to be your lover. In fact, I'm looking forward to it."

He took a step back. His smile widened and after giving her a confident nod, he turned and walked off.

Asia's arms fell to her side, and as she watched him walk away she knew that she hadn't seen the last of Lance Montgomery.

11

Sam and Tina

Sam released a long whistle as he switched the phone from one ear to the other while slipping into his pants. "She was just seventeen!"

Marcus raised his eyes heavenward and couldn't help but grin. Sam's words reminded him of the opening lyrics to a classic Beatles song. "Yeah, she was just seventeen. Do you know what that means?"

"That you could have gotten arrested." Sam shook his head, not wanting to believe what had happened, but the young women today looked a lot older than they really were. Kathie's daughter Maury had looked a lot older than fourteen. She could have passed for a twenty-year-old.

"I'll never try Internet dating again."

Sam couldn't help but smile. He could tell Marcus was pretty teed off. "Hey, don't give up on it. A couple of people I work with have had great results with it."

"Good. I'm happy for them, but for me I'll stick to the traditional form of dating."

"So what's your next move?"

"Don't know yet but I need to come up with something fast. I had worked up a case of the hots for Francine, and it's hard to get out of the mood if you know what I mean."

Sam smiled. Yes, he knew exactly what Marcus meant. In fact

he was looking forward to his date tonight with Tina Arnold, and from their conversation last night she was looking forward to it as well. "Look, man, I got to finish getting dressed. We're still on for next weekend, right?"

"Yeah, you said Lance is coming into town."

"Right, and I thought we could all get together here at my place. It's kind of iffy whether Phillip can make it. He might have baby-sitting duty."

"Well, I'll be there but I won't have bells on. I'll have a hard-on," Marcus said in a voice that was dead serious.

Sam chuckled. "Sounds like a personal problem you ought to take care of, and keep it to yourself how you go about it."

Less than thirty minutes later, Sam had grabbed his jacket to walk out the door when he heard the doorbell ring. He crossed the room to open it. "Falon?" he said, surprised yet pleased to see her.

"Sorry if I caught you at a bad time," she said, smiling and turning those gorgeous honey brown eyes on him. "But I wanted to share some of this with you. It's an Italian dish I made."

"Why, thanks," he said, eagerly taking the dish from her hands. He tried to ignore the heat that settled in his stomach when their hands accidentally touched.

"It's real easy to make if you want the recipe."

"Hey, I'm game so pass it on." He slumped back against the doorjamb, finding it hard to get his bearings. He was on his way to have dinner with one woman and was standing here having the hots for another.

She laughed. "Okay, I'll drop it off tomorrow. I see that you're on your way out and I don't want to hold you up. Good night and enjoy your evening."

"Thanks." He expelled a thick breath as he closed the door. Boy, she had looked good in those jeans and top. Yeah, he was hot all right but knew he had to have things under control when he saw Tina. Besides, he had already decided that Falon was off-limits. She wasn't the type of woman he was looking to get involved with now or ever.

But as he glanced down at the container in his hand he couldn't help thinking that it was nice of her to remember his interest in Italian food and to share something she'd made.

Walking to the kitchen he couldn't help but inhale the delicious aroma. He couldn't wait to get into whatever it was. And just to think she had offered to share the recipe with him. He hoped it would be something quick and easy that he could prepare for Tina one night. He still entertained the idea of having Tina over for dinner.

Tina.

When he had talked to her on the phone earlier she seemed really excited about seeing him again and he was just as excited about seeing her. He smiled as he headed for the door. Things were looking good for him and he felt blessed.

Falon stood at the window and watched Sam cross the parking lot to his car, slowly letting out a breath she hadn't known she'd been holding. There was something about the man she had liked from the first, although there was a lot that she didn't know about him. But he really seemed like a nice guy.

She smiled. Her cousin Marcy had gotten the lowdown on him from Ms. Candy, a woman in her mid-fifties who lived down the hall and who thought she knew everybody's business. The first day that they had moved in, Ms. Candy had arrived with a welcoming package and a lot of gossip to share. Not wanting to be a party to such nosiness, Falon had excused herself and gone to her room to read, knowing if she was interested about anything she could always get it out of Marcy later.

And she had.

According to Marcy, via Ms. Candy, Samuel Gunn was divorced and worked as an urban planner with the city of Gary. He basically kept to himself but went to the gym at least three to four times a week. Falon had to admit that his body was definitely in good shape.

Another thing Marcy had relayed via Ms. Candy was that so far no woman had spent the night at Sam's place. No man had spent the night there either, which was a possibility you couldn't overlook these days. In fact, according to Ms. Candy, she had never seen him with a woman, but he did have two good-looking male friends who came over occasionally to watch a football game, drink beer and get loud and boisterous.

"When are you going to stop drooling over the guy and do something?"

Marcy's words startled her. She thought her cousin was still taking a nap. She turned around. Marcy was an attractive, shapely, full-figured woman with coffee-colored skin and dark brown eyes. Her fiancé, Wayne, was presently in Iraq and had been there for almost a year. There was no doubt in Falon's mind that when Wayne returned to the States the two would be getting married.

"I like the packaging but I still haven't gotten to really know him," Falon said, moving across the room to the sofa to sit down. She knew how easy it was to get caught up in appearances instead of getting to know the real person. Guys always looked at her, saw the outside packaging and immediately wanted to get with her without really trying to get to know her at all. She no longer indulged in the sensual side of her personality for that very reason.

"And you won't get to know him unless you become more aggressive," Marcy said, interrupting her thoughts. "You've always been the reserved type, even with Donnell, and that's probably why he thought he could screw around on you the way he did."

"I don't want to talk about him," Falon said, not wanting to think of Donnell Robinson and the pain he had caused her.

The two of them had met four years ago while obtaining a degree in culinary arts at Kendall College in Chicago. It was then that they had decided to take their relationship to another level and moved in together.

It wasn't long after that when she discovered just how insecure and immature Donnell was. One day she had come home early to find him in bed with another woman. Hurt and humiliated, she had moved in with Marcy. It had hurt her to no end that he had betrayed her and destroyed what she had thought were their nice, neat plans for a future together.

That had been almost a year ago, and Donnell's actions had made her leery of another serious involvement with a man. It seemed that most of them out there wanted to be cheaters, players or opportunists. Not risking another heartbreak, for the past year she had turned down men's advances to concentrate at excelling at Blakes. She worked in the evenings and often took the weekend duty the other chefs didn't particularly care for. It helped for her to stay and kept her mind occupied. Things had been going just fine until she and Marcy had decided that they needed a bigger place and had moved into this particular apartment complex with Sam Gunn as their neighbor. And it didn't help matters that Marcy was constantly reminding her that she didn't have a love life.

"He's probably involved with someone," she said, thinking how good he had looked when she had dropped off the sampling of chicken cacciatore. Tonight he was wearing dress slacks and a dark pullover sweater. The first day they had met, he had been wearing tattered jeans and a been-around-a-long-time T-shirt. Even then she had thought he looked good. Then another time she had seen him when he had come home from the gym. The brother had looked so toned and built that her body had gotten hot. The man with him had looked good, too, but it had been Sam who had caught her eye.

"Every man is involved with someone, Falon. The question is how serious is the involvement? Unless he's committed, married or engaged, there's nothing wrong with a sistah putting the move on him," Marcy said, meaning every word.

That was the one word that men didn't like to use—committed, Falon thought. She had believed that she and Donnell were committed to each other but he had proved her wrong. In trying to explain his actions, he said most men didn't want to get tied down to one woman these days. She wondered just where that left her and other women who wanted a commitment, love, marriage, family . . . the whole nine yards?

"I prefer not putting the moves on anyone," Falon said, shaking her head. Their mothers were sisters but sometimes it was hard to believe that she and Marcy were related since their personalities were so vastly different. Since they shared the same birthday—although Marcy was twenty-seven and Falon twenty-six—they had always been close while growing up in Portage, Indiana, a stone's throw from Gary.

Falon loved her cousin to death and used to envy her for being so outgoing. Marcy never met a stranger whereas Falon had the tendency to keep people at arm's length until she got to know them. Even the way they went about hooking up with guys was totally different. Before Marcy had become engaged, she was the dating queen. To say Wayne Aiken had taken off her crown was an understatement. Now her cousin was happy and content with being a lady-in-waiting, but then Wayne was to die for. An officer in the Marines, he was one gorgeous brother.

"Even if you aren't ready to get into a serious relationship with a man, then you should consider hooking up with a guy just to have some fun. And Sam Gunn looks like he could be a lot of fun."

Falon contemplated Marcy's words and decided her cousin was right; Sam Gunn looked like the sort of guy you could have fun with. But she wanted more and wouldn't settle for being any man's fun girl.

Tina Arnold was definitely a gorgeous woman, Sam thought as he stared at her from across the table. And he liked what she was wearing, a form-fitting black dress that hugged every curve on her body. She came off as self-confident and he liked that, especially after the time he had spent with Kathie Wilkins. He bet Tina was not a woman who would constantly ask a man how he thought she looked while they made love. She would know that she looked good without asking.

Still on the cautious side, which was something he could appreciate, she had agreed to meet him at an Italian restaurant in Chicago that was known for its good food. The waiter had given them a table in the back and the lights were dim, providing a somewhat romantic atmosphere.

Over dinner they talked about a lot of things as they got to know each other better. She was a transplant who moved to Chicago due to her job. Her home was in Kansas. Her family was still there and she went back to visit whenever she could.

When he had talked about his family, she appeared attentive, interested, something that pleased him. And they had discovered that they were both Aries. It didn't mean a whole lot to him but it apparently meant something to her.

"You wouldn't believe what our horoscope said today," she said excitedly, after taking a sip of her wine.

He met her gaze over the rim of his wineglass, thinking she had a gorgeous pair of lips. "What?"

"Unexpected doors will open today. Be ready to have fun and do something that's not in the norm for you. And don't be afraid to travel on the wild side," she said softly, leaning toward him.

Sam blinked. The intensity of her gaze made his temperature go up a few notches. Was he imagining things or was she hinting at something? He swallowed thickly. Was it only wishful thinking on his part or had she really tried coming on to him?

There was only one way to find out. If he was wrong, he would back off. And if he was right, it would be full throttle ahead. "Do you think these unexpected doors could be bedroom doors?" he asked smoothly, remembering the chapter from *The Playa's Handbook* on how to run a game and get the best results.

He expelled a deep breath when she licked her lips slowly. His gaze then moved to her eyes and saw a build-up of desire there. And then, suddenly, he had a vivid image of her naked and spread-eagle on a bed under him.

"Possibly," she said, not breaking eye contact with him. "There's only one way to find out." She smiled and he felt his body immediately get harder.

"What way is that?" he asked, barely able to get the words out.

She gave him a considered look, smiled again and said softly, "Follow me home and let's see what happens."

Good Lord, Sam thought as he followed Tina back to her place. He never would have thought things would move this fast. But it looked as if he'd been wrong.

She lived in a pretty nice house, he thought as he pulled in the driveway behind her. The neighborhood was pleasantly quiet, and he could see the residents on her street had immaculately manicured lawns. By the time he got out of his car she was standing on her porch under the light, looking through her purse for the keys. The light cast a golden glow on her and that sexy turn-you-on dress she was wearing. "Nice neighborhood," he said, coming to stand beside her.

She looked up at him and smiled, and once again her smile almost took his breath away. "Thanks. I've lived here for a little over a year and love it. It's quiet and the homeowners take pride in the community."

She opened the door, then before they crossed over the threshold, she looked at him and said, "Well, this is it, the first unexpected open door, since I definitely didn't expect to bring you home with me tonight."

He looked at her, studied her face. He wanted to say that he hadn't expected it, either, and if she wasn't comfortable with him being there he would leave. She was the one who was into that horoscope mumbo jumbo, not him. "Are you sure this is what you want?" he decided to ask so there wouldn't be any sort of misunderstandings later.

She met his gaze. "Yes, I believe it's what's in the stars."

He wondered what would happen if she picked up the paper later and discovered that she'd read the wrong horoscope? Thinking that tonight was a night that he would take his chances, he followed her inside and she closed the *unexpected* door behind them.

She put her hand on his. "Wait. I need to turn off my alarm system."

He watched as she switched off the porch light before disappearing around a corner. When she returned moments later, she had turned on a lamp in the foyer. He noted that she had also taken off her shoes and removed her jacket.

"It's safe to come into the living room now. Would you like something to drink?"

What he really wanted was for them to get down to business and open some more doors—namely her bedroom door. "Sure. I'll take a beer if you have one."

She grinned. "One beer coming up. Please make yourself at home."

She walked off toward the kitchen, and he removed his jacket and sat down and settled back against the soft cushions of her leather sofa. Her furnishings were nice. Evidently she was doing well for herself.

"Here you are. I figured you would want it straight from the bottle, but here's a glass in case I was wrong," she said, handing the bottle of beer to him along with a glass.

He placed the glass on the table in front of him and tipped the neck of the bottle toward her and said, "Thanks, and you weren't wrong."

She nodded and wet her lips with her tongue again. The gesture caused his stomach to clench. "I want you to know that I've never done anything like this before," she said softly.

He lifted a brow, smiling after taking another swig of beer. "What? Serve a man beer from a bottle?"

She shook her head grinning. "I've never brought a man home after a first date."

He'd figured as much. He reached out and closed his hand over her wrist. "This is our second date. We met that night for drinks at Slaughter's. If you're not sure about this, Tina, I can leave. There will be other times because I definitely want to see you again."

He was saying one thing and wanting another. All the way from the restaurant while following her here, he couldn't help but imagine how it would be to kiss the corners of that mouth he liked so much. He also looked forward to burying his face between her breasts as well as removing her panties to find her wet and ready for him. The thought of that made him so hot that he finished off the rest of his beer in one huge swallow and placed the bottle on the table next to the empty glass.

After an awkward silence, she slanted a glance at him and said, "I'm sure about tonight, Samuel."

He nodded. Then who was he to argue? He reached out and smoothed his hand down her arm, needing to touch her. "Then it's time for us to open the next *unexpected* door, don't you think?"

She smiled as desire blazed in her eyes. He saw it and his body responded. "Yes, I think you're right."

"Samuel?"

Tina was stretched out, naked and waiting for him on the bed. He had yet to remove his clothes. He had been so caught up in the striptease act she had just performed. No woman had ever put on a striptease for him and his body was still responding in kind. He had stood there, glued to the spot as she had removed every piece of her clothing. And when she had inched a pair of black thong panties down her legs, followed by the slow, daring removal of a matching bra that exposed a pair of gorgeous breasts, he had almost swallowed his tongue. As he took a slow, steadying breath, he thought she was simply stunning; the sort of woman that affairs were made for.

She wouldn't have to call his name twice, he thought, as he quickly removed his clothes and made his way toward the bed.

He placed a pack of condoms on the nightstand, and as he did so, she leaned up and gripped his erection. She licked her lips and lowered her head to him. When her mouth closed around his aroused flesh, he knew he was in deep trouble.

Oh hell.

She might never take a man home on the first date but there was nothing inexperienced about what she was doing with her mouth. The woman was a pro. He knew he should make her stop before it was too late for the both of them. But not now. He would just let her have her way with him for a while longer.

Moments later, reluctantly pulling away, he gently pushed her back on the bed and quickly covered her body with his and immediately took one of her nipples into his mouth, licking and sucking until he heard her whimpering. He slid his hand down, needing to feel her heat, and when he eased his finger inside, she shivered beneath him.

He was about to shift his body to taste her like she had tasted him when she whispered, "No, some other time. I can't wait. I want it in."

He wanted it in, too. He also wanted to see her expression when he put it in. The eyes staring at him were glittering with heat and desire, so much so that they nearly stole his breath. He leaned down to nibble on her lips and she began whimpering again. He felt her nails dig into his shoulder blades but he knew what he had to do before they went any farther.

Leaning up he reached out and grabbed the foil packet off the nightstand and when he had completed the task of putting on a condom, she leaned on one elbow and pushed him backward against the pillows. Her confident smile made him swallow but when she slid atop him the only thing he could do was go still as he remembered one of the handbook rules—beware of women who prefer the "on-top" position all the time.

He swallowed again. Did she want to use the on-top position this time, or did she prefer it all the time? He didn't have time to think about it anymore when she took his erection into her hand and eased down on it, sliding him inside of her to the hilt. It felt good. She felt good. And when she began to ride him with the same know-how and expertise as when she had gone down on him, he knew the answer to his question. She was a woman who evidently liked having sex this way, and for now he couldn't do anything but go along for the ride.

Sam lay beside Tina. She was asleep but he was wide awake. Wow! They had made love three times, and with all three times she had preferred using the on-top position. Although he had suggested they use another position, she had told him that being on-top was her favorite.

Although she had given him the ride of his life all three times, he couldn't help but remember what the handbook had said about women who preferred the on-top position. They tended to be domineering, forceful women who always wanted to be in control. Although he didn't see such behavioral tendencies in Tina, he couldn't help but wonder if such a thing was possible. But then, he wasn't into this for the long haul, and as long as he was having a good time he wasn't going to worry about it.

"Samuel?"

Tina's sleepy voice invaded his thoughts. He leaned toward her and kissed her forehead. "Sorry, I didn't mean to wake you."

"Umm, that's okay," she said sleepily.

He glanced at the clock on her nightstand. It was almost two in the morning. "It's time for me to go," he said, kissing her forehead again. She was tired and she damn well ought to be. The woman could very well have been a horsewoman in another life. She was certainly skillful at riding and he had enjoyed every moment of it.

She yawned and nodded. "Will you please lock the door behind you?"

"All right. What about your alarm?"

"Please set it for me. The code is my birthday."

He frowned. He didn't know exactly when that was. The only thing he knew for certain was that she was an Aries. He rubbed a hand down his face. They had made love three times and he didn't even know the day she was born.

Evidently sensing his dilemma, she lifted her head and looked sleepily at him. "March twenty-fifth, so enter the code zero-three-two-five."

He smiled. "Thanks." He stroked her naked back, thinking an affair couldn't get as good as this. "Call me later when you wake up."

"Okay."

He slid out of the bed and began putting on his clothes, thankful that he had brought enough condoms with him tonight. He had had no idea that he would get so lucky. Having sex with her had been a lot better than the time with Kathie. Tina had practically wiped out the memory of both Kim and Kathie.

He blinked as the image of Falon standing in his doorway, smiling, surfaced. Damn! Not even the recent memory of sex with Tina could banish it.

He glanced over at the bed and Tina's slow, easy breathing let him know she had drifted off to sleep again. She had flipped on her back and his gaze moved slowly across her body. For the longest time he stood there letting his eyes linger on her breasts, thinking that with their fullness and roundness they were definitely the real thing. He'd been absolutely sure after cupping them in his hand and feasting on them like a starving man.

He sighed. He had to leave. But he definitely intended to see her again.

12

Phillip and Marcus

Phillip looked over at Marcus as he drove his Mercedes down the interstate, clearly disgusted. "Why the hell am I going along with this?"

Marcus smiled. "Because you're just as horny as I am and this is one way we can possibly eliminate the problem."

Phillip frowned. "Yeah, but is it legal? The last thing I need is to have my picture plastered across the front page of any newspaper for buying sex."

Marcus rolled his eyes. "You aren't buying sex, Phillip. There's a chance we might not make a hit tonight. The women might take one look at us and decide we aren't what they want. All I'm saying is that if you're nice and grab their interest, then get ready to have a good time. Dylan took me into his confidence and mentioned he was going to a place called Fantasyland and asked if I wanted to come along. I couldn't turn down the chance to see what it was about and he agreed to let me bring you."

Dylan McClain, a devout bachelor, was a fellow engineer who worked on the same floor as Marcus. He had gone on to explain that Fantasyland was a private club that hosted what was called a *fantasy party*, a very private affair arranged by a group of women who wanted to play out their fantasies. Everyone wore masks to protect their identity. Arrangements were made in secret, no names were passed and the only way there could be a hook-up later was if the two individuals agreed and removed their masks in private.

The party was by invitation only and although drinks were served, no drugs were allowed and everyone present was of legal consenting age. Although the things that occurred at Fantasyland were eccentric and oftentimes outlandish, everything was legal. This was a private club and what adults did behind closed doors was their business.

"Hey, this is a nice club," Marcus said as Phillip drove through the huge iron-wrought gates. It was obviously high-class and the other expensive cars parked out front gave credence to that fact. It resembled an upscale country club, but there was nothing country about it.

"I bet there's a bunch of old women inside whose fantasies are to have boy-toys," Phillip grumbled as he straightened his tie. The dress was black tie. If nothing else, he and Marcus definitely looked good.

Getting out of the car he touched his pocket and felt the packets of condoms he had put there. "Hey, you brought protection with you, didn't you?" he asked Marcus as they walked toward the heavily lighted building. Marcus was right. This was definitely an upscale place.

Marcus chuckled. "I brought as many as I could jam into my pockets. Both of them. I plan to make up for lost time." He chuckled again when he heard Phillip mumble something about him being a "greedy ass."

They were met at the door by a huge guy who looked like he wouldn't hesitate to break some bones. As tall as he was big, he was a brotha who was fortunate, or unfortunate depending on how you looked at it, to resemble Mr. T, minus all the gold chains.

"Your invitation," he said in a deep voice that brooked no resistance as he glared at them through fierce, penetrating dark eyes.

Joking around with this guy seemed risky so Marcus decided to do what he was asked and immediately handed their invitations over to him. He felt a tad uncomfortable when the man gave him and Phillip a thorough once-over. Then evidently deciding they were invited guests, he asked, "Full-face or half-face masks?"

Marcus shrugged. He thought that it didn't matter to him then quickly changed his mind. A full face might become a nuisance later. "I'll take a half face."

"I want a full face," Phillip said. Marcus rolled his eyes heavenward. Leave it to Phillip to want to be different.

The man then handed them their masks. "Put these on," he instructed, and after they had done so he stepped aside and said, "All right, you can go on in."

Marcus nodded as he opened the door to go inside. He couldn't help but notice that Phillip was right on his heels, which meant he hadn't wanted to get on the man's bad side any more than he did.

"Wow." That was the one word from both his and Phillip's lips when they stopped inside the lobby and glanced around at the elegant surroundings. Soft music was playing and several couples who were milling about in the lobby didn't even glance their way when they entered. Everyone, like them, was wearing a mask. The women were elegantly dressed in formal wear, some more daringly revealing than others, and the men were either wearing suits or tuxedos.

It seemed like a lot of clothes to take off when it came time to get naked, Marcus thought, as he and Phillip walked along the corridor toward the room where the music was playing. They were again stopped at the entrance but this time it was a woman who guarded the door, and from the way the half-face mask was situated on her face, it was obvious that she was a young woman. By the smoothness of her skin and the curve of her smile, he felt he could safely assume that she was in her early or mid-thirties, not a year older.

"Welcome to Fantasyland, gentlemen. Here are your name tags; you are to continue to use these names whenever you're invited here."

Marcus and Phillip both raised their eyebrows as they glanced down at the items the woman had handed them. Seeing their confusion, she decided to explain. "Real names aren't used here. These will be yours."

"Oh," Marcus said, glancing down at the name he'd been given. His name was High Intensity, and the name that Phillip was given was After Dark. Marcus lifted a brow, wondering where in the heck the idea for the names had come from but then quickly decided he was better off not knowing.

"Once you've placed your name tags on your jackets, you are free to enter."

He smiled at their hostess as they put on their name tags. "Thanks." They opened the door and entered.

Phillip looked around. The room was huge. There was an open bar on one side of the room, and not far away was a huge table filled with hors d'oeuvres. There were more women in attendance than men and again it wasn't hard to see, even with their masks in place, that these were young women. Another factor was the way the gowns fitted some of the women's curves. It made a man want to take a deep breath and holler. He had to admit he'd been wrong. Old biddies didn't have bodies like the women here tonight. A hot sensation flickered over Phillip's skin. This had to be heaven. Hell, he wouldn't mind being any woman's boy-toy tonight.

"Too bad I didn't think to invite Sam," Marcus said glancing around. He widened his eyes when a woman passed right in front of them in a gown that left little to the imagination.

"Hey, don't feel bad," Phillip said. "With the way Sam's luck has been lately, he's probably somewhere getting laid as we speak."

Marcus nodded. "So, do you want to split up and return to this spot later?"

Phillip nodded. "That's not such a bad idea. It might take awhile to circulate."

Marcus nodded again, knowing they intended to do more than just circulate. "And remember, man, playa's have sex, they don't make love."

Phillip smiled. "Yeah, and I don't think I'll have a problem with that tonight."

Marcus grinned as he glanced at his watch. "Let's say we meet up here again at midnight. That gives us three hours."

"Okay, and be back here on time."

Marcus chuckled, thinking of a number of reasons why he could get delayed. "And if I'm not?"

Phillip glared at him. "You just better make sure that you are or I'm going to leave your ass. I promised Chandra that I would get up and take her to Sunday school in the morning."

The two men split up and each hoped like hell that when they met up again at midnight they would have something to smile about.

"Oh, my goodness, they gave you the name High Intensity for a reason," the woman said as she wrapped her legs around Marcus's waist, angling her body as she urged him to go for another round.

And Marcus didn't mind obliging. He was long overdue and was certainly putting his condoms to good use. He had put on a double just in case. He began thrusting harder, going deeper, increasing the pace and driving them both over the brink toward their third orgasm of that night.

Cries of pleasure were torn from their lips and he collapsed against her, his head coming to rest between breasts that he knew weren't the real thing. At the moment, he could care less since he was certain the rest of her had been.

"Wow, that was incredible," the woman, whose code name was Breathless, whispered into the silence. He leaned up slightly, withdrawing from her and smiled as he looked at her face . . . at least the part that the half-face mask didn't shield. He knew she was twenty-six with a birthday coming up in a couple of weeks. She said that she had been a good girl all her life and wanted to let her hair down for once. She had said that much about herself but nothing else. Oh, and she had also shared that her hidden fantasy had always been to do a black man. And boy she had really done him . . . three times. He'd always heard that white women had mouths made for blow jobs and he was inclined to believe it.

"Yeah, that was incredible," he said, levering up onto his elbows and thinking about all the things they had done together so far. He sighed deeply, knowing what he had to do. "Excuse me for a minute while I use the bathroom."

"Sure."

He knew she was watching him as he grabbed another condom packet off the nightstand and waked naked toward the bathroom. To his surprise, the huge clubhouse had private rooms that took up five entire floors, and he figured that at one time the place had probably been a hotel. He shook his head. People with money could do just about anything, even live out their sexual fantasies.

He couldn't help but smile while he changed condoms. What he'd told Breathless was true. What they had shared had been incredible. At first when he was about to enter her, he realized that this was the first time he would be making love to a woman since Dottie, and for a brief moment he had frozen. But then, a calm had settled over him and he knew that he had to get on with his life. Besides, Dottie would understand that if he didn't get *some* real soon he would go stone raving mad. For him going sixteen months, eight days, twelve hours and twenty minutes without sex was way too long.

When he walked out of the bathroom, he found Breathless reclining in bed waiting for him. He paused in the doorway, admiring her nakedness as she admired his. He knew without a doubt that her fantasy had been fulfilled, and the way she was licking her lips, she wasn't through with him yet.

But then, he thought as he slowly moved back toward the bed, he wasn't through with her either.

Just his luck to get a woman with issues.

Phillip watched as she nervously clasped her hands together. She was wearing a full-face mask and her code name was Brazen, but so far he couldn't find anything brazen about her.

They had been in the room for over an hour and they still hadn't made it to the bed yet. This was her first time at Fantasyland and her fantasy was to unleash her sexuality and get over the embarrassment of her desires. From what she was saying, he knew she and her husband were no longer together, and during the time they had been married he was very unexciting in the bedroom. The missionary position was enough for him and the suggestion that they try anything else would have shocked him. So she had suppressed her desires for something "more."

As Phillip listened to her talk, there was something about the sound of her voice that he found oddly familiar. A part of him felt like he had heard it before but at the moment he couldn't remember where. He started to ask her if there was a possibility that they had met before, then quickly decided that wouldn't be wise since anonymity was one of the key elements at Fantasyland.

He watched through lowered lashes as she took a sip of her wine. They were sitting opposite each other. She was sitting in a loveseat completely naked, and he was sitting in a wingback chair shirtless, barefoot and ready to roll whenever she was. Her being comfortable with her nudity at least was a good thing, he thought.

"I decided to see a therapist and after a few weeks of counseling, she suggested I come here and let everything out," she said, leaning slightly forward in the seat. "So here I am."

"I'm your fantasy man for tonight, sweetheart," he said softly, soothingly, deciding that he had heard enough to get a pretty good picture of what she needed. A part of him couldn't understand some men's opinion that it was okay for them to unleash their innermost sexual desires but for a woman to do so meant she was less than a lady. A couple, especially a married one, should feel free to indulge in every aspect of the sexual experience. Besides, in his book, a man had an obligation not only to himself but to his woman to make sex romantic and mutually pleasurable.

Phillip slowly stood and crossed the room to her, and his heart clenched at the look of uncertainty he saw in her eyes through the mask. He stopped, inhaled gently and said, "I think couples should make sex more interesting by varying the sexual positions, using lotion, oils, candles, even toys if that's what they want. I don't consider a woman who's willing to explore new methods a freak but someone with the common sense not to rely on an orgasm as the ultimate sexual outcome.

He slowly reached out his hand to her. "Come and let me show you that some men like having a wild woman in their beds."

He watched as she stared at him through her mask; the same way he was staring at her through his. Then he felt it. The way the atmosphere in the room shifted, the way the temperature seemed to rise. He watched as she took a long sip of her wine, finishing it off. Leaning forward, she placed her glass beside his empty one on the table. She then lifted her gaze back to his and said softly, "I don't know you but for some reason I feel that I can trust you."

Phillip inhaled deeply. He knew it had taken a lot for her to say that. "And I won't let you down, Brazen." She smiled. "I'm depending on it, After Dark."

She slowly stood and placed her hand in his, and he gently tugged her to him. Something deep within pulled at him and he knew, without a doubt, that he had to kiss her. He lowered his mouth to hers.

Since they were both wearing full-face masks, kissing wasn't easy, but because of the soft material the masks were made of, they managed it.

He continued kissing her and rejoiced when he heard her whimper of pleasure. He captured her tongue with his and a slow, sensuous mating began. He loved her taste and knew he could lose himself in it.

He slowly pulled back. He didn't want her to feel rushed, but God he was anxious to unleash that sensuous sexual being inside of her. He wanted to be the one to experience her wild side when she lost control. For all the years she had suppressed her desires, she damn well deserved it. "Tell me," he whispered softly. "Tell me what you want to do."

She leaned into him and placed her arms around his neck, bringing their bodies close even though he was still wearing his pants. But the feel of her breasts, firm, high, beautiful, pressing against his bare chest sent a sizzling sensation all through him. He knew she felt it and she met his gaze through the eye openings of the masks, held it and said, "I want to finish undressing you."

The way she'd said it let him know she had never undressed her husband before. Reaching out he gently smoothed his hand up her thigh. Because of the mask, he couldn't watch her reaction to his touch but he could hear her swift intake of breath. He also felt the tremor that ran through her, and her response sharpened every nerve of desire within his body.

"All right, take off the rest of my clothes."

He watched her hesitate briefly before reaching out to slowly slip his belt from his pants. He inhaled deeply. The anticipation was about to kill him but he was determined to let her remain in control.

"Umm, looks like I'm having a little trouble here," she said, tugging at the zipper, trying to pull it down. He understood her dilemma. He was hard. He was huge. And his erection was straining against his fly, making it difficult.

"Is it possible for you to suck it in?" she asked.

Her question, as serious as it was, amused him. "Trust me, sweetheart. There is no way I can suck it in. Here, let me help."

Together they were able to make it work and finally got his zipper down. He then took a step back and eased his pants down his legs then tossed them aside. That left him in his underwear and she seemed fascinated that he was wearing a pair of black bikini briefs that clearly showed why zipping down his pants had been difficult.

She looked down at him, studied him with all the intensity of a would-be-shopper who was buying fresh fruit at the market, and then she reached out and touched him, as if to make sure it was real and that it wouldn't bite. As if totally fascinated, she continued to stroke him and for a moment he wondered if she realized just what her touch was doing to him. It was arousing him even more and he watched as her eyes got larger when she saw his shaft do likewise.

"I wish I could let you stand here and play with me, but I don't think it would be a good idea," he said, barely able to get the words out through clenched teeth as he tried to hold on to what little control he had left. "I think we should get into the bed, don't you?"

She released him, met his gaze and nodded her head. He then swept her into his arms and carried her over to the bed and gently placed her on it. He watched as she scooted back against the pillows and lay on her back, watching him. And waiting.

He backed away and slowly removed his briefs; he then reached toward the nightstand and picked up the pack of condoms he had placed there earlier. He glanced over at her. "Do you want to cover me?"

She licked her lips like he had just asked her to share a bowl of strawberry ice cream with him. "Umm, what if I don't do it right?"

He chuckled. "Trust me. I'll be your backup. I'll make sure its done right."

She nodded and leaned over toward him. Taking the condom packet from his hand, she, with painstaking slowness, rolled the condom onto him. He held his breath during the entire process. Her hands on him felt so damn good.

"There. What do you think?" she asked, leaning back to admire her handiwork.

"I think, that if I don't get in that bed with you soon, it would have been all for nothing."

She chuckled and he knew that she understood his meaning. When she scooted back in the middle of the bed, nonchalantly presenting her back to him, his breath caught when he saw the tattoo of a star near her shoulder blade. He blinked. He had seen that same tattoo on a woman before, but when? Where?

Star.

Suddenly he gulped in a deep breath of air as he remembered. He blinked thinking he was surely mistaken but knew it was true. She wasn't a divorcée but was a widow.

"You okay?"

His gaze met hers and he inhaled deeply. No, he wasn't okay. He wanted to get the hell out of there. He took a few steps back.

"What's wrong?"

He slowly closed his eyes. This was the woman who had been haunting his dreams for the past month. The woman who had come across as a self-assured, confident female and it felt like a punch in his stomach to know she had issues like everyone else.

He shook his head. No, her issues weren't like everyone else's. They were personal and were hers alone.

And they were issues that he could help her resolve tonight.

"After Dark?"

He was beginning to hear the panic in her voice. He stepped back closer to the bed, needing to reassure her. "For a moment there, I was almost in a daze. I've never seen a more gorgeous body before," he said truthfully.

He saw her relax. "Thank you."

He leaned over and kissed her lips. "Are you ready for me?"

"Yes."

Without saying another single word, he slipped into the bed beside her and gathered her into his arms. He felt her initial slight resistance and then he began talking to her, telling her how special she looked, how much he wanted to be with her, make love to her, get inside of her. He knew she was listening. He knew she was taking it all in and letting her mind and body respond to his words. He held her close, kissed her through the mask and continued to kiss her even more when she began withering under him. What they were about to share was supposed to be pure fantasy and he was making doubly sure that it was.

"After Dark!"

He wanted her to call him by his real name like he wanted to call her by hers. But he knew he couldn't do so. He couldn't ruin the moment for either of them. He drew her mouth back to him and kissed her again and when he knew they needed to breathe, he released her mouth then lowered his hand past her stomach to the area between her legs. She was wet. She was hot. And she had the most arousing scent that had ever come from a woman. It teased his nostrils, making him itch to get inside of her.

"I want to get naughty."

Hearing her words, he slowly pulled back, needing to see her eyes. They were staring at him and he read the anticipation in them. "And I want you naughty," he said.

She didn't say anything for a few moments and then she scooted to the other side of the bed and said, "Move to the middle of the bed and lay flat on your back."

He didn't hesitate to do what she asked. He saw her smile, satisfied that he had done what she'd requested without asking questions. Her gaze then traveled over his naked body and burned everywhere it touched. She dropped her gaze for a second to his middle, zoomed in on his aroused shaft before meeting his eyes with hers once more.

She leaned over and touched her lips to his. "I've always . . ."

When she hesitated, as if not sure she could tell him what she wanted, he said softly, "We'll do things whatever way you want, Brazen. Don't be afraid or ashamed to tell me. When making love, nothing a couple feels comfortable in doing is wrong."

She met his gaze and he wanted her to believe he would give her anything she wanted and would let her do anything she wanted. To-night, for her, there was no limit.

"I've always wanted to be made love to . . ." She cleared her throat and said quietly, "Doggie style. I—I've never tried it that way before but I've always wanted to. Can we?"

Phillip swallowed deeply. She'd made such a simple request. She didn't want to bring out the whip, handcuffs or blindfolds as he'd assumed. "Yes, if that's what you want then that's what it's going to be." He scooted to the edge of the bed. "You'll need to get in the middle on all fours."

The bed dipped slightly as she did and he couldn't recall a time he had seen any woman in this position who looked so desirable. He wanted her so bad. He would be giving her what she wanted and in the process he would be getting what he wanted as well.

"Ready?" he asked, feeling himself get harder by the second just looking at her and the position she was in.

"Yes."

He slowly moved behind her on his knees and snaked a muscled arm around her middle and pulled her tightly against him. He sucked in a deep breath when his staff came in contact with her body. Her scent, one of a woman in heat, filtrated his nostrils, causing his already heightened senses to become electrified.

"I just want to make sure you're ready for me," he whispered as he leaned close to her ear, letting his warm breath stir heat on her neck. He felt her shiver when he took his finger and dipped inside of her. Oh, yeah, she was ready all right.

"You sure you want this?" he asked, letting his fingers stir inside of her for a while, liking the purring sounds she was making.

"Y—yes, I'm sure."

"Good." He licked a path across her shoulder blade, where her tattoo was, while leading his body inside of hers. They both sucked in a sharp breath when he began entering her this way, his pulsing length going deep inside of her. He felt her tight body stretch to accommodate him, and he pulled her closer against his where they connected in such a way they appeared as one being.

When he had gone in to the hilt, he slowly began to move, skin against skin, the slapping of flesh. The sensations sent intense pleasure through all parts of Phillip. This wasn't his first time making love to a woman this way but to him this was the first time it had mattered. He heard her breath catch and hitch with his every thrust. He closed his eyes as a muscle twitched in his jaw and his hands tightened around her waist, pulling her back closer to him. And when he felt her shudder he knew what was happening and increased the pace and depth of his thrusts.

Violent shudders tore through their bodies. Deep tremors snatched their breaths. He experienced it, an orgasm like no other. And as a warm sensation filled his chest, he blasted across the stars, paid a visit to the moon and took a peek at Mars. What he felt was shattering. Explosive. A towering inferno.

And a part of him wondered if he would ever be able to return to earth as a normal man.

Hours later, Phillip eased away from Terri. Getting out of bed, he stood and began putting his clothes back on. When he had gotten completely dressed, he walked over to the bed and looked down at her. It was best if he left before she woke up.

The mask was still in place and leaning over he gently pushed it aside enough to kiss her cheek before putting it back in place. Now that he knew her identity, he wasn't sure what he would do. One thing was for certain, he would never forget this night and all the different lovemaking positions they had tried. Any man in his right mind would be thrilled to have such a wanton and sensuous woman in his bed every night. Inhaling deeply he turned and left the room, closing the door behind him.

He saw Marcus just where they had agreed to meet. "Ready?" he asked when he reached him.

Marcus frowned. "Hell, yeah, I'm ready. I've been standing here for thirty minutes. You're the one who was adamant about us leaving at midnight."

"Sorry."

For a few moments neither man said anything as they walked out of the building toward their car. "Hey, I had a good time tonight," Marcus said into silence. "I intend to come back if I can get an invitation. What about you?"

Phillip shook his head as he unlocked the car doors and slid into the driver's seat. "No, I won't be back."

Marcus shot a quick look at him. "Why not? Were you disappointed?"

Not by a long shot, Phillip thought. But he knew he couldn't explain things to Marcus. It was something he couldn't even tell Sam. What had happened tonight was his secret and his alone. "No, I wasn't disappointed," he said honestly. "In fact I was totally satisfied with the way things turned out."

"Then what's the problem?"

He glanced over at Marcus. "There isn't one and I don't want to talk about it." He knew his tone was a little sharper than he'd meant for it to be.

"Hey, man, there's no reason to get testy."

Phillip sighed deeply, thinking, If only Marcus knew.

13

Lance and Asia

"Ms. James is waiting for you so you may go right on in, Ms. Fowler."

Asia smiled at Julia Palmer, her agent's secretary. "Thanks, Julia."

She opened the door to Melissa's office, expecting to find her agent buried knee deep in manuscripts, but stopped abruptly when her gaze lit on Melissa, another man and, of all people, Lance Montgomery. The two men were sitting around Melissa's desk chatting like the three were old friends. Everyone looked up, saw the surprised expression on her face and all conversation stopped.

Asia's gaze locked on Lance when the two men stood. She remembered the last time they had been together in Dallas and the kiss they had shared. That had been three weeks ago but she recalled it like it had happened yesterday. Her mouth still tingled whenever she thought about it. That kiss had blindsided her.

"Hello, Asia. It's good to see you again."

Lance's voice, low and deep, sent heat throbbing in her stomach and started her heart pounding in her chest. She inhaled deeply, forcing back a full-fledged desire attack. What on earth was Lance doing here in Melissa's office?

She tried not to notice how good he looked wearing an expensive-looking business suit and white dress shirt. The man dressed like the money he made.

"Lance." She acknowledged his greeting but refused to lie and say that it was good seeing him again, too. She shot a glance at her agent, giving her a look that clearly said, *You better tell me what's going on.* She watched Melissa nod perceptively.

"Come in and join us, Asia," Melissa said cheerfully, standing and coming around her desk, taking her hand and all but yanking her into the room and closing the door behind her. "You know Lance Montgomery, and this is his agent, Carl Kilgore."

"Mr. Kilgore," Asia greeted, offering the older man her hand.

She watched him study her under dark bushy brows while saying, "Ms. Fowler, this is my pleasure. I've heard a lot of wonderful things about your book."

She fabricated a smile on her lips thinking the man was full of it, just like the author he represented. "Really, Mr. Kilgore, and who gave my book such a glowing review? Certainly not Dr. Montgomery since we see things totally differently."

"And that's what makes our plan so wonderful," Melissa said excitedly.

Asia cast a quick glance at her agent. "What plan?"

When the room got completely quiet again, Asia frowned. "I think someone should tell me what's going on." She gave Melissa a "and I mean now" look.

"Asia . . ." Melissa began in a placating tone, picking up on her mood, which at the moment wasn't a good one. "Dr. Montgomery and Mr. Kilgore have approached me with a wonderful publicity idea for the book."

Asia crossed her arms over her chest, clearly annoyed and agitated. "Whose book?"

"Both yours and mine."

Asia wished that Lance hadn't spoken. The sound of his voice washed over her, turning her inside out. She turned and stared at him for a long, uncomfortable moment and he returned her stare.

"Yes, both books," Melissa piped in enthusiastically. "If you'll take a seat, I'll explain everything."

Asia inhaled slow and deep. She didn't want to take a seat. She didn't want to be within a hundred feet of Lance Montgomery, much less in the same room.

"Come on, Asia, and sit," Melissa said jovially, almost pushing her down in the extra chair Mr. Kilgore had suddenly produced. She glanced around the room and saw the enthusiastic looks on Melissa's and Carl Kilgore's faces. Lance was still staring at her, saying nothing.

"Okay, what's this publicity idea?" she asked. Melissa never got excited about anything, and Lance's features were unreadable.

"I'll let Dr. Montgomery explain everything," Melissa said, hurrying back to take the seat behind her desk.

Asia looked at Lance, waiting. He leaned back in his chair and met her gaze. She saw something in his eyes that the others weren't privy to. It was a look of predatory coolness. "What you said earlier was true. Our books are vastly different because of our opinions on how people should handle relationships."

She lifted a brow. "And your point?"

The corner of his mouth lifted into a smile, and as much as she didn't want it to happen, his smile sent full sexual awareness through every bone in her body. "My point, Asia, is that those differences in opinions oftentimes cause controversy, and controversy equals sales."

She nodded; no wonder Melissa was all giddy. Although her book was doing well, Melissa would try anything to make it do even better. "So what are you suggesting?"

Lance leaned closed to her chair. "We're suggesting that you and I do a televised talk show together, giving our individual take on things, stirring up talk, questions and opinions. This will tantalize the viewers who will want to purchase both books to see what all the hoopla is about."

"I've already ran the idea by your publisher, Asia, and their marketing department thinks it's a wonderful idea," Melissa piped in.

Asia sighed. They would since they wouldn't have to deal with the likes of Lance Montgomery on a professional or personal level.

"Lance's publicist has already spoken with several television networks who are undeniably interested," Mr. Kilgore was saying. "The finer details can be discussed later. All we need now is for everyone to agree."

"No, I won't agree." Asia's response was quick, automatic and firm. It also had two of the three people in the room looking at her like she had lost her mind. The third person was just looking at her. And . . . she noticed something else; he was smiling. He'd known she would be difficult and refuse the offer. She had a feeling that he had been expecting it, which made her wonder what the hell he was trying to pull.

"May I speak with Asia alone for a moment?"

Lance's request, spoken in a voice that tantalized her senses and heightened her awareness of him more than ever, sent a sensuous charge through her. She was about to open her mouth and tell him that no, he couldn't talk to her alone, when she decided it was best to have a face-off with him once and for all. His pursuit of her was only a game to him; a predatory game he was hell-bent on continuing. In the process, her peace of mind was taking a direct hit and her body was getting pummeled as well. She was feeling things and thinking things that she hadn't in years. And she wanted things. Things she didn't need to have; things she would regret desiring later.

"Of course you may," Melissa said, and Asia recognized that the excitement in her voice was not as high as it had been earlier. Melissa knew her well enough to know that she didn't like surprises, and better yet, that she didn't like being backed up against a wall about anything.

Asia watched as Melissa and Mr. Kilgore quickly left the room, leaving her alone with Lance. Deciding not to sit any longer, she stood and crossed the room to the window and looked out. It was early fall and the city of New York looked chilly on the outside, but here in this office she felt heat, a sizzle and slow-stirring blaze.

"I knew you would be difficult." The sound of Lance's voice behind her stirred that blaze even more.

She turned around. "Then why did you bother?" she snorted

indelicately. She was angry with him but more so with herself. She knew what Lance Montgomery was all about yet she was being drawn to him anyway. However, she was determined to fight the attraction with everything she had.

Moving with predatory grace, he came to stand in front of her. His gaze held hers. "Because I refuse to give up on you."

Lance sighed deeply, knowing he had just spoken the truth. Never in his life had a woman made him take leave of his senses like this one had. He wondered what there was about her that was making him act so irrationally. He didn't know the answer but whatever it was, it went beyond his scope of comprehension. She was beautiful—he would give her credit for that. But he had been involved with beautiful women before so it couldn't be just a physical thing, although he had to admit that she was one of the most innately sexual creatures he had ever met. And what was so intriguing was that she didn't flaunt it, use it or apply it to her full advantage. He would bet the millions he'd made from the sale of all his books that she wasn't even aware it existed.

But he was aware, as fully aware as a man could be about a woman he wanted. Still, there was something else that kept him coming back, made him determined to hear his name flow from her lips in the heat of passion—passion she had denied herself from experiencing for a year. Yes, Asia Fowler was a challenge but deep down she was becoming more than that. He just couldn't figure out what.

"Then that proves something to me, Dr. Montgomery," Asia said, breaking into his thoughts.

He continued to hold her gaze. "And what's that, Dr. Fowler?"

"That you aren't as smart as you look."

Lance couldn't help but laugh. That statement coming from any other woman would have been an insult, but coming from Asia it meant he was getting to her since she wasn't into sheer rudeness. He saw something beyond the façade she was trying to display. He had been with enough women to know the signs. Regardless of how much she wanted to deny it, regardless of how much she didn't want it to be so, she was as unequivocally hot for him as he was for her.

He could actually feel her wanting and her longing. A year was a long time to deny the things that made you a sexually feminine, very sensuous woman. And more than anything, he wanted to be the man who brought her back around, made her see things, feel things, experience things. His back was the one he wanted her to scratch when she reached her first orgasm after a full year. He wanted to be the one inside her when the explosion hit, an entire year's worth of pent-up passion. A thrill raced through him at the thought.

It also pushed him to use another approach.

He tilted his head and studied her for a moment, then said, "You're actually afraid of me, aren't you?"

He watched her lips slip into a frown at the same time that he heard her derisive snort. "Afraid? Why would I be afraid of you?"

"Because I remind you that you have needs."

Asia's heart began to race under the weight of his words. As much as she wanted to deny what he had just said, she couldn't. He had just stated the truth. Oh, she knew she was a woman with needs but he had a way of making that fact monumental whenever she saw him. He had a way of making her feel sexy without saying a single word. His look alone spoke volumes, and most times she was able to read him loud and clear whenever she saw him.

"You're making a mistake, you know, turning down my offer for us to do a television show together. I think once you really think about it, you'll agree it's a good idea—an opportunity of a lifetime. You're a businesswoman as much as I am a businessman, and a key to book sales is good marketing and promotion. You have to be ready to capitalize on the hype, take advantage of whatever publicity can be generated."

Asia frowned. Deep down she knew he was right, but still . . .

"However, I can understand if you're afraid of me, afraid of the things I make you feel."

She watched as a sexy smile touched his lips—lips that she knew were capable of giving her pleasure. They were lips she wanted to feel on hers again, lips she wanted to reacquaint with their taste. She wanted him with a fierceness that was downright uncharacteristic for her, but which was becoming second nature when it came to him.

Asia sighed deeply. Her sensual reaction to him disturbed her, but she was never one to run away from a challenge. She had to prove to herself once and for all that she was strong. She had overcome the pain David caused her and she was determined to overcome Lance Montgomery's need to break down her defenses.

Needing distance from him she walked across the room and settled her bottom on the edge of Melissa's desk, ignoring the way Lance's gaze shifted to her legs when her skirt eased up a few inches. Clearing her throat to reclaim his attention, she lifted her chin and met his gaze. "I am not afraid of anything and, you're right, I know a good business deal when I hear one. But we need to get a few things straight, Lance."

"What?"

"I understand this is a game you need to play out and that I'm a part of it. But be forewarned, I've told you my position on things. I like my life just the way it is. I don't need you to change it nor do I need you to worry about me missing out on some great sexual experience. I live my life the way I choose, with or without a man in it. I intend to one day have a relationship with a man, but it will be with a man who wants me with a passion above all else and especially above anyone else. He will be a man who is ready to commit his life to me, to be mine exclusively, and place me not only above all other women but make me his *only* woman. That's the only man I will sleep with. Are you willing to step up to the plate and be that man?"

There, she had laid her cards on the table. He knew where she stood and she knew just as sure as it was Thursday that she had placed him in a corner, a corner that he had no intention of remaining in. It was his nature. Men like him didn't know the meaning of exclusivity. They wanted to have their cake and eat it, too, and unfortunately some women, those who were still vulnerable, gave them a huge slice with all the icing. She had been that type of woman once, but refused to be one again.

She watched as something flickered in his eyes and knew his answer before he spoke the word. "No. I refuse to give any woman that."

His words were almost a snarl and suddenly she knew. Some woman . . . possibly even more than one . . . had hurt him, and a part of her felt his pain. He was safeguarding his heart the same way she was safeguarding hers. They were survivors but their approach to living was vastly different.

She stood and met his gaze unwaveringly. "Then we understand each other. We want totally different things out of a relationship and I suggest we always remember that. I'll do that televised show with you and will have our publicists work out the necessary details. There is no reason the two of us will need to contact each other."

Without giving him a chance to say anything else, she walked out of the office.

Hours later, back in Chicago, Lance stood in front of the window in his living room and looked at the lake, drinking a glass of wine and trying to get his bearings. Asia thought she was calling the shots in this game but he had news for her. He had yet to play his hand.

He wondered how much longer it would take to break her resolve and make her see reason. All this restrained lust he was feeling for her had him at a disadvantage, but he would deal with it because the fruits of his labor would be well worth it.

He turned when his attention was drawn to the door at the sound of a key being inserted. Then it opened.

"I wasn't sure you would be here, Lance," the woman said softly, entering his home and closing the door behind her. She removed her coat and tossed it across the sofa.

Lance shook his head as he gazed at the strikingly beautiful woman who, although twenty-four looked barely twenty-one, and dressed accordingly. She was wearing jeans that could have been painted on her body and a midriff top that was outright ridiculous for the chilly Chicago weather. Half of her belly was showing for heaven's sake, and she was proudly displaying a ring in her navel.

"Why didn't you call to let me know you were coming, Carrie?" he asked, taking another sip of his wine.

She smiled. "Logan thought I should surprise you."

"Figures." He crossed the room to refill his wineglass.

His sister shook her head then walked slowly over to him. She wrapped her arms around his neck and smiled up at him, brushed her lips across his cheek. "I'm glad to see you but I want to know why you're in such a grumpy mood? If I didn't know better, Lance, I'd think you have woman problems."

14

Sam and Falon

Sam smothered a frustrated growl as he looked at the meal in front of him. He had tried the recipe twice and it still didn't taste anything like the one Falon had prepared. He'd thought he had died and gone to heaven when he had dug into the sampling she had dropped off that night, and the next day he had come home to find the recipe in an envelope she had slid under his door.

He planned on preparing a home-cooked meal for Tina this coming Wednesday night. Since their first night of sexing, they had gone out two other times and each time the evening had ended with him going back to her place.

He actually liked the way their relationship was going, which he considered hassle-free. She wasn't looking for a serious relationship and neither was he. She was one of those women who enjoyed being a playa as much as men did. She didn't question him about what he did when they weren't together and he didn't question her. They were both into safe sex and that was what was important.

All of that should have satisfied his mind since he wanted nothing more than a casual affair, no strings and no commitment. However, the traditional man in him that had always dated a woman exclusively often wondered if she was seeing someone else— although it was her business if she was. But still, he couldn't help but wonder, especially since she had asked him not to call her on certain days of the week, saying those were days for herself. He had a gut feeling that those were actually her days with someone else. And the only other uneasiness he had . . . if you called it that . . . was a minor one, her obsession with the stars. Each time they were together she would quote their horoscope like it should be as important to him as it was to her. Although he wasn't seeing any-one other than Tina, he knew he could if he wanted to without feel-ing like a cheater. That was the beauty of being a playa.

Returning his thoughts back to the meal that sat in front of him, he wondered what he had done wrong. It tasted good but he knew something was missing. He wondered what Falon's secret was since the recipe was pretty straightforward. Evidently he had gone wrong somewhere, but for the life of him he didn't know where. Tonight was only Saturday but he believed in planning ahead. He was not a last-minute kind of guy.

He wondered if Falon was busy tonight and if she would be will-ing to come over and possibly walk him through the recipe? There was only one way to find out. Since she had included her phone number at the bottom of the recipe, saying if he had any questions about anything to give her a call, he thought this was a problem that constituted a call.

Leaving the kitchen he walked across the room to the phone. For some reason her number was locked into his memory. He tried to convince himself that was because he had been working with the recipe so long it had put her phone number constantly in his face.

He was satisfied with that reasoning. Now if he could only come up with a good reason as to why he couldn't shake the feeling of excitement flowing through him at seeing her again, holding a con-versation with her, looking into those beautiful honey brown eyes of hers.

"Hello?"

He recognized her cousin's voice. He and Marcy had met one evening when they had both been coming in from work. In fact, over the past month, he had seen more of Marcy than he had of Falon. Whenever he asked about Falon, Marcy would say that she was at work. He wondered just how many hours she put in during a given week since she was practically never at home. Didn't she have a social life and if she didn't, why not?

"Hi, Marcy, this is Sam, your neighbor down the hall. I was wondering if Falon is home?"

"Yes, she is, Sam. Hold on."

He heard a couple of doors opening and closing before Falon came on the line. "Hello?"

The sound of her voice made his skin tingle and he had to admit, even to himself, he liked the sound of it. "Hi, Falon, this is Sam. Thanks again for the recipe but I seem to have run into a problem."

He took the next couple of minutes to tell her what he knew, or what he didn't know, about making chicken cacciatore, and how after following the recipe, his did not taste like the one she had prepared.

He could hear her chuckle on the other end. The sound sent heat all the way up his spine. "When will you try preparing it again?"

"I'm game now if you're not busy. I wouldn't want to take you away from anything."

There was only a moment of hesitancy before she said, "I'm not doing anything but reading. I'll be over in a second."

He smiled. "Thanks, Falon. I appreciate it."

He sighed deeply after hanging up the phone. She was definitely the sort of neighbor to have around, one who wouldn't mind helping you in a pinch. She was also good to look at. He sighed again, remembering that all she was and could ever be was his neighbor, even if he was honest enough to admit that he was attracted to her.

He moved around the living room, picking items up so the place wouldn't look sloppy. Marcus and Sam had dropped by earlier that day. Marcus had told him about how they had spent last Saturday night at a private club called Fantasyland, and had had a lot to say about the white woman he had spent his evening with. Phillip, Sam noticed, hadn't had a whole lot to say about the woman he'd been with, and Sam couldn't help but wonder why.

He also wondered about Lance. He was supposed to come up this weekend but had called and grumbled about some acquisition giving him problems and he had to rethink, regroup and conquer. Sam shook his head. He had known Lance long enough to know he was talking about a woman.

When he heard a knock on his door, Sam breathed in deeply. He glanced around one more time to make sure the place looked decent, then made his way toward the door. The moment he opened the door and saw Falon standing there, he took another deep breath and expelled it slowly. She was wearing a pair of well-worn jeans and a black V-neck T-shirt. A cute pair of glasses was propped on her nose. Her face was free of makeup and her hair, all that glorious honey blond hair that he liked flowing about her shoulders, was pulled back in a ponytail. But still, nothing took away from her attractiveness. Nothing.

"Come on in," he said, and once she had walked into his apartment and he had closed the door behind her, the place suddenly felt smaller and the air a lot warmer.

She glanced up at him. "I'm ready to roll up my sleeves and start whenever you are," she said smiling.

He chuckled. "Then follow me." He led her into the kitchen and after washing her hands in the sink, she immediately went to the pot he had on the stove. She picked up a spoon and tasted.

While washing his own hands he couldn't help but study her. He watched how her tongue darted out of her mouth to taste the food she had scooped out in the spoon. He liked the way the sunlight that flowed in through the kitchen window caught the flecks in her eyes and wondered if they glowed when she made love.

"You're right, something is missing."

He blinked when her words captured his attention. "I don't understand. I followed your recipe."

"And you didn't use any substitutes?"

He dried off his hands. He had to admit there had been a couple of substitutes, but none that he thought would have mattered.

"When I made the marinara sauce, I used regular canned tomatoes instead of imported Italian ones, and I substituted vegetable oil for olive oil. I figured what the heck? Oil is oil."

He watched a teasing glint shine in her eyes when she folded her arms across her chest and tilted her head back and looked at him. "Excuse me, I hate to tell you this but oil isn't oil, especially with Italian foods. If the recipe calls for olive oil, you have to use olive oil. And as far as tomatoes are concerned, imported Italian tomatoes are the best and can be purchased at most major grocery stores. Those tomatoes enhance the flavor more than just regular tomatoes. You're in luck. I have both olive oil and a can of imported Italian tomatoes at my place, and if you want, we can work together and prepare a dish."

"I don't need to serve it until Wednesday night," he said, thinking of the blunder he'd made with the substitutions.

"That's fine. One thing about Italian foods is that they taste even better after staying in the freezer a few days and being reheated. It gives a chance for the spices to settle and seep in, so if you prepared it tonight, it will be even better on Wednesday."

"And you have time to help me tonight?"

She smiled. "Yes. Lucky for you this is my night off."

"No date on a Saturday night?" he asked.

He watched her stiffen. "No, no date and I'm offering my help if you want it."

He leaned back against the counter and wondered what that was all about. It was obvious that his question had rattled her. Women who looked like her didn't usually have free weekends. Now she had him curious. He gave her a warm look and a smile, then said, "Then I'd love to have your help."

If Sam thought she would be doing all the cooking, he was dead wrong. Once Falon returned with the ingredients, she put him to work. First they began on the marinara sauce and she made sure he had chopped the basil leaves. Another mistake he'd realized he had made was that she used fresh basil leaves . . . just like the recipe called for instead of the one found in a bottle in the seasoning section of the grocery store like he'd used. He regretted taking the recommendation of a woman shopper who'd told him no one would know the difference. Once they had finished the sauce and had it simmering on the stove, they started on the cacciatore.

He smiled as he watched her move around his kitchen. Although he knew the layout of their kitchens were probably similar, she seemed so much at home in his. Sharing kitchen space with her seemed so intimate. He couldn't recall the last time he and Kim had cooked together.

"I would think," he said, breaking the silence, "that the last place a chef would want to be on her day off was in a kitchen."

"Logical thinking," she said, smiling over at him while cutting the three pounds of chicken into bite-size chunks. He was amazed at how she handled a knife and was glad he wasn't that chicken she was expertly slicing.

"But when it comes to me there's not much logic," she said. "I could stay in a kitchen day and night and it wouldn't bother me. I love to cook, always have. I blame my parents for buying me one of those Easy Bake Ovens when I was only four. My life hasn't been the same since."

He chuckled. "Your parents are still alive?"

She smiled. "Yes, they're still alive and still very much in love after thirty years," she said proudly. "With me and my brother Ron living away from home, they spend their time doing things together. Both retired at fifty-five, and neither Ron nor I can keep up with them. They're forever traveling and doing things they enjoy doing. However, they make sure they're in place for Christmas since that's when Ron and I always come home."

"And where is home?"

"I grew up in Portage."

"His smile widened as he took a spoon and sampled the sauce they had prepared. Hers definitely tasted a lot better than his had. "Hey, we're real neighbors then."

She took the spoon from his hand, reminding him the sauce was to be used later and was not for his pleasure no matter how good it tasted. "So I take that to mean you're a Gary native?"

"Yes, born, bred and raised here. I left for a little time while attending Howard in D.C., but as soon as my four years were over, I headed straight back here. I work for the city as an urban planner where I get to do a lot of fun stuff."

"What about your parents? Are they still living?"

"Yes. They retired to Florida a few years ago. I have a sister who lives in Philly. There's no particular day that we all get together; we usually drop in on my parents anytime. My sister Carolyn and I always look for a reason to take a vacation and visit Florida."

Falon nodded. "Hey, I can understand that." She slanted a look at him. "Are you one of those people who hate their jobs?" she asked as she handed him a large onion to chop.

He grinned. "No, I actually love mine. It pays well and I enjoy doing things that make Gary grow and prosper, like that park we're developing. Michael Jackson didn't forget his roots and we appreciate all the land he donated to the city."

Falon nodded. She recalled reading an article in the paper about it some months back. Placing the chopped chicken aside she began slicing the mushrooms. Typically while cooking at home, she preferred the kitchen to herself, but for some reason she felt comfortable with Sam sharing her space. She enjoyed listening to him talk. He spoke with confidence but wasn't arrogant and she appreciated that. In her occupation she encountered plenty of arrogant men who felt only a male was good enough to wear a chef's hat, and unfortunately she would have to bring them down a notch or two by proving otherwise. She'd always kept on her toes around men. But she felt easy around Sam. Relaxed.

"So what's a nice-looking girl like you doing stuck in my kitchen on a Saturday night instead of out wining and dining with some special guy?"

She glanced over at him. He appeared busy chopping the onion but she knew he was listening, waiting for her response. She reached over and picked up her glass of wine. The recipe called for sherry and they had decided to indulge in what was left. "First of all," she said after taking a sip, "there isn't a special man, and secondly, I can't think of anything I enjoy doing more. Now it's time to mix everything," she said, not missing a beat and bringing to an end the discussion on her love life, or lack of one.

Sam watched as she added the chopped chicken to the olive oil that was heating in a large frying pan and how she expertly browned all sides of the meat. Next were the onion and mushrooms. While they were waiting for the ingredients to cook the two or three minutes as required, he leaned against the counter, took a sip of his own wine and said, "I'm divorced and have been for six months."

Why he chose that moment to announce his marital status he really didn't know. Maybe it was because he wanted to share it with her.

"Yes, I already know."

He lifted a brow and caught the gleam of a smile in her eyes and smiled. "Can I assume that I've been the topic of the apartment complex's gossip vine?"

"Umm, it happens," she said, ignoring his chuckle to lean against the counter. "Especially since you're single. That makes you popular. The women living here outnumber the men."

He watched as she proceeded to drain the oil from the frying pan. Then she handed him the salt, pepper and wine to add. He liked the way they swapped duties with ease. She was making it possible for him to brag about preparing this meal without actually lying.

After doing his task he watched as she added the marinara sauce and chicken broth. "Now it has to boil, and then simmer for thirty minutes," she said, placing the top on the pot.

Sam nodded. Already his entire apartment was filled with the aroma of something mouthwateringly delicious. "Come join me in the living room," he invited. "Kick your heels up. You deserve it."

She chuckled. "So do you."

Grabbing their wineglasses, they moved from the kitchen into the living room. He settled down on the sofa, then propped his feet on the coffee table. Falon chuckled as she sat in the chair opposite him and followed his lead.

"So, how long were you married?"

Sam crossed one ankle over the other before he answered. Meeting her gaze he said, "Two years."

She lifted a brow. "Two years? That wasn't very long."

He fought back a frown. "Long enough to find out she was cheating on me."

"Oh." Falon didn't know what else to say. It had taken her almost a year to come to terms with the way Donnell had betrayed her.

"I'm sorry," she suddenly felt the need to say, "that you had to find out something like that."

He lifted his gaze and met hers. "It would have been much worse if my friends hadn't been there for me. I couldn't bring myself to even tell my family because they thought the world of my wife. She was like another daughter to them. I just told them recently. They thought the divorce was my fault."

Falon's hand tightened around her wineglass. He had taken heat from his family to protect the reputation of a woman who hadn't been loyal to him.

"That was very noble of you," she said truthfully. "I doubt that I could have done it. In fact I know that I couldn't. My boyfriend and I broke up a year ago when I came home from work and found him in bed with another woman. After breaking everything that wasn't nailed down and throwing everything within my reach at the two of them, I called my brother and male cousins to come break a few of his bones. Luckily my dad intervened before they got the chance to. But before nightfall, everyone in my family knew what a bastard Donnell had been and everyone wanted blood—and we weren't even married. Had he been my husband cheating on me, then my brother and cousins would have filled him with cement and tossed him into Lake Michigan. Long marriages run in my family. Wedding vows are taken seriously."

"I'm glad that most people still do," Sam said.

Falon was about to say something else when the timer went off, letting them know the food was ready. Pulling her legs off the table, she stood and took another sip of wine before saying, "Umm, I think you're going to love this batch."

He inhaled the air knowing that he would and followed her into the kitchen. He watched as she transferred the cacciatore to a serving dish, and then she stood back while he poured sauce over the chicken then sprinkled it with parsley as she instructed.

"It looks too good to eat . . . almost," he said, pulling out a drawer for two forks.

"But you will eat it, right?" she asked smiling, as she took one of the forks from him.

"Hell, yeah, I'm going to eat it and if there's not enough left for Wednesday, oh, well, I won't lose any sleep over it."

"Hey, you'll do just fine if you have to make some more on Wednesday," she said easily, taking some of the cacciatore and putting it into a smaller dish. She slid her fork through the dish and held it up to him. "Now open up and tell me what you think."

He opened his mouth and she brought the fork to his lips. His gaze held hers as she fed him. It tasted delicious, but standing so close to her, watching her, made him think of another delicious treat.

"Well, what do you think?" she asked and he noticed her voice was low, almost quiet, as she watched his mouth while he chewed.

"Incredible," he said, holding her gaze. "Delicious. Delectable. Now it's your turn," he said, taking the fork from her hand. Sam knew he could just as easily use the other fork that was lying on the counter, but watching her feed him had been intimate, a total turn-on, and he had lost himself in the depths of her honey brown eyes. She had removed her glasses earlier, sometime while they had been making the marinara sauce and slicing the chicken. Her honey brown eyes were so rich, sensuous and sexy, it almost made his breath catch. But he had to breathe. He needed to breathe.

He kept breathing and stared straight into her eyes as he

brought the fork to her lips. Lips that he noticed were quivering slightly. Slowly, deliberately, in the quiet stillness of the room, he watched as those quivering lips parted, saw the tip of her tongue when it met with the fork to swipe the food, then watched as she gently chewed, making his stomach muscles tighten. She seemed to enjoy the meal they had prepared, and watching her devour it heightened his senses and made him want to share the sensations and the taste with her by joining their mouths together.

When she finished the bite and used her tongue to wipe around her mouth, his stomach tightened even more. Watching her eat had been a totally sensuous experience.

"You want more?" he asked quietly, and watched as she took a sip of her wine.

"No, that was enough," she said after taking a paper napkin to wipe her lips.

"Let me do that." His gaze flicked from her mouth to her eyes as twinges of desire ripped through him. He started to take the napkin from her hand but decided to do it another way. Driven, pushed, compelled, he returned his gaze to her lips as he stepped closer and lowered his head letting his mouth slant over hers. Taking the tip of his tongue first he outlined her lips, removing any lingering sauce and then when she made a breathless sigh, he went inside her mouth to explore fully, completely.

Falon was convinced that everything feminine in her sprang to life at that moment. She suddenly felt a hot sensation from the top of her head to the bottom of her feet. Her breasts felt full, heavy, and her nipples tingled as Sam continued to kiss her in a way that no man had ever kissed her before.

Each stroke of his tongue was causing heat to infuse between her legs, and she was helpless to do anything but press her body closer to his for the contact. She was being blindsided by lust and single-mindedly driven to do something she hadn't done in over a year—enjoy the attention, the workings, the "get-down-with-it" kiss of a man. And she would enjoy it until her senses kicked in and her world returned to normal. Right now it was tilting on its axis, almost out of control, and she wanted the experience. She needed it.

Sam deepened the kiss. Besides feeling an erection that was growing harder by the minute, he felt an odd sensation develop in his chest, almost making it impossible for him to breathe. This was a kiss like none other. Never had he wanted to devour a woman's mouth like he was doing now. Oh, he had enjoyed kissing Tina but for some reason this was different. At the moment he couldn't name the difference or even explain it, but the difference was there. It was as if Falon's taste was his and his alone and he wanted it all, to shape, mold and conform her mouth into one that belonged to him.

He heard the sound of the phone ringing and ignored it. But neither of them could ignore the sound of the feminine voice leaving a message on his answering machine. They broke off the kiss as Tina's voice said, "Sam, this is Tina. Looking forward to the surprise dinner you're preparing for me over at your place Wednesday night. You know how I love Italian food. I can't wait to get into it, just like I can't wait to get into you. So rest up. Our horoscope for today says to jump out of your routine and look for new opportunities. Be passionate with everything you do. Try exploring a foreign culture or meeting people different from your usual crowd. Hey, and wouldn't you believe it but today during a business meeting I met a woman from France. She's convinced me that one way to broaden my horizon is trying out French food. I am so excited. I'll tell you everything when I see you on Wednesday. 'Bye."

Sam inhaled deeply when surprise followed by disappointment flitted across Falon's features. He knew what she was going to say before she opened her mouth and he wanted to stop her.

"That kiss should not have happened, Sam." Her expression was unreadable.

"Why not?" he asked, lifting his hand to cover hers, but wasn't surprised when she pulled her hand from his and took a step back.

She nodded her head in the direction of his answering machine. "You're obviously involved with someone."

Her voice was filled with disappointment. He wanted to take the few steps to her and smooth a hand down her bare arm; touch her, pull her to him and kiss her again. He wanted to erase the sound of Tina's voice that had shattered the special moment they had shared. He inhaled deeply and said, "Tina and I are involved but not seriously."

He watched as Falon's frown deepened. "Oh, you're involved in one of those."

This time he frowned. "One of what?"

"A meaningless, no-strings, no-commitment affair."

She'd said it like the thought of it was something nasty. "And what if I am?" he asked defensively. He didn't have to explain himself to anyone.

"Then I guess it's your business. Look, I'd better go," she said and moved to walk around him. He reached out and touched her arm. He felt the heat sizzle; heat neither of them could deny feeling.

He quickly dropped his hand. "Look, aren't you the same woman who sat in my living room less than an hour ago and told me that her boyfriend had screwed around on her? Maybe you can jump back into another serious relationship after experiencing something like that but I can't. What my wife did to me nearly ripped out my soul. So if you're pissed because I've decided to enjoy life but not get seriously involved with anyone then that's your problem."

When she didn't say anything but continued to stare at him, he rubbed the back of his neck to relieve the tension that had suddenly gathered there. He had to inwardly admit that it wasn't just her problem, it was also his since for some reason what she thought mattered.

"Falon," he said, breaking into the silence that encased them.

She quickly held up her hand. "No, don't, and you're right. It's my problem. Like I told you earlier, long marriages run in my family. I was raised to believe in forever-after and if someone breaks your heart, you should give it plenty of time to heal and then move on. I believe in love and commitment, Sam. What Donnell did hurt me badly but it didn't destroy me. It would be a waste of my time to begin dating a man for the fun of it while I mend a broken heart. I don't want to be known as a woman who has slept her way to Mr. Right."

"It might be easier for a woman," he said softly, wanting her to understand.

"No," she said quietly, "I don't think it matters whether you're male or female. However, I do believe that the amount of time it takes a person's heart to heal depends on how deep the relationship was that you were in. How can you heal if you're jumping into bed with different women all the time, being a playa, a no-commitment kind of guy?"

She stared at him, at the angry look that appeared on his face and knew he was pissed at her words but she didn't care. They had shared a kiss, a kiss she had enjoyed and she knew that he had enjoyed it as well. It had meant nothing to him but she had hoped it would be the start of everything. Oh, she hadn't expected a proposal in a few weeks, but she had thought that after tonight, they would start getting to know each other better and things would escalate from there. But according to him, there wouldn't be a "from there." Anything they shared would ultimately lead to nowhere.

"I have to go, Sam."

He knew she was right. She had to go. At the moment thoughts of her were consuming his senses. He couldn't think straight and the best thing would be for her to leave. He took a step back. "All right."

Before she reached the door he called out to her. "Falon?"

She turned around and met his gaze and smile. "Yes?"

The radiant smile she'd worn all night was gone, yet her honey brown eyes were warm as she gazed at him from beneath long lashes. And there were those dimples that were denting her cheeks that couldn't help but pull you in. The time they had spent together working in his kitchen had been special and he didn't want things to end this way.

He crossed the room to her and stood awkwardly for a minute. Usually, he was a man who was never at a loss for words but tonight it seemed as if he was. His eyes met hers, trying not to remember that her mouth tasted as soft and as sweet as it looked.

"Can we at least be friends?" he asked quietly.

A part of him wished he was as strong as she was and that his attitude about getting back into another relationship, a serious one, was something he could handle. But he knew that it wasn't. The pain of Kim's betrayal was still there and a constant reminder of how vulnerable his heart was.

He watched as she gave him a long thoughtful look, a look that even now was stirring his blood. He liked her. He respected her values. Now that they had cleared the air, so to speak, and he knew there was no way he could have her for a lover, he would be more than honored to have her as a friend.

Falon considered Sam's request. Could the two of them be just friends when a part of her wanted more? There were a million reasons why she should put distance between her and Sam, and one of them was the kiss they had shared earlier. It hadn't been an ordinary kiss. At least for her it hadn't. But then, there were other things to consider. She could use a friend and she had a feeling that so could he. She had plenty of female friends but not guy friends that she felt close to, and for reasons she couldn't begin to fathom, it suddenly seemed predestined that they were meant to be friends, and she would be okay with that.

"Are you sure that's what you want, Sam?" she asked.

"Yes." *And nothing more,* he added silently. He knew it would be difficult but he intended to make it work.

"All right, Sam. We can be friends."

Sam blew out a breath he hadn't realized he'd been holding and said, "Thanks."

BOOK THREE

Happy is the man that findeth wisdom,
and the man that getteth understanding.
Proverbs 3:13

15

The Gang

After finishing his workout at the gym, Sam glanced over at Marcus who was still lifting weights. Phillip was finishing up on the treadmill.

"Hey, that's enough for today," Marcus said. He breathed heavily as he lay back on the bench press.

"That's not too bad for a punk like you," Phillip said grinning. At six feet, Marcus was the shortest of the three of them and weighed the least. After Dottie's death he had lost a lot of weight, but now it seemed his appetite had picked back up and he was working out consistently, putting meat back on his bones.

Marcus glared at Phillip. "A punk? Hey, man, kiss my—"

"I saw your mama the other day at the grocery store," Sam interrupted. The last thing he wanted to hear was Marcus and Phillip going at it. "She's worried about you."

Marcus snorted as he moved aside to let Phillip try his hand at the weights. "I talk to Mama at least once or twice a week. She just can't understand why I won't go to church."

Sam nodded. Everyone knew that Ms. Essie practically lived in the church. Hell, he remembered that when he and Marcus had become friends whenever he stayed over at Marcus's house on a Saturday night he had to bring his church clothes because he was going to church on Sunday morning. Even when they had gotten older, no matter how late he and Marcus had stayed out Saturday night, they were expected to be ready and dressed for Sunday school the next day. But then his parents had been the same way. Sunday was for going to church. It was something you understood and accepted. No back talk. No lip. You just did it.

Sam knew that since Dottie's death Marcus hadn't been inside a church. "Sometimes you have to do stuff just to please your mama," Sam said grinning, even though he had known that Ms. Essie was dead serious. Marcus's mother had lectured him for a good fifteen minutes. He had gone in there to purchase a pack of condoms, had seen her and grabbed a bottle of mouthwash instead.

"Yeah, yeah, but I'm not letting anyone, not even my mama, shove religion down my throat, man," he said angrily. He grabbed a towel and wiped the sweat from his face. "Look, I'm out of here. I'm going home, shower and head over to Fantasyland."

Phillip raised a brow. "Again?" he asked. He was aware that Marcus had been back to the club several times.

Marcus chuckled. "I have a lot to make up for and I'm going to get all that I can while fulfilling Breathless's fantasies."

Phillip frowned. "You're still screwing *her*?" Marcus had told him and Sam about the white woman whose fantasy had been to have sex with a black man.

A grin tugged at Marcus's mouth. "When something is good, you get as much of it as you can. I know the nights she's going to be there and she requested that I be her man during those visits. I'm more than happy to oblige. See you guys later."

Sam shook his head as he watched Marcus walk away. "I'm worried about him, man," he said to Phillip.

Phillip glanced over at Sam as he lay back on the bench press. "Why?"

"I think he's getting too caught up in this Fantasyland thing. He's been back four times already."

"And you think there's something wrong with that?" Phillip asked as he began to pump iron. He didn't want to admit it but he thought something wasn't right with it as well.

"Hell, I don't see you going back for more, although you claimed you weren't disappointed."

Phillip sighed as he effortlessly put the weights back in their holder. He needed to talk to somebody, and since their college days he and Sam had always been able to talk to each other about anything. He trusted Sam. He trusted Marcus, too, but Marcus was not as serious-minded as Sam, and at the moment he needed someone who was serious-minded.

At first he hadn't planned on sharing what he'd found out that night at Fantasyland with anyone, but his deceit was eating him alive and he could barely go through each day without guilt weighing him down. He had to talk to someone about it.

"You got a second, Sam, for us to talk?"

Sam glanced over at him. "Sure, shoot."

Phillip glanced around. "No. Not here. Let's shower, change and go someplace. Do you want to go to O'Neal's and grab a few beers?"

Sam studied Phillip. He really needed to get home to tackle the work he had brought home from the office, but from the look on Phillip's face and the tone of his voice, he could tell something was bothering him and he was curious to know what. He had been curious for the past couple of weeks.

"Sure, man, let's go grab a couple of beers and talk."

Sam's eyes widened. "Are you telling me that the woman you had sex with at this Fantasyland place was actually that attorney?"

Phillip grimaced as he took another gulp of his beer. "Hell, yeah, that's what I'm telling you, Sam. I knew who she was but she didn't know who I was." Not exactly something he wanted to admit, but he had done so anyway.

Sam cleared his throat then asked, "Could you be wrong, Phillip? A number of women could have a tattoo star on their shoulder blade."

"It was her, man. There was no mistake about it. After listening to her story I put two and two together and it all makes sense." He decided not to mention that the sex between them had been incredible. He had never responded to a woman like he had to her. What they'd shared had been off-the-meter, earth-shattering, and downright toe-curling. There hadn't been a single night since then that he hadn't gone to bed and thought about it, dreamed about it, yearned for it again.

"So you think that night was her first and last time there? That she hasn't turned into another Marcus who can't seem to get enough of the place?" Sam asked curiously.

Phillip shook his head. "I honestly don't think so, Sam. The only reason she was there was because her therapist suggested that she go."

Sam nodded. "I thought you were going to tell me tonight that you had started sleeping with Rhonda again."

A strangled laugh bubbled up in Phillip's throat. "Not hardly. Rhonda met some guy on that cruise she went on and is all into him . . . not that I'm complaining mind you. It was time we started acting like a divorced couple."

Sam nodded again. He leaned back in his chair and gazed at Phillip. "So what's the next move regarding the attorney? Are you going to try to see her again?"

Phillip sighed deeply. "I'd like to. I feel guilty as sin because I know what we did. That night as Brazen she poured her heart and soul out to me. She wanted me to know why she was there and that sleeping with a stranger was not her norm, and that once she fulfilled her fantasy she wouldn't be back. So, if I want to see her I'm going to have to do so as Chandra's father and not let her know about that night."

"And you have a problem with not letting her know?"

"Yes. I'll feel like I'm being dishonest with her; like I was telling her a lie."

Sam sighed. He knew women hated anyone deceiving them. Hell, men hated anyone lying to them as well. "Yeah, and the worst way to start off any relationship, whether long-term or short, is with a lie."

Phillip nodded in agreement. "Yeah, a lie is a lie. And a lie of omission is still a lie."

After the waiter delivered more beers, Sam glanced over at Phillip. "So, I'm asking again, man. What's your next move?"

Phillip took a long swig of his beer. "I don't know." Moments later he met Sam's gaze. "Ahh, hell, man, I want her again. The sex was the best I've ever had but it's more than that, Sam. I felt more. I felt some sort of a connection. And I may as well confess that I don't feel like I had sex with her that night. I actually felt like I was making love to her."

"Shit."

"Yeah, tell me about it," Phillip chimed in after Sam's one-word statement that basically said it all. Sleeping with Terri had been more than him finding release that night . . . although he had sorely needed it. And it had been more than him filling a hunger. It was different when you cared and that night he had cared.

"Hey, man, take a step back," Sam was saying, sitting up straight in his chair. He had placed his beer bottle out of his hand, giving Phillip his full attention. "Remember playas have sex; they don't make love." He said it like reminding Phillip of it would zap some sense back into him.

Phillip nodded. He remembered exactly what *The Playa's Handbook* had said but with Terri Davenport things had been different, and as much as he wished they hadn't been, they had. "I know, man. But I can't take that night back or how I felt."

He glanced over at Sam. "What about you and Tina? You never feel like you're making love to her instead of having sex?"

Sam knew the answer to Phillip's question without even thinking about it. "No. It's strictly a sex thing, hard and heartless. I enjoy making out with her but I don't feel anything emotional."

And he often wondered about that. All the times he'd made love to Kim he had loved her so he'd always equated sex with love. But now as far as he was concerned, he and Tina were two people who had needs that were being fulfilled. It had gotten to the point where they both knew how the evening would end. He took her to dinner on Wednesday nights then they would go back to her place for a night of sex. Afterward, he would get dressed and tell her he would see her the next Wednesday. She would call him once or twice during the week to give him their horoscope, but other than that they didn't see each other. Very seldom would she call and invite him to do something on the weekends, which was just as well since he hung out with Marcus and Phillip on the weekends anyway.

"What about Falon?"

Sam blinked. His thoughts were immediately seized by the mention of Falon's name. "What about Falon?"

"I know you told us that the two of you decided to just be friends but wouldn't you want more with her if you could get it? Do you think you would feel differently if you were to sleep with Falon?"

For a moment, Sam figured he looked like someone had punched him. Phillip had thrown out the very scene that he had been fighting in his mind for weeks—ever since that night he and Falon had decided to be just friends. He still wanted her. He was enjoying getting to know her as a friend but he wanted her the same way a man wanted a woman. Now, that was *his* fantasy.

"Sam?"

"Yes?"

"You haven't answered my question. Do you think you would feel differently if you were to sleep with Falon?"

Sam took another sip of beer. He could probably look Phillip in the eye and say, *Nah, man, it wouldn't be different,* but he knew he would be lying through his teeth. Besides, Phillip needed to hear the truth in order to deal with his own issues involving the attorney. "There's no way I can think of Falon and sex in the same sentence, man. She's a special woman and I appreciate her as a friend," he said, thinking of the time they were beginning to spend together.

They had given themselves time to come to terms with this

friendship thing and then, after avoiding each other for a week, they had run into each other when they came home from work at the same time. He had invited her over to his place to show her a couple of paintings he had purchased from this African-American vender at the mall. She had agreed to come by later and she had. She had hung around and helped him hang the pictures in his living room, and then afterward they ended up just sitting and talking about how their day had gone. That had helped to break the ice with the friendship thing.

Last night they had walked to the corner store together to get her an ice cream cone. She had shared with him a couple of things that had happened at work. There seemed to be no tension on her part over their growing friendship but there was certainly tension on his. He still couldn't get over the fact that he wanted her.

He met Phillip's gaze again. "If Falon and I ever slept together, emotions would definitely be involved. I really like her, Phillip, in ways Tina can't touch."

Phillip nodded and forced a smile on his lips. "Maybe some men aren't cut out to be playas, Sam, and we fit that category."

"Yeah," Sam agreed, taking another sip of his beer as something warm shifted in his chest. His lips tilted into a smile.

"What are you smiling about?" Phillip asked.

Still smiling, Sam sat there for a few moments not saying anything. Then he said, "I think that tonight you and I have faced some profound truths." He chuckled at the blank look on Phillip's face. "If you can't figure out what I'm talking about now, I bet you will later. And my advice to you is this: If you want that attorney then go after her."

Now it was Phillip's time to smile. "Thanks for the advice, man, and I think I will."

Tonight had been another good night of sex, Marcus thought, as he lay there flat on his back and stared up at the ceiling, trying to get his breathing back to normal.

Beside him Breathless slept. He glanced over at her, at the mass of blond hair spread across the pillow. She still had her mask on like he still wore his. That was the one thing that had remained constant—the masks.

And the good sex.

He could get used to this, he thought smiling. No worries, no hassles, no commitments.

"High Intensity?"

He lifted a brow. He'd thought she was asleep, resting up for another round. "Yes."

"I've been thinking about us."

Marcus's brow lifted a little higher as panic slowly creeped up his spine. When it came to them there wasn't an "us." "Us?"

"Yes. Don't you think it's time we take off our masks and reveal our true identities?"

He quickly rose to lean on his elbows and stared at her like she was stone crazy. Hell, no. He didn't think that way at all. Why would they want to do something like that? One of the things he liked most about Fantasyland, not to mention the good sex he got, was the mystery of not knowing just who he was getting it on with. "Why would we want to do something like that?"

"Because we like each other."

He frowned. Yes, he liked her but, so . . . ? "I thought the reason you were fulfilling your fantasy this way, Breathless, was because you always wanted a black man, and you knew your parents would probably kill you if you dated one."

Over the past few times they had been together she had shared that with him. He knew her parents were well-off, high-society snobs and she was their rich, spoiled daughter who did whatever they said to get her monthly allowance. An allowance that was more than his monthly salary and he thought he made good bucks as an engineer.

"Yes, but when I turn twenty-seven in a week, I'll get the trust fund my grandparents left for me. I'll do fine without my parents' money and can do whatever I want. I think it's time for me to get liberated."

He nodded. She could get liberated all she wanted but without him. Personally, he liked things just the way they were. "I prefer keeping things this way," he said. "I don't want a relationship with you beyond these four walls, this bed. I'm single and I like it that way. I don't want a relationship with a woman other than for sex."

"And I want more."

Marcus sighed. She could want all she wanted. If she had him pegged as the man she wanted more from, he needed to pull back and haul ass. "Then I wish you all the best in your endeavors," he said, sliding out of bed and putting on his clothes.

She sat up in bed. "Where are you going?"

"I'm leaving and it was nice knowing you. I enjoyed the time we spent together but I like things the way they are now." *No worries, no hassles, no commitments*.

"I'll pay you."

Marcus stopped in the process of putting on his pants and glanced over at her. Anger clouded his face. "Thanks, but no thanks. There are some things money can't buy and I'm one of them." He continued dressing and she didn't say anything. She didn't have to. He could tell she was pouting. The little spoiled rich kid in her was coming out.

"I want you, High Intensity."

He sat down to put on his shoes and glanced up. She sounded serious. "You've had me several times over. I've given you enough memories to last quite awhile. I fulfilled your fantasy, didn't I?"

"Yes."

"Then I've delivered." He picked up his jacket from the table and headed for the door. He glanced back over his shoulder. "It was nice knowing you." He opened the door then walked out without looking back.

———

A short while later Marcus walked into his house. He felt hard and heartless and wondered exactly when he had become such an unfeeling and uncaring bastard. Instead of feeling flattered that Breathless had wanted him, he had felt aggravated, pissed and annoyed. He had somehow gotten wrapped into this "being a playa" thing a little too tight. Where was the man he used to be? The man who used to cherish the thought of love and commitment? The man who used to treat a woman with love and respect, not like she was just a body to hump? When did he start feeling that all he wanted from a woman was what he could get for himself? That made him sound selfish and uncaring and at the moment that's exactly how he felt.

He began removing his clothes, feeling the need to take a shower and deciding that he wouldn't be rereading *The Playa's Handbook* for a while.

16

Lance, Asia and Sean

Asia glanced out at the audience and knew Lance had been right. People liked controversy. The studio, she was told, usually held thirty to forty people but today it held a packed house of close to one hundred.

The show's director, Robert Gerard, was talking to the cameraman, and Asia was trying to pay attention to the last-minute instructions the man who identified himself as Troy was giving her. He was a member of the production staff. "Remember to look at the monitor and not the audience," he was saying. "And when in doubt follow the cameraman's lead."

She nodded then glanced at her watch wondering where was Lance? There wouldn't be much of a debate if he didn't show up, and they had less than five minutes to airtime. And what annoyed her the most was that she was anxious to see him; she actually felt anticipation in her body and she didn't like that at all.

"You're frowning."

She glanced up at Troy. "What?"

"I said you're frowning. Remember this is television and unlike radio people will be able to hear *and* see you. They will know what your response is before you open your mouth. Do what you can do to hide your emotions."

That was easier said than done. Lance had a way of pushing her buttons.

"You look beautiful, Asia."

Asia's gaze moved toward the direction of the familiar voice and a huge smile automatically formed on her lips. "Sean! What are you doing here?"

He walked closer to her. "I happened to be in Chicago on business and heard you would be taping today; I called Melissa and she made arrangements for me to get in. I thought you'd like to have a familiar face in the audience."

Her smile widened knowing that she did. The last time she had seen Sean had been a few months ago, the night he had asked her to marry him, and she knew he was giving her space while waiting patiently for her answer. Whatever decision she made she wanted it to be the right one. Sean Crews was a handsome man. He was also a warm, loving and caring person.

"Thanks for coming, Sean," she said, truly meaning it. Even when she had been with David, it was Sean and not David who had actually looked out for her. It had been Sean who had tried to shield her from his brother's duplicity, and later it had been Sean who had come to her and told her the truth about David's betrayal. She had cried in Sean's arms for loving a man who had done nothing but cause her pain.

That particular night had been the one and only time that she and Sean had slept together. It hadn't been anything planned but had been something that just happened. The next morning she had regretted what they had done and had told Sean that it couldn't ever happen again.

He reached out and took her hand in his, bringing her thoughts back to the present. "You don't have to thank me for being here, Asia. You know if it was my choice, I would always be there for you."

"Interrupting something?"

Asia glanced up when Lance suddenly appeared, seemingly out

of nowhere. She met his gaze. His features were unreadable, but for some reason she felt he was tense, somewhat angry, annoyed.

"No, you aren't interrupting anything," she said. "Lance, this is Dr. Sean Crews, a good friend of mine. Sean, this is Dr. Lance Montgomery."

Sean eased his hand from Asia and extended it to Lance. "Dr. Montgomery, it's a pleasure to meet you. I've worked with your brother Lyle Montgomery several times."

Lance nodded as he took the man's hand in a firm handshake. "You're a medical doctor?" he asked coolly, deciding he hadn't liked the fact that the man had been holding Asia's hand when he walked up.

"Yes, and like Lyle's specialty is the heart, mine is orthopedics. However, he and I have teamed up to do several surgeries around the country together. I've even met your other brother Logan."

Lance again nodded. He watched as Sean's hand automatically went to Asia's shoulder. He found the move annoying and when he met the man's gaze he knew it had been done deliberately, as a way to stamp his claim. But as far as Lance was concerned this man—no matter what part he played in Asia's life—didn't have a claim. If he did then she wouldn't be celibate after a year. No man in his right mind would let a woman he cared about forgo passion of the richest and most rewarding kind without doing something about it.

"We roll the tape in five minutes!" someone shouted.

Sean slowly removed his hand from Asia's shoulder. "I guess I need to find my seat. And don't get all nervous about this," he said softly. "You'll do fine and no matter what, remember like always, I'm here for you."

Asia smiled. "Thanks, Sean."

"Unfortunately, I'm going to have to leave as soon as the show is over to catch my plane. I have an important surgery to perform in Miami . . . on a child, a little boy."

Asia nodded. "I know he's in good hands."

"Thanks." Sean smiled and then leaned over and placed a kiss on Asia's lips. "Take care." He glanced over at Lance. "It was nice meeting you."

Lance nodded. "Likewise." He then watched him walk away before turning his attention to Asia. "He seems like a nice enough fellow."

Asia's gaze softened as she watched Sean walk away. "He is. Sean is a wonderful person."

Lance shrugged. It was hard for her to convince him of that. The eyes that had looked at him hadn't depicted *wonderful*. He had seen jealousy, possessiveness and something else that Lance recognized as love. There was no doubt in his mind that Sean Crews was in love with Asia. How the man felt toward Asia wasn't his business, but what was his business was how Asia felt toward the man.

"Is a wedding being planned?" he asked casually as he took his seat across from her.

She lifted a brow. "A wedding?

"Yes, yours and Crews's."

She frowned. "At the moment Sean and I are just good friends."

At the moment . . . Lance's lips tightened. Did that mean the two of them were contemplating marriage? Her response had not been what he had wanted to hear.

Remembering what Troy had told her about hiding her emotions, Asia tried to look at Lance with an unreadable expression when she asked, "And you're admitting that some men only want women for sex?"

The smile he gave her was contagious and without shame when he said, "You won't get an argument from me."

He then shifted in his chair, presenting his best side to the audience, something she knew he wasn't even aware he was doing. "But seriously, why are women getting upset over the entire "playa" issue? There are just as many female playas as there are men. Women are going for it. Some aren't looking for a serious relationship any more than some men are."

And that's how they continued for thirty minutes, presenting their sides, debating, diving into racy topics, proving they were experts on relationships and sex, both in theory and practice . . . although Asia conceded to everyone that she was sure Dr. Montgomery was definitely far more practiced than she was. He smiled and didn't deny it and even offered to give her all the practice she needed if she was interested. It had been more than a mere sizzling innuendo. It had been an outright invitation made on television—one she expertly skirted around.

By the time the taping ended, Lance knew the sale of their books would increase once the show was aired. He also knew he would probably stay aroused for life. On the airwaves, Asia's voice always managed to turn him on; seduce his mind and escalate his breathing pattern. And sitting across from her for thirty minutes, he had been hard pressed to concentrate. He had been hard period and was glad his jacket had kept the state of his body well hidden while he was sitting down.

He inwardly admitted, unashamedly, that the woman certainly did things to him. He was certain everyone in the audience, including her friend Sean, had felt the chemistry that flowed between them, had felt their sexual attraction even while they'd been in heated discussions, presenting opposing views.

Unlike good fellow Sean, Lance was a man of action. He had no intentions of hanging around waiting for Asia to decide where she wanted their relationship to go. He wanted to sleep with her and would do everything to make it possible before her plane left in the morning. She was on his turf now and the battle lines were drawn. He would be the one to give her everything he knew that she craved even though she was trying not to hunger for it.

"A limo is standing by to take the two of you to the private dinner party," some woman with a notebook was saying.

Asia lifted a surprised brow. "What private dinner party?"

The woman shrugged. "Don't know the details. All I know is that the two of you are expected to be there, and I was asked to make sure you arrived on time as the guests of honor."

Asia looked uncertain, not sure she wanted to spend any more of her time in Lance's presence. "I don't know," she said slowly.

"What's wrong?" Lance asked in a low, soft voice. "Surely you aren't afraid of sharing a limo ride with me? You've done it before and seen how completely harmless I can be."

His insinuation, like he'd known it would, raised Asia's ire. "I thought I made it clear that you don't scare me." She then turned to the woman who was standing patiently, waiting for them to move. "Where is the limo?"

"It's waiting out front."

Asia nodded. "I'll be ready after I go to the dressing room to grab my coat and purse." Without glancing over at Lance, she turned and walked away.

Jealousy, Lance thought disgustedly, was an annoying sonofabitch.

The thought that Asia was thinking about marrying Sean Crews didn't sit well with him. He couldn't erase the memory of how the man had touched her with a familiarity that bordered on intimate. He wondered how that was possible if she'd been celibate for over a year. Unless it had happened *before* she went on her sex strike.

He wondered why he even gave a damn. He'd had plenty of women; more than he could count or cared to remember. Some of them had been more beautiful than others. Most of them intelligent— although he had to admit he had dated some whose IQ he'd felt had been questionable. But all of them had definitely been desirable.

And he'd never been jealous of any of them.

Asia Fowler had quickly become an obsession. She shook his control, weakened his resolve and made him think of things he had no business thinking about. Like today for instance, while taping the show when she'd said that she wanted marriage, a home, children . . .

In the darkest recesses of his mind he had actually imagined her tucked away in some house in the suburbs, in a brightly decorated nursery with a child cuddled in her arms as she breastfed.

His child.

Lance glanced down at his hands. They were actually shaking at the thought. He had never thought of any woman giving birth to his child. But he had today.

He inhaled deeply as he glanced over at her. She had put distance between them and was almost hugging the window. It would be so easy to slide over there, corner her and capture her mouth in his for the kiss he knew they both wanted. Even now the back seat of the limo was sizzling and since a privacy glass kept the driver from knowing what they were doing, he had the opportunity. But he knew he didn't have a willing partner just yet. He had to continue to break down her resolve.

And he needed to find out more about her relationship with Sean Crews so the jealousy that was gnawing at his insides could go claim another victim.

"He loves you," Lance decided to say, without any explanation, any forewarning.

She glanced over at him, her brow raised slightly. "Who?"

"Sean Crews."

She inhaled deeply and continued to meet his eyes. "And I love him, too, in a very special way. He was there for me during some of my darkest moments."

Lance nodded. What she was feeling was gratitude and not love. He knew it and was sure she knew it as well, which was probably the reason she and Crews hadn't gotten together. But he wanted to hear her admit it.

He shifted his body and leaned back against the seat, spreading his arm across the back. His hand itched to reach out and snag her and bring her to him. He wanted to devour her mouth, kiss her senseless, taste her between her legs.

"If you love him then why not marry him?" he asked, needing to take his mind off how bad he wanted her.

She broke eye contact and glanced out the window. The vehicle was no longer in traffic but was easing down the freeway. "It's complicated."

"How so?"

She met his gaze again. "He's David's brother," she said softly. A part of Asia wondered why she was telling Lance anything, especially that.

"Who's David?"

She saw the anger that lined his lips; heard it in his tone. If she didn't know better she would think he was jealous. But she did know better. And for some reason she decided to answer his question.

"David Crews was my lover, the man who taught me a lot about life." She glanced back out the window.

Lance nodded slowly. He remembered hearing her speak that day at the Betty Shabazz Center, and how she'd told the audience what she had endured to bring her to this point in her life. Evidently this David had been the romantic culprit in her past and being David's brother wasn't earning this Sean guy any brownie points.

When Asia met his gaze once more, he saw remembered pain and unwavering determination so profound that it made his breath catch.

"And David being the asshole that he still is," she continued, "is the reason I'll never let another man use me for his pleasure."

Lance glanced down and studied his manicured and neatly trimmed nails. Lifting his head, he met her gaze; held it. "But will you allow a man to treat you to yours?"

She lifted a brow. "My what?"

"Pleasure. What if a man wants to make love to you, not for his pleasure but solely for yours?"

Asia's brows rose a little higher. "Most men aren't willing to make that kind of sacrifice."

"I would."

Asia frowned, not believing it for a second. "I doubt that."

Lance doubted it himself. He knew that if he ever got between her legs, he'd come before he buried the first inch.

"I don't want to talk about this anymore," Asia said. Once again their conversation was getting out of control. Visions of them together in bed with him nestled between her legs, giving her the pleasure of the most profound kind flooded her mind. She sighed deeply. All she wanted to do was make an appearance at this private party and then return to her hotel room and rest. She would be flying out of Chicago in the morning and as far as she was concerned tomorrow morning couldn't get here quick enough.

"All right. So what do you think of our weather, Asia?"

She glanced down at her hands, wishing she could do something with them. They were itching, actually throbbing, to reach out, grab hold of Lance's tie, pull him to her and kiss him as she so desperately wanted.

Instead she met his gaze directly. "Not as cold as I expected for October." She hoped he didn't hear the husky longing in her voice.

"It knew you were coming and wanted to impress you."

She couldn't help but smile. "And I appreciate that. Although I live in New York, I was born and raised in the South and more often than not I find that I don't handle cold weather very well."

She inhaled deeply. His agreeing to drop the subject wasn't keeping her mind off the idea of him between her legs, giving her all the pleasure she could stand. The imagery whetted her appetite, made her wet.

Damn him.

She sighed again when the limo pulled to the curve and came to a stop. Evidently they had reached their destination.

17

Lance and Asia

"Did the woman at the studio say who is expecting us?" Asia asked as she and Lance stepped into the elevator. The huge group of condos had a stunning view of Lake Michigan and she could tell they were costly as well as classy.

She'd felt like royalty entering the building and had been totally aware of her surroundings while walking across the elegant lobby. She had also been intensely conscious of Lance's hand at the base of her back.

"Yes, she told me," he said quietly, once the elevator door closed shut. "We're going up to the twentieth floor."

They were alone and for the moment it seemed that neither had much to say. It was as if they were giving their bodies time to cool down from all the heat they had generated in the limo.

However, Asia's body was far from cool since Lance's hand at her back was gently stroking her through her clothing. His touch felt good, soothing, and it was sending small ripples of desire through her.

She let out a deep breath when the elevator door opened to the twentieth floor and allowed Lance to lead the way. They walked all the way to the end of the hall and he knocked on the door. Within seconds a uniformed waiter opened the door, smiled at them and then stepped aside. Before the man could say a single word, Lance ushered her inside.

Asia glanced around seeing no other people, but she did see a beautiful dinner table set for two, with lit candles, a bottle of wine and a breathtakingly beautiful view of Lake Michigan as a back-drop. She was almost too caught up in the stunning view to hear the waiter say to Lance, "Everything is as you ordered, sir." Followed by Lance's, "Thank you, Stuart. That will be all."

She quickly turned around in time to see Lance close the door behind the man and lock it. It then became crystal clear who was giving the private party, and that she and Lance were the only ones attending.

Lance held Asia's gaze. He could see the anger growing in her face and the scowl that quivered at her lips. Evidently she was not impressed with the way he had manipulated things. She was livid. She was also the woman he wanted with a passion and he would do anything to have her right here, right now.

"You have incredible nerve," she said in a voice filled with so much anger it seemed the room shook even though she hadn't actually raised her voice. It was the tone that added the special effects. He watched as she tossed her hair back, away from her face, letting it flow down her shoulders, not aware of the beautiful picture she made as the sun, a very rare oddity this time of the year, shined through the floor-to-ceiling window and blazed through her hair, making it appear more luxurious, glossier.

There was also the powerhouse business suit she was wearing, fuchsia in color, short in length. It was a shade that captivated her features and the length showed off her gorgeous legs. When he had first seen her in it, all he could think about was getting her out of it.

"Well, don't you have anything to say?"

"I think of myself as a man of action rather than words," he said, taking in her haughty look and loving it, wishing he could bottle it.

"Could have fooled me with the type of books you write," she said coolly, glaring at him. "What if I said I wanted to leave? Now."

He leaned back against the door. "Then I would appeal to your logical side and suggest that you at least let me feed you before departing. Stuart is not only a good waiter but occasionally he moonlights as a chef; an excellent one. I had him prepare a few dishes that I think you might enjoy."

From the aroma that was floating from the kitchen, Asia knew that she would. But still, she refused to let Lance get off easily. She didn't appreciate his underhandedness. She detested being tricked. "Why did you do it?" she asked, as curiosity replaced her anger for the moment.

"I think it should be obvious. I've asked you to dinner several times and you refused me. So I decided to take matters into my own hands."

She narrowed her eyes at him. "Don't women ever tell you no?"

He smiled. "Not usually."

Asia could believe that. "Fine, I'm glad I was the first then." She glanced over at the table again; she sniffed and smelled the tantalizing aroma and made her decision. "Well . . . I hate for all of Stuart's hard work to go to waste, and since I'm here I may as well eat. But I want you to call me a taxi as soon as I finish my meal."

"If that's what you want."

"It is."

"Then that's what you'll get." He came away from the door to stand in front of her. "But I hope you'll at least let me treat you to dessert before you go."

She glared up at him. "It depends on what it is."

He smiled again and she didn't want to admit that the smile was sending ripples through her, the same ripples she had experienced in the elevator. "I'm sure you'll like it. Come sit down, let's get started," he said, taking her hand and leading her toward the table.

Asia removed her coat and watched as he placed it across the back of the sofa. She then sat down in the chair that he pulled out for her at the table. Warning bells inside her head went off, signaling that she should leave, not later but now; that she wasn't ready for this, she wasn't ready for the likes of Lance Montgomery. He would play on her weakness, feed on her hunger—the sexual one.

It had been well over a year since a man had made love to her, brought her to the point of no return, sent sensations racing through her body, mind and soul. But here, sitting at this table that was elegantly set for two, impossible as it seemed with the delicious aroma filling the air and taunting her nostrils, her mind was dominated by another scent.

The scent of a man.

He was a man who wouldn't hesitate to prey on all the obvious signs of a woman in heat. Yes, she was definitely in a danger zone.

She sat back in her chair and watched moments later as Lance came out of the kitchen pushing a dining cart. He unloaded several sterling silver trays and placed them in the middle of the table, then lifted the lids to reveal baked chicken, wild rice, a medley of vegetables, macaroni and cheese and sweet potatoes.

"I heard since you were really a Southern girl that you liked soul food and didn't eat it often enough, so I thought I'd do the honor and give you what you wanted."

She looked up and met his gaze, genuinely impressed, and although she didn't want to, she felt touched. "Thank you."

"You're welcome. Would you like a glass of wine?"

"Yes, please."

She watched as he reached across the table and grabbed the bottle of wine and poured a generous portion into her glass. He then poured himself a glass as well. She observed further when he took the seat across from her. "It's okay to dig in," he said.

After bowing her head and saying the grace, she did just that.

Lance leaned back in his chair and studied her while he slowly sipped his wine, savoring, relishing and appreciating the woman sitting at his table. He seldom shared his home with any woman. It was his usual mode of operation to take them out somewhere, occasionally to a hotel, but never here, his private quarters, his sanctuary, his refuge from life as he knew it.

She glanced over at him and asked, "Are you going to eat anything?"

He smiled. "No, soul food doesn't thrill me like it does you. I'll just sit here and patiently wait for dessert."

She shrugged, wondering what kind of dessert he had on the menu. She glanced around the room after taking another bite of food. He'd been right. This waiter-chef Stuart was an excellent cook. "You have a very nice place. I bet it costs you a fortune each month."

He smiled. "It's paid for. Gaining ownership to it was at the top of my list when I got my first royalty check."

She grinned. "Must have been some check."

He chuckled. "It was." At times it still amazed him that some people felt they needed to know about the art of staying single—a code he lived by. It wasn't like he had invented it; men had been footloose and fancy-free for years and so had some women. He could only guess people liked hearing how to remain that way from someone else.

He watched as she ate—saw how she savored each piece she placed in her mouth knowing the taste was satisfying her palate cravings. Stuart would be pleased to know she had enjoyed the meal he had prepared.

"Wow, that was delicious," Asia said a short while later, fully aware that all the time she had been eating Lance had been watching her. But she had been too busy satisfying her taste buds to care. When her wineglass had gotten empty he had stood to refill it. Otherwise he had sat there, across from her, watching her, saying nothing.

"Ready for dessert now?" he asked quietly. His voice seemed strained with patience; low, sexy.

"Umm, before I have dessert I think I better walk off what I just finished eating," she said. Taking her wineglass in her hand she stood and walked over to the window. Again she thought the view of the lake was magnificent. She turned to find him still sitting at the table, watching her.

"How long have you lived here?" she asked, not liking how the room was drenched in silence. It had been okay while she'd been eating but now she found the silence vexing.

"Five years. My father still lives in Gary, Indiana, which is a stone's throw away from here. Since he refuses to move to Chicago, at least he's close enough so that I can check up on him periodically."

"And you have brothers?" she asked, remembering his conversation with Sean earlier.

"Yes, actually two. They're both doctors. Logan is a plastic surgeon who lives in Florida and Lyle is a heart specialist living in Texas. The three of us are close, even in age, and it was hard for my father to raise three sons after my mother left."

Asia raised a brow. "Left?"

"Yes, she left when I was only eight. Lyle was ten and Logan twelve. She took off one day without looking back. Evidently motherhood got to be too much for her." He decided not to go into the sordid details of his mother's affair and the newborn baby girl she'd taken with her when she'd run off with her lover.

Asia nodded, wondering how any woman could do such a thing, just up and leave their family, especially children who needed her and not to mention a husband who Asia assumed loved her. "It was her loss since the three of you are now successful men."

"Yes, thanks to my father," he said, knowing he would be giving his dad credit for the way he and his brothers had turned out for the rest of his life.

"Are your brothers playas, too?"

Lance chuckled. "They aren't married if that's what you're asking. But they are involved in relationships."

"Serious ones?"

He chuckled again. "As far as serious goes for now I guess. But I don't see either of them getting married anytime soon."

Asia nodded and turned back to the window. It was late afternoon; the sun, which had been shining bright when she'd first arrived, was now going down. Boats were sailing on the lake, looking like little toys. It had been a good day for it, if that was the sort of thing you were interested in.

"It's a beautiful view from here, isn't it?"

She almost jumped. She hadn't heard Lance get out of his chair to come stand behind her.

She inhaled deeply. "Yes, it's gorgeous," she said, not turning around. Gauging their proximity, they were standing close; too close. She could actually feel the heat of him on her back, her butt, the back of her legs. And the warmth of his breath was on her neck. She wondered if the temperature had suddenly gone up in the room . . . or if it was just her.

She felt hot. Very hot. Unbearably hot.

She was tempted to take off her jacket but thought that wouldn't be a good idea. Especially now.

"Yes, it's gorgeous, just like you, Asia."

Asia sighed. He shouldn't be saying those things and most importantly she shouldn't be listening, taking it all in, basking in the words. Suddenly, it seemed that her back ached and she wanted to lean back against him and his solid chest. She was tempted.

Giving in to temptation, she closed her eyes and leaned back, getting more than she bargained for; felt more than she expected. Besides his chest being solid, the area that was below his belt felt large, hard. She knew what that meant and knew it was time for her to go.

"I think I'll pass on dessert. It's time for me to leave," she said softly, meaning it, although she didn't make a move to depart.

"Are you sure about that? You haven't asked what's on the menu," he murmured, and in a smooth move he wrapped his arms around her waist and gently pulled her back to him, letting her feel how much larger and harder he had gotten in just that short time. His erection felt wonderful pressed against her butt.

Her fingers tightened on the stem of her wineglass as sensations began ripping through her, slow, easy, deliberate. While one part of her mind was telling her not to give in to the enticement and the lure of temptation, another part of her, that part that always seemed to come alive whenever Lance was around, told her it was okay to experience those things she had shut the door on a year ago. After all, she was a woman and women had needs just like men. And why should a woman have to be the one to keep her panties on when a man certainly didn't know the meaning of keeping his pants zipped?

Her head began spinning at the mixed signals, the varied messages her mind was receiving. Needs and wants versus plain old common sense were battling it out, and at the moment, needs and wants were winning. "Okay, you got me curious. What's for dessert, Lance?"

"Something called Chocolate Temptation," he said throatily. "And it's something we'll both enjoy." Before she could take her next breath, he turned her in his arms and captured her mouth with his.

At that moment, that instant, that very second, needs and wants conquered Asia's spirit, broke her resolve and made her open her mouth. Lance slipped his tongue inside and began a mating ritual that nearly brought her to her knees, made her light-headed with desire and stole her breath.

Her empty wineglass fell noisily to the carpeted floor as her eyes fluttered closed and her arms surrounded him, clutched his neck, tight, to hold his mouth in place although it didn't seem to be going anywhere. But she still held it in place anyway, just in case. She intended to get her fill and deal with the consequences later.

This is what had ruled her dreams since the last time they had kissed. Pleasure mixed with heat combined with an awakening that started a molten sensation all through her body. She knew her panties had to be drenched. Now she understood why some women claimed to take an extra pair with them on dates. This was one situation where a spare pair would definitely come in handy.

Then it seemed as if with deliberate precision he began rubbing his chest against hers, using the same rhythm as his tongue inside her mouth, the contact to her breasts was electrifying, tantalizing, driving her mad. She felt sexual, sensual, starved. Her body was reminding her of the healthy sexual drive she'd once had, the one that was returning full force.

With a harsh breath Lance pulled his mouth away and swept her into his arms. He swiftly moved toward his bedroom. After placing her on the bed she drew him down to join her and he went willingly, kissing her again, devouring her mouth.

Moments later, needing to breathe, he pulled back, studied her mouth. He had left his mark. She looked like a woman who had been thoroughly kissed.

"I've never been kissed the way you kiss me," she murmured, gazing into the darkness of his eyes.

A surge of pleasure rammed through him with her words. She hadn't seen anything yet. Before she left she would discover just how good he was with his tongue. But now, he wanted to touch her, see the naked flesh he had dreamed about, thought about, craved. His hands moved, patiently and with extreme care; he began undressing her, peeling off each item, and he didn't stop until every stitch was removed.

He sucked in a deep breath when she lay before him nude; every curve revealed and the beauty of her exposed. She was more than Chocolate Temptation, she was a dark, pleasurable delight and he intended to savor her the way she was meant to be savored.

"Aren't you going to remove your clothes?"

Instead of breaking into his concentration, her question only heightened it. "No, this isn't about me, it's about you, Asia. Remember in the limo when I asked if you would allow a man to treat you to pleasure? You insinuated that such a thing wasn't possible because men were inconsiderate bastards."

"I didn't say that."

He smiled. "Not in so many words but it was obvious you thought it." He held her gaze. The sun was going down, and remnants of it were coming through the window and touching her exposed flesh. Flesh he wanted to taste all over.

"But I do want to pleasure you, Asia. Will you let me?" he asked as blood, hot, heavy, surged through his veins. He had left his mark on her mouth and now he wanted to leave his mark on her body. "When you leave here you will still be celibate but completely satisfied."

His words and the intense look in Lance's eyes shot heat up Asia's arms. His voice held a huskiness, yet at the same time a degree of tenderness she would never have expected from him. Once again he was proving that Dr. Lance Montgomery was a very complex man . . . but a very generous one if his offer was real. She'd never known a man who wanted to cater to her pleasure and her pleasure alone. "Will one-sided pleasure be enough for you?" she asked, her voice barely a whisper.

He smiled. "Yes, but it won't be as one-sided as you think. Just looking at you like this makes me want to come. I'm going to get as much enjoyment out of what I'll be doing as you will. Tasting you is going to drive me mad."

His words were making her body feel heated, deliriously weak. But she found the strength to reach up and encircle his neck with her arms. "Then go mad, Lance Montgomery, and take me with you."

A smile touched the corner of Lance's lips, then his mouth hungrily covered hers, claiming it his as he intended to do the rest of her, every inch. Moments later, he pulled back, but his mouth smoothed over her lips, nipping at them, licking from corner to corner and then he nudged her mouth open again in another long, soul-stirring kiss.

The next time he pulled back, his lips began moving lower, slowly, down her throat to her breasts. His mouth hung slightly open, over a nipple. His breath, hot and urgent, meant to heat the hardened tip, tease, taunt, claim, and then his tongue stalked out, grasped, licked, sucked and he heard the moan that rippled deep in her throat as he continued to trace lazy circles around both nipples, enjoying what he was doing to her; how he was making her feel.

Then it came time to go lower, move farther south and he felt his erection harden and thicken even more. He moved to her navel and skimmed the outskirts with his tongue, felt the quiver of her body beneath his mouth. He licked her softly over and over again and when she purred, sensations raced through him. "Do you like this?" he asked, barely able to get the words past his lips.

"Oh, yes. Yes," she responded in a deep guttural voice.

"Good." Deciding it was time to take on the real treat he moved his mouth lower.

Lance's warm mouth coming so close to that intimate part of her stole Asia's breath. She closed her eyes and pressed her head back into the pillows and grabbed hold to the bedspread, tight. If he kissed her there, the same way he kissed her mouth, she would die from extreme gratification. She would like to hear him explain her death to the paramedics when they arrived to take her body away.

"Oh." The word escaped her lips when she felt his mouth close over her and felt the entry of his teasing tongue. He soothingly nipped her and before she could take another breath, he began exploring her as intimately as any man had ever done. Shamelessly, she lifted her bottom off the bed and pressed against his mouth, and as if knowing just what she wanted, he grasped her hips and greedily devoured her.

Lance's full concentration was on what he was doing. Asia's womanly scent inflamed his nostrils and her taste drove him over the edge. Her moans were music to his ears and her nails that dug into his head was pain he gladly endured. Her moans got louder as he tongued her harder and faster.

And then he felt it. A violent spasm tore through her and a loud scream was hurled from her lips. Then suddenly, passion, the likes of which he'd never known before poured through him, alerting him to what was about to happen. He was ready; had gotten prepared. Earlier, in anticipation, he had used the half-bath off from the kitchen to put on a condom so that when this happened, he wouldn't embarrass himself. Her taste alone was making him come. He didn't want to think how it would be when he actually made love to her.

He accepted the explosion that ripped through him as he continued to take Asia over the edge. He was right there with her and he knew from this moment on that his life would never be the same again.

Hours later, Lance stood in front of the window in his living room staring at the lake as he drank a glass of wine. What the hell had happened to him in that bedroom with Asia? He was a man accustomed to being in charge but he had relinquished that control to her. He had almost lost his mind while absorbed in the sensuous sweet taste of her body.

It had been an experience that he wouldn't forget. He had wanted to hear her scream but had fought back from screaming himself. What he felt in giving her pleasure had been potent and earth-shattering. And afterward, after throwing a blanket over her, he had taken her in his arms and held her while she slept. And she was still sleeping.

And he was thinking.

He had never been driven to give a woman that much pleasure. What was there about her that made her so different from the others? And why had he been so obsessed with having her? And still was. What he'd done today was just a prelude to the actual lovemaking act. Why did the thought of making love to her throw him into a state of turmoil and unrest? Suddenly, out of nowhere, he knew the answer. With Asia he had felt something he had never felt before.

Emotions.

That realization caused panic to surge through him and fear engulfed his world. For several moments he struggled with the thought, the slightest possibility, that any woman could make him feel emotions. He was a playa of the third degree. He was a man who didn't commit, no matter how hot the sex was. He didn't do emotions. Nothing had changed.

But deep down he felt the threat of change and knew it could actually happen if he didn't do something to stop it. A woman like Asia Fowler could strip him of everything, his peace of mind, his self-respect, his pride. The last thing he needed was a woman coming into his life to screw it up again. He sighed deeply. He could see only one solution to his problem. He had to end this madness. His survival depended on it.

"Lance?"

He turned slowly at the sound of Asia's voice and met her gaze. She was completely dressed but he couldn't help but remember how she had looked naked; how incredibly responsive she had been to his touch and his mouth. Her gaze was searching his and he saw the questions logged there. He knew what she wanted: an assurance that she hadn't made a mistake in the liberties she had given him. She had shared a part of herself that she hadn't shared with another man in over a year. Although they hadn't made love in the actual sense, they had made love in the carnal sense.

But now it was time to pull back. He had played this game long enough and it had backfired on him. He knew what he had to do, although a part of him didn't want to. However, there was no way around it.

"So, do you now understand what can happen when a woman denies herself pleasure?" he asked, then took a sip of his wine. He had meant his words to cut her when all he wanted was to cross the room and take her into his arms and hold her and . . .

He inhaled deeply, then said, "I hope you learned this lesson well." He saw her flinch, and saw the anger that began spreading from one side of her face to the other.

"Lesson? What are you talking about?" she asked, speaking in that tone that told him she was pissed off.

He smiled in a way he knew was downright chilling, convincingly so. "I'm talking about the fact that I had you just where I wanted you. I could have ended your little sex strike here; tonight. What advice would you have given to the sistahs in your next book had that happened, Asia? You were lucky I decided not to take things that far. I wanted dessert instead of the full-course meal, but next time I—"

"Next time!" she exclaimed, as anger consumed her body with a vengeance. "There won't be a next time, your bastard!"

At that precise moment, their attention was drawn to a knock at the door. Needing distance from the reality of the moment, Lance crossed the room and opened it.

Rachel Cason from V-103. He wondered what the hell she was doing showing up at his place. He quickly decided that whatever the reason her timing was perfect. In true playa form he needed to prove that no one woman could get under his skin. He needed to prove it to Asia and to himself as well.

"Rachel, come in," he said, stepping aside for her to enter, then closing the door behind her.

She stopped when she saw Asia. "Dr. Fowler?" Her gaze then went to Lance. "Sorry, I didn't mean to interrupt anything."

He smiled. "You aren't interrupting anything important. She was just leaving," he said, pulling Rachel into his arms and kissing her with a hunger that he really didn't feel.

He released Rachel's mouth long enough to watch Asia cross the room to pick up her purse off the table and her coat from the sofa. Without saying anything else she walked to the door.

Before opening it she met his gaze and what he saw in the depths of her eyes made his heart clench. He had effectively destroyed any chance of them ever connecting.

She then opened the door and closed it shut behind her.

18

Sam and Falon

"Nice party."

Falon glanced up at Sam and smiled. "Thanks, but Marcy did most of the work. Having Wayne back from Iraq, even if it's only for two weeks, has done wonders for her attitude. She was becoming a nervous wreck and an absolute grouch with all the unrest going on over there. And hearing that a soldier was getting killed every day wasn't helping. I just wish he could stay in the States awhile longer."

Sam nodded and glanced over at the couple who were on the dance floor wrapped up in each other's arms. It didn't take much to see that the two were very much in love. He remembered a time when he had danced with Kim that way.

"Want some more punch, Sam?"

He glanced at Falon. She was being a thoughtful hostess and although she didn't want to take credit for how the party was going, he knew she was the person responsible for all the food. Everything looked and tasted good, and he was glad that she and Marcy had thought to invite him. "No, thanks, I'm fine."

He glanced back at Marcy and Wayne. They were still on the dance floor. After being separated for eight months, it was obvious the two would definitely be making up for lost time during the two weeks that Wayne was here. He agreed with Falon that it was a pity that he had to go back. But the good thing was that his full year would be over in about four more months and he would be coming home permanently. He first met Wayne earlier that day and had found him to be a real nice guy. He had also met Falon's brother Ron and her cousins and had found them likeable as well.

"Hi, Sam. Falon."

Sam glanced around to see his other neighbor, who everyone referred to as Ms. Candy, approach them. He'd learned that the woman was in her mid-fifties and worked out of her home transcribing doctor's records. He also knew she was one of those neighbors who seemed to know everybody's business. "Hello, Ms. Candy."

"Nice party, isn't it?"

"Yes, it is."

The woman then turned her smile to Falon. "Sweetheart, everything was simply fabulous, and you must give me your recipe for that shrimp salad. It was so delicious."

Falon smiled graciously. "No problem. I can have it for you next week."

"Wonderful." Ms. Candy then turned her attention to the couple on the dance floor and stated the obvious. "Maybe we should end the party so those two can finally go to bed."

Falon chuckled. "Hey, maybe we should. I think I'll pass the word in a few moments that the party is officially over."

Ms. Candy nodded her agreement and then walked off. Sam thought besides being nosey, the woman was very astute. "Are Wayne and Marcy planning on checking into a hotel tonight?" he asked Falon curiously.

She grinned. "No, they're staying here."

He lifted a brow. "I think three might be a crowd . . . especially in their situation," he said grinning as he took another sip of his punch. "It's obvious that the heat is on."

Falon took a sip of hers, chuckled, then said, "Yeah, I know and that's why I offered to check into a hotel tonight. It's easier for me to throw a few things in an overnight bag than it would be for Marcy. She doesn't know the meaning of packing light."

Sam nodded. By the way the couple was all into each other on the dance floor, he figured that Marcy wouldn't have to pack anything at all and it would be just fine with Wayne. He glanced over at Falon and saw her watching the couple and he could see the longing in her eyes as well as the happiness. She was happy for Marcy but a part of him knew, especially after the conversation they'd had that night in his apartment, that she wanted the same thing for herself. She wanted love and commitment in her life.

Hell. He wanted those things himself one day. But not now. With all the garbage he would bring to the table, he didn't know when he would be marriage material again, if ever.

"Well, I guess I'd better start putting a bug in everyone's ear that the party is over so I can begin putting the food away and straightening up before I go."

Sam nodded again. For some reason, the thought of Falon in a hotel room, even though she would be alone, didn't sit well with him and out of the blue he asked, "Would you like to stay over at my place tonight?"

Her brows lifted and the look on her face was total surprise. "What?"

He sighed, wondering how he could have suggested such a thing. But the offer was out there and he couldn't take it back, and a part of him didn't want to take it back. "Instead of going to a hotel, you can stay at my place tonight. I don't have any furniture in my guest room but my sofa makes into a bed."

Falon pondered Sam's invitation. She figured she had become acquainted with him well enough to know his offer had been made out of kindness and nothing more. She knew where he stood on relationships and affairs and he knew her position as well. They had decided to be friends and nothing more and so far things were working out better that way. She respected his decision not to become involved in a committed relationship, but she longed for the day she would meet a man who would want to commit his life to her. "I hate being a bother, Sam."

"You won't be."

She thought on it some more then asked, "What about that woman you're seeing? She might not like the idea that—"

"Tina and I aren't seeing each other anymore. We ended things a couple of weeks ago."

"Oh. Sorry."

"Don't be. It was for the best and it was a mutual decision."

Sam sighed. Falon didn't know how close to the truth what he'd said had been. Surprisingly, he had gotten tired of the sex-only relationship and could no longer put up with Tina quoting him their horoscope every time they were together. She had become outright obsessed with it to the point that sometimes the positions they took while making love were based on the stars.

On those nights where the angle of Pluto to the sun was good, he got the on-top position; and on those nights when Neptune was having a mellowing effect on Venus she was on top; then if there was a waxing full moon they did it from the back or on the side.

At first it had been fun trying out different positions but it had quickly gotten downright annoying that they couldn't just roll with the flow and do whatever suited them whenever it suited them. Besides, he hadn't been able to get the kiss he and Falon had shared out of his mind.

"And you're sure it won't be a problem?"

Falon's question interrupted his thoughts. "Falon, I'm positive. I'll be up late tonight so when you're finished here all you have to do is grab your overnight bag and come over."

She seemed to ponder his invitation some more, then said, "All right, as long as you're sure."

"I'm positive."

She smiled. "Okay then, you've got a deal. Thanks."

"You're welcome. Besides, that's what friends are for."

Her smile widened. "Yes, you're right. That's what friends are for."

———

"I may be out of line for asking but why did you and Tina decide to split?"

Sam glanced over his shoulder. Falon, armed with a stack of linen, was about to tackle the job of turning his sofa into a bed, and he was sitting at the kitchen table eating some of the Swedish meatballs she had graciously brought with her. Evidently she had known how much he enjoyed them at the party and brought him what was left.

Since he never thought of Falon as being the nosey type, he figured that the reason for her question was due to her concern for Tina. Because of her ex-boyfriend's betrayal, Falon saw any breakup as a heartbreak. He could tell her that, yes, she was out of line for asking but a part of him didn't mind her knowing the reason . . . at least the part he didn't mind telling her.

"Like I told you at the party it was a mutual decision. Tina and I decided it was time for things to end. She hadn't wanted a serious relationship any more than me and we decided the relationship we shared had run its course."

"And she was okay with it."

Sam smiled. "Yes, Falon, she was okay with it and I'm okay with it, too. Everybody's happy." Wanting to change the subject he asked, "How are things going at work?"

She smiled as she continued making up the sofa. "Things are going fine. I haven't told anyone but Marcy but I received a call from Paris last week. A hotel there is looking for an American chef and my name was given to them."

Sam suddenly felt a sensation oddly akin to panic invade his chest and when a meatball nearly went down the wrong pipe he began choking. Quickly he grabbed his water.

"Sam, are you okay?"

He waved off any of her concerns and took another huge swallow of water. "Yeah, yeah, I'm fine." He took another swallow then asked, "Paris? Don't you think that's a long way from home?"

"Yes, but it's a good opportunity and a chance of a lifetime. I'll only be gone for a year."

A year! Why did a year sound like forever to him? "When do you have to let them know?"

"I have to be interviewed first but I plan to talk to my parents about it tomorrow. I believe they will be okay with it if I got the job. I think my leaving town for a while will do me good."

He nodded, not knowing what else to say.

"But then, it's not a definite that I'm the chef they want. They've invited me to fly to New York for the interview. I understand they will also be interviewing four other chefs."

Sam nodded. No matter what Falon said, the job would probably be hers if she wanted it. He had eaten enough of her food to know she was an excellent chef. "Well, I think you have a good shot at it," he said truthfully. And he wasn't sure how he actually felt about that.

The next morning the aroma of eggs cooking and bacon frying teased Sam's nostrils. He turned over in bed and opened his eyes. He then remembered that he had a houseguest.

Falon.

He closed his eyes again when he recalled the bomb she had dropped on him. There was a possibility that she would be moving to Paris for a year. Like she'd said, it would be a good opportunity for her but still a part of him knew he would regret her leaving. He also knew he couldn't have it both ways. He had decided he wasn't ready for a serious relationship and Falon was the type of woman who was.

Sighing deeply, he slipped out of bed and went into the bathroom to brush his teeth and take a shower. Moments later, wearing a pair of jeans and a pullover shirt, he walked into his kitchen and stopped dead in his tracks. Falon was fully dressed like she was going someplace and damn but she looked good. She was wearing a two-piece suit that was red in color and her shoes, a pair of pumps, were the same shade of red as her outfit. And those legs of hers made him do a double take. Her makeup, the little he detected she had on, was flawless, and her hair was flowing in a mass around her shoulders.

He must have made a sound, probably the sound of his guts clenching, and she glanced over her shoulder. "Good morning, Sam, I was just about to leave you note. I left eggs, bacon, sausage and toast warming for you in the oven."

He didn't care about food warming in the oven, he wanted to know why she was dressed the way she was. "Where are you going?" he asked, as if it was his right to know.

She picked her purse up off the table and smiled at him. "To church. I'm used to getting up early on Sundays whenever I'm not working to go to Sunday school; an old habit and one I enjoy."

She chuckled then added, "My parents always had this rule that no matter how late we stayed out and partied on Saturday night, we were expected to make church on Sunday. And they didn't care if we slept through the whole service, just as long as our bodies were accounted for."

Sam nodded. He couldn't help but smile. His parents had been the same way and Marcus's mom had been the worse. "You look good."

Falon smiled as she checked her purse for everything. "Thanks, and I would have invited you but I figured you wouldn't want to get up so early on Sunday."

She lifted her gaze and met his. "However, if you like, you can come to our morning service that starts at eleven o'clock."

He nodded again. He just might take her up on that. He did go to church occasionally but not as often as he knew he should. Even while married to Kim they had gone what they considered enough, but they had gone more regularly when their marriage had been in trouble and had needed counseling from their minister. It had been counseling that hadn't done any good since Kim had decided to do what she wanted to do anyway.

"Thanks. I just might do that. Where is your church located?"

She gave him the directions. "Don't be surprised if you see me," he said smiling.

She smiled back. "I won't."

Sam really enjoyed the service at Falon's church and then afterward, she invited him to her parents' house for dinner. Now he knew where Falon had gotten her cooking skills from. Both her parents, who appeared to be in their early fifties, were whizzes in the kitchen, and they seemed to enjoy working together to deliver a mouthwatering feast.

He noted Falon had been careful when introducing him to everyone; making sure they understood the two of them were friends and nothing more. After dinner, he and her father enjoyed a rather lengthy conversation about the Chicago Bulls and he discovered the man had season tickets. Falon's father also told him about a men's retreat the church would be hosting next month and invited him to attend the two-day affair. It sounded interesting and Sam promised to think about it.

"Your parents are great," he told Falon while he helped her wash the dinner dishes. She had volunteered to do the task while her brother Ron, she said as usual, ate and ran.

"Thanks. I think they're great, too, and they have been wonderful role models for me and Ron."

Sam didn't say anything for a moment while he dried the dish she had handed to him. Now he understood why she felt the way she did about love and commitment. It was evident that Mr. and Mrs. Taylor enjoyed their lives together. He knew his parents had had a long marriage, too, and that was one of the reasons why he had never shunned the thought of marriage like a lot of other guys did. He had embraced it and knew that was the way things were supposed to be done. A guy found the girl of his dreams and married her, they had children and then lived happily ever after. Unfortunately for him, Kim had shown that's not how it always worked.

"Well, that's it."

He blinked when Falon's words pulled him out of his reverie. "What?"

She smiled. "That was the last dish. Kitchen duty is officially over. Now we can leave."

"Oh." Since they had come in separate cars he knew they would be leaving that way and for some reason he felt a little disappointed. He wasn't ready to part from her company. "How would you like to play a game of cards at my place?"

She lifted her brow. "Tonight?"

"Sure. If Wayne and Marcy are interested they can join us."

Falon nodded. "No one has heard from Marcy all day so we can only assume they are still too much into each other for company, but I can certainly call and ask."

"Okay."

A few moments later when he was about to leave, Falon came out of the house grinning and whispered for his ears only, "Marcy said thanks for the invitation but she and Wayne have more to do with their time than play cards."

He laughed. "Okay."

"But I'd love to play if the invitation is still open."

He nodded and smiled. "It is."

The next morning at work Sam tried to concentrate on the report he was reading and found it impossible. He finally tossed the papers aside and leaned back in his chair. He had really enjoyed Falon's company this weekend. And he had discovered last night she was as much of a sneak at playing cards as he was.

He smiled. He hadn't been able to pull anything on her and she had proven to be a worthy opponent. Later that night Wayne and Marcy had finally decided they needed a break from the bedroom and had come over to join them. What ensued after that was a game of the guys against the girls and he couldn't remember the last time he'd had so much fun. To give Marcy and Wayne another night together, he had offered Falon the use of his couch again and when he'd left this morning, she was still asleep.

The ringing of the phone on his desk caught his attention and he quickly crossed the room to pick it up. "Yes, Alice?"

"It's a call from Mr. Lowery."

"Thanks, and please put him through." A few moments later he heard Marcus's voice. "Man, I called your house this morning and a woman answered. She sounded kind of sleepy so I hung up on her thinking I had the wrong number but when I checked my call-back button I saw that I had dialed the right number."

Sam chuckled. "Oh, that was Falon."

"I see."

Sam raised his eyes to the ceiling knowing what thoughts were probably going through Marcus's mind. "It's not what you think, man. Falon and I are still nothing more than friends. Her cousin's boyfriend came back into town from Iraq and I invited Falon to crash over at my place . . . on my sofa . . . to give them privacy."

"Umm, that was real kind of you."

"Thanks. I'm a nice person. Is there a reason you called me so early that you woke up my houseguest?"

"How was I to know you were going into the office early? You're usually still at home around seven. Besides, I tried calling you yesterday afternoon and couldn't reach you."

"I had dinner with Falon and her parents."

"I see."

Sam frowned. "Will you stop saying that?"

"What?"

"That you see."

Marcus chuckled. "But I do see even if you don't."

Now that statement pissed Sam off. "You don't see a damn thing, Marcus."

"Okay, I don't see. Look, are you going to the gym after work today?"

Sam sighed deeply. Leave it to Marcus to ruin a perfectly good day. "Yes, are you?"

"Yes, and I just talked to Phillip. He'll be there, too," Marcus said. "I decided to take a vacation day today. Mom needs me to do a couple of chores around her place and that's where I'll be most of the day, so I'll see you guys later at the gym."

"All right." Sam hung up the phone. No matter what Marcus thought he saw, things were not going that way with him and Falon. They were friends and nothing more.

19

Phillip and Terri

Phillip inhaled deeply as he reached for the telephone for the third time that morning. It was barely nine o'clock but he couldn't put it off any longer. He had to call Terri Davenport and ask her out before she left her office for the courthouse. And he hoped that this time around she wouldn't turn him down.

"Baker, Smith and Reynolds," the professional speaking voice said a few moments later.

"Yes, I'd like to speak with Terri Davenport, please."

"Who may I say is calling?"

"Phillip McKenna."

"Thank you and please hold."

He inhaled deeply again and nervously drummed his fingers on the edge of his desk. What if she wouldn't take his call? What if she—

"This is Terri."

He swallowed hard. "Terri, this is Phillip McKenna."

There was a brief pause on the other end, and then she said, "Yes, I know. My secretary told me. How are you?"

"I'm fine and yourself?"

"I'm okay and how is Chandra?"

He appreciated her asking about his daughter. "She's fine, and since we've gotten her professional help she hasn't bitten any more kids."

"That's good."

"And how is Star?"

"Star is doing fine. Thanks for asking."

"You're welcome."

After a few seconds that were leading to dead silence, he thought he'd better say something since he was the one who had initiated the call. "I was wondering if you're free this coming Wednesday evening?"

"Wednesday evening?"

"Yes. I'm taking Chandra to the UniverSoul Circus that's coming to town and was wondering if you and Star would like to join us. I thought the four of us could do dinner at Outback Restaurant and then be ready to enjoy the show at seven."

After thinking about it, he figured it would be best if their first date included the girls. Once she saw that he was an okay guy, hopefully she wouldn't hesitate to go out with him the next time alone.

"Dinner at Outback and seats at the UniverSoul Circus?"

"Yes."

"Wow, sounds wonderful. We'd love to join you and Chandra."

Phillip smiled as he leaned back in his chair. "Great. I'll pick you and Star up around five. Will that be okay?"

"Yes, that will be fine and thanks for inviting us."

He smiled. "It was my pleasure. Good-bye."

"Good-bye."

He let out a deep breath. Even over the phone, the sound of Terri Davenport's voice stirred everything inside of him to life. And all he had to do was close his eyes to remember how he had made love to her. The memories could make him hard as iron and hot as fire.

Seeing her again wouldn't cure everything that ailed him, but it was definitely a start.

Gripping her coffee cup tight in her hand, Terri got up from her desk and walked over to the window. She had thought about Phillip

McKenna a lot over the past month and had often wondered if she would ever hear from him again, considering she had turned down his dinner invitation the last time he'd called.

She smiled as she took a sip. This time he was using a new strategy by including the girls. The attorney in her couldn't help but admire the way his mind operated. One sure way to get to the mother was to win over the child. Although he had initially suggested the girls were the reason he had wanted to see her again, she hadn't believed him for one minute. But even so, at the time she hadn't been ready to go out with anyone so it would not have mattered even if she had believed him.

But now all that had changed, thanks to a wonderful therapist who had helped her worked through an issue that had been bogging her down for the past seven years . . . and with the help of a wonderful man whose name she didn't even know.

She closed her eyes, remembering a night she would never forget. She thought of her secret lover often, wondering how he was doing and doubting he knew just to what extent he had helped her that night.

She took another sip of coffee thinking of those erotic kisses, that tongue that knew how to inflict pleasure to a degree she hadn't known existed, than anything she knew, thrusts that gave as much as they took, and seeking fingers that stroked her flesh until she'd felt drugged. He had proven to be just as adventurous in bed as she had.

And when she had awakened he was gone; slipping out of her life with the same ease that he had slipped in.

But because of him and the unselfish gift he had given her, she knew that her life would never, ever be the same again.

20

Marcus and Naomi

"What are you doing here?"

Naomi, whose face had been buried in the refrigerator while looking for eggs and milk, whirled around, almost bumping her head. Shocked, she placed her hand over her heart to keep it supported in her chest, thinking if she didn't it would most certainly drop to the floor. "What are *you* doing here?" she countered.

Marcus leaned back against the closed door and frowned. Naomi looked flustered and surprised as hell. "I asked you first. Besides, I don't owe you an explanation. The last time I looked, this was my mother's house and I'm welcome here anytime."

With clenched teeth she slammed the refrigerator shut and crossed her arms over her chest. "So am I."

He glared at her, trying not to stare at her mouth, specifically her bottom lip. For some bizzare reason he wanted to suck on that lower lip. "Maybe so but that doesn't answer my question," he decided to say. "What are you doing here?"

Naomi returned his glare. "Would you believe me if I said I was stealing the silverware?"

"From inside of the refrigerator? No. Come up with something else." He continued to study her. This was the first time he had been this close to her in a long time, and he could see just how clear and smooth her skin was, a silky texture and a smooth shade of dark brown.

"I don't have to come up with anything. I'm here because Ms. Essie called and asked me to come over. She forgot that she had a doctor's appointment this morning and had arranged for some man to come over to repair her washing machine. Evidently she promised this person breakfast because before she left she asked for me to whip him up some bacon and eggs."

Marcus lifted a brow. Puzzlement showed on his face. "My mama actually told you that?"

Annoyance lined her features. "Yes. Why would I make up something like that? Now if you'll excuse me, I have to fix eggs and bacon." She turned back around to the refrigerator and reopened it.

"I don't want any."

"What?" she asked over her shoulder.

"I said I don't want any."

"Any what?"

"Eggs and bacon. I've eaten already."

Naomi turned back around. "Who gives a flip that you've already eaten?"

Marcus laughed. All the years he'd known Naomi, he had never known her to give off any lip. "You should if you believe that cock-and-bull story my mother concocted," he told her.

Confusion showed on her face. "What are you talking about?"

"I'm the man who's fixing my mother's washing machine. She set us up."

Naomi closed the refrigerator and leaned against it. "Why would she do something like that?"

"Why do you think?"

He waited. It wouldn't take long for her to figure it out. When she did, she met his gaze, apologetically. "I'm sorry, Marcus. I had no idea what Ms. Essie was doing."

He shrugged. "It's not your fault. Neither is it mine. But maybe it's time we both had a long talk with her."

Naomi nodded. "Yeah, maybe it is."

"But I doubt it would do any good. She's determined to play matchmaker." Then he thought of something. He hadn't noticed another car in the driveway when he had arrived. "Where's your car? I only noticed my mom's car when I pulled up."

"That's because she has mine. When I arrived, she said she couldn't find her car keys so I offered to let her use mine so she wouldn't be late for her appointment."

Marcus raised his eyes to the ceiling. "Yeah, misplacing her keys sounds like another tall tale to me."

Naomi inhaled deeply. "Well, I'll call a cab."

He cocked his head. "Why?"

"Why what?

"Why are you calling a cab?"

"So that I can leave."

"What's the hurry? Why can't you wait until my mother returns with your car?"

Naomi sighed in frustration. "Look, maybe you've forgotten our last conversation but I haven't."

She would never forget that he told her not to call him again. He didn't want to have anything to do with her, and if that was what he wanted, she was fine with it. She had prayed about it and didn't intend to worry about it any longer. In time the Lord would either make it possible for him to love her back or would remove him from her heart.

"I remember what I said to you that day and I owe you an apology. I know I came on rather strong. My only excuse is that at the time I was going through some things. In a way I still am, but that was no reason to be rude to you, especially when you had been kind enough to invite me to dinner. You also apologized for what happened that day you came to my house and I should have been willing to accept your apology and let it go."

She met his gaze. "Yes, you should have. Now if you'll excuse me I think I will call that cab." She walked off and he couldn't help but stare at her long legs that were showing beneath her short denim skirt.

The problem with his mother's washing machine didn't take long to fix and in less than an hour, Marcus was back in the kitchen. He grabbed an apple off the kitchen table and had just taken a huge bite when he glanced out of the window. Naomi was sitting outside on the steps. Evidently the cab she'd called hadn't arrived yet. It would surprise him if it did. From what he'd heard, due to the increase of robberies, cabs weren't going into certain areas of town any longer.

Hell, he'd heard the pizza man's car had gotten hijacked while delivering an order to the Turners last week. This neighborhood was the same one where he used to live and where he would stay outside and play with his friends until dark. As a child he had considered it the safest place in the world. Now the neighbors, those who were still left, had banded together and formed a coalition to keep drugs, gangs and violence out of the community.

He had tried talking his mother into letting him buy her another house, one in a nicer and safer neighborhood, but she had staunchly refused saying her church was in walking distance and all her friends lived close by. He had let the subject rest. Maybe it was time to bring it up again.

Opening the back door he walked out on the porch to join Naomi. "I see you're still here."

She glanced up at him. "Yeah, the cab never came."

He nodded as he sat on the steps beside her. The air was chilly but she wasn't wearing a jacket. Evidently she felt warm enough in the pullover sweater she had on. "That doesn't surprise me. This neighborhood isn't what it used to be."

"Yeah, I guess you're right." She glanced over at him. "So what are you doing home today?"

He smiled. "I decided to take the day off to spend it with Mama—to do whatever she needed me to do around here."

She leaned back on her arms. "That was thoughtful of you."

He chuckled. "Yeah, but if she wants me to continue to be thoughtful she needs to stay out of my business."

Naomi smiled. "I'm sure she meant well. You're her only child, Marcus. She loves you and worries about you."

He frowned. "I'm thirty-two, Naomi."

"And I'm sure she of all people knows your age since she's the one who gave birth to you. But I've heard that once a mother then always a mother. It's in her makeup to worry. She can't help it. And it's also in her makeup to want you to be happy. She can't help feeling that way, either."

He nodded again. A part of him wished what she'd just said didn't make so much sense. But it did. "So why aren't you at work today?"

She shifted on the step. "Sundays and Mondays are my days off. On Sundays I go to church and on Mondays I usually volunteer to help any senior citizen at church who needs it. I'm part of the pastor's senior ministry."

He lifted a brow. "When do you have time for yourself?"

She grinned. "I make time for myself."

He had to conclude what she said was true because whenever he saw her she looked good. Like now. Even dressed in a skirt and pullover sweater she looked fantastic. Her hair was short but styled in a neat cut, her nails were always polished and by the shape she was in it was apparent that she cared about her health.

"Do you date, Naomi?"

At first she didn't respond, but then he heard her take a deep breath. He sighed. What right did he have to ask her that considering how he'd treated her this past year?

"Sometimes," she said softly. "We have a singles group at church and once in a while we all get together and do things."

He nodded. He remembered his mother mentioning the group after Dottie had died, thinking he might have been interested. At the time the only thing he'd been interested in doing was wallowing in his grief.

"Why do you want to know if I date?"

He shrugged. "Just curious."

A few moments passed and then she said, "We're having Family and Friends Day at church this coming Sunday. I'd love to invite you to attend, Marcus."

Marcus inhaled deeply, refusing to even consider the invitation. It had been during Family and Friends Day at his mother's church over five years ago that he'd met Dottie.

Moving on, letting go. Wasn't that what he was supposed to be doing? But still, some things were easier to do than others. "Thanks for the invite. I'll think about it."

They both glanced around when they heard a car pull in the yard. It was his mother returning and they could easily see that the sight of them sitting together on the steps had her smiling from ear to ear.

Marcus glanced over at Naomi and whispered, "Should we get into her case now for what she pulled or should we wait until later?"

Naomi met his gaze and smiled. "Wait until later. Let her gloat for a while. No harm's been done has it?"

He shrugged as he stood. "No, I guess not." He reached out and extended his hand to help her up. The moment their hands touched, he felt it. It was that same sensation that had hit him the moment she had touched him before; that time on his thigh, but the sensation had been the same.

A sensation of new awareness.

21

Sam and Falon

Falon glanced over at the man behind the wheel of the SUV as he drove through the chilly Indiana night to the grocery store. "Thanks, Sam, I guess I haven't been anything but a nuisance to you lately, but I really needed to pick this item up for tomorrow's presentation."

He glanced over at her and smiled. "Hey, no problem. I hadn't planned on doing anything tonight anyway. After spending time with Phillip and Marcus at the gym this evening all I intended to do after my shower was grab a beer and chill. Besides, I think you being a part of career day at that high school tomorrow is awesome."

"Thanks, and I'm looking forward to doing it. A lot of kids don't think about a career as a chef and I want to enlighten them as to the benefits." She not only planned to enlighten them but she planned to feed them by baking a batch of brownies and making them part of her presentation. She had already started mixing all the ingredients when she remembered she was low on sugar due to all the baking she'd done for the party last weekend. To make matters worse, Marcy had her car since Wayne had Marcy's. She had asked Sam if he would be willing to drive her to the store and he had been gracious enough to do so.

When they arrived at their destination, she quickly got both her seat and shoulder belts unfastened. "I promise not to take long.

I'm going to run in and run right back out," she said, smiling over at him.

He grinned. "Hey, no hurry. Like I said, I'm not pressed for time." He watched as she walked briskly across the parking lot toward the store's entrance and couldn't help noticing the way the guys she passed would turn and take a second look at her. She was definitely a looker with her mass of honey blond hair blowing in the wind, and even wearing a pair of jeans and a T-shirt and a short leather jacket she looked fantastic. He continued to watch her and the thought slowly crept into his mind that he would give anything to run his hand over every inch of her body in male appreciation. But another thought followed that one and reminded him that with Falon Taylor came requirements he wasn't ready to buckle down to.

Sam's mouth suddenly felt dry and he couldn't wait to get back home to get a beer. He took a deep breath. He had promised himself that he wouldn't think about Falon that way; after all, they were just friends. But hell, he was also a man and just the thought that she had spent two nights under his roof didn't help matters.

He blinked when he watched her come out of the store swinging a small bag in her hand. She opened the truck door and got back in. "See, I told you I wouldn't take long," she said, refastening her seat and shoulder belts.

"And I told you that time didn't matter." He stared at her several long moments before turning the ignition in his truck.

She raised an arched brow. "What?"

"I just remembered that of all the people who got on the dance floor Saturday night, you weren't one of them."

She chuckled. "I was too busy to dance."

"Then you owe me one."

"One what?"

"A dance."

She glanced over at him and saw he was dead serious. A warm feeling flowed through her from the way he was looking at her. His gaze seemed to burn right through her clothing. Not good for two people who were supposed to be just friends. "Okay. I'll remember that the next time Marcy throws a party."

He grinned. "Yeah, you do that."

They returned back to the apartment complex in no time. On the way back, she told him about a new recipe she would be trying out later in the week and invited him over to sample it.

"When are you leaving for New York?" Sam asked as they walked side-by-side back to their apartments.

"Friday morning and I won't be returning until Sunday evening."

"Do you need a ride to the airport?" he asked as he guided her through the building's huge glass doors.

"I was going to drive myself and leave my car there, but an extra car will come in handy for Marcy and Wayne, so I'm going to ask Ron or one of my cousins to take me."

"I'll do it."

She glanced up. Surprised. "You will?"

"Sure," he said, taking her hand and holding it while they walked.

For a moment she didn't respond, and then finally she said, "Thanks."

By now they had reached her door. "You're welcome."

She slowly pulled her hand from his. "I guess I better go on inside and finish the brownies."

"All right." He took a step back and watched as she unlocked the door. She stepped inside the apartment and was about to close the door behind her. "Falon?"

She glanced up and met Sam's gaze. "Yes?"

"Will you save a couple of brownies for me?"

She laughed that warm sound that made him yearn for more than friendship. "Yes, Samuel Gunn, I will save a couple for you. Good night."

He smiled. "Good night."

Later that night while lying awake in bed, Sam found his thoughts filled with Falon. He had tried the "just be friends" thing with her but it wasn't working. He wanted more and that was the crux of his problem. He wanted more but he wasn't sure he wanted the depth of a relationship that she did and he knew she wouldn't settle for less. She wanted exclusivity, and sharing an exclusive relationship with any woman was out of the question for him.

When he heard his phone ring he glanced over at the clock. It was almost midnight. Who would be calling at this hour? "Hello."

"Sammy?"

He rose up in bed. "Mom?" He felt a sudden lump in his throat. Why would his mother be calling him this late?

"Yeah, Sammy, this is me. I couldn't sleep. I had you on my mind."

He blew out a breath of relief, glad nothing was wrong with his parents. "Oh."

"You okay, Sammy?"

"Yes, Mama, I'm fine. How are you and Dad?"

"We're fine, too. We woke up this morning thinking about you, knowing what day it was."

He blinked and then he remembered. It was Kim's birthday. How could something that used to mean so much to him completely slip his mind? "To be quite honest, Mama, I had forgotten about it."

"And here me and your father thought you were probably all depressed today, thinking about her."

He took a few moments to let his thoughts dwell on his mother's statement and it then occurred to him that lately he hadn't thought of Kim at all. "No, I was fine today. I'm doing good, Mama. There's no need for you and Dad to worry about me."

And then only because his parents were miles and miles away and couldn't drop in at any time, he decided to say, "I've met someone." He didn't question why he wanted to tell them about Falon when he hadn't ever considered mentioning Tina to them.

"You did? Oh, Sammy that's wonderful," his mother said happily. It felt good to hear such happiness in her voice. "We're only friends, Mama. It's nothing serious. After what Kim did I'm not ready to take any such big steps yet."

"I understand, son. Now tell me about her. Does she go to church?"

Sam laughed. "Yes, Mama, she goes to church. In fact she believes in going to Sunday school and I attended morning service with her yesterday. The service was good."

"Already, I like this girl," his mother said, and he could hear the smile in her voice. "Bring her home the next time you come."

Sam shook his head. "We're just friends."

"Well, I hope by the time you want more that she's still around."

Sam frowned. "What do you mean by that?"

"What I mean, Sammy, is that good women, and I mean real good women, just like good men, are few in numbers and hard to find. I thought you had found a good one in Kim but I was wrong." With a sympathetic sigh of regret, she continued. "But I don't want you to make a mistake in thinking that all women are like Kim and possibly miss out on a blessing."

Several long moments passed before Sam said anything. "I loved Kim so much."

"I know you did. But you must continue to move forward and don't miss the forest for the trees. Gifts from God come in all kind of packages, and when they come we have to be ready to receive them. And there're times when we think we aren't ready, but the Father knows what's best because he knows *us* best. Think about what I've said, son."

"I will."

"Good night, Sammy."

"Good night, Mama."

22

Marcus and Naomi

Marcus raised his eyes to the ceiling. "Mom, I'm sure Naomi has more than one jacket." His mother had left a message for him at work asking that he drop by on his way home. She needed him to do an errand for her. After yesterday, he should have figured that the errand had something to do with Naomi.

"You don't know that for sure, Marcus."

"Then why don't we call her and find out?"

"And why can't you just do as I ask?"

He sighed heavily. There was no doubt in his mind that like yesterday, this was another setup. His mother had mentioned that his cousin Connor, who was two years younger than him and an officer on the Gary police force, had dropped by earlier today. He wondered why she hadn't asked Connor to take Naomi the jacket. "Mom, we need to talk."

"Not now, honey, Oprah is about to come on. We can talk some other time? Just call me later . . . after you've done this errand for me."

He watched as his mother shifted her attention from him to the television, tuning him out, outright dismissing him. "I'll be calling you tonight," he said, deciding to put in the last word. He grabbed the jacket off the chair and walked out of the house, locking the door behind him.

Essie Lowery breathed a sigh of relief when Marcus left. She loved her son but there were times when he could get on her last nerve. He thought he was so smart but she intended to show him that, no matter what, mothers were a lot smarter.

She grinned as she settled back in her chair to watch Oprah. Today was Naomi's day of beauty: the day she got her hair done, her nails polished, her feet and toes treated—all that stuff women did to themselves these days to get pretty. And no matter how much Marcus might not want to notice Naomi as a woman, Essie knew that eventually he would have no choice but to notice. After all, he was still a man.

Marcus clutched the jacket in his hand as he rang the doorbell. This was only the second time he had been to Naomi's house. The first time had been last year when he had dropped his mother off for some type of prayer meeting.

She lived in a nice subdivision that had only been established a few years ago. The houses were sturdy with a nice patch of yard. Naomi's house was one of the few with a huge porch and a rail that wrapped around both sides. He could imagine sitting on this porch on the less cool days to enjoy the outdoors while sipping a can of beer. According to his mother, Naomi lived close to the post office where she worked, and considering the cost of gas he figured that was good.

Marcus swore under his breath as he leaned against the porch railing. His mother had manipulated him for the last time. He intended to have a long talk with her tonight, something he should have done yesterday, but she had complained about the rough time she'd had at the doctor's office and the last thing he had wanted to do was add to her misery.

"Who is it?"

"It's Marcus."

The door opened slowly and a surprised expression crossed Naomi's face. "Marcus? What are you doing here?"

Marcus pushed himself off the railing to stand upright and opened his mouth, but for a split second, no words would come out. The first thing he noticed was that Naomi's hair was fixed differently. Curls were sprinkled all around her face and her eyebrows were arched in a fine line. He liked this new look on her.

"You hair looks great," he couldn't help but say.

She shrugged. "Thanks. I decided to try wearing it differently." She lifted one of her arched brows and asked again, "What are you doing here?"

Her question jogged his mind and made him remember. "Oh, here," he said, handing her the jacket. "You left this over to my mother's house yesterday."

She took the jacket. "Thanks, but you didn't have to drive out of your way to bring it to me. I have others."

He nodded. "Figured you did. I even told that to Mama but she was sort of persistent."

"Oh, I see."

And he knew that she really did. She was now as aware of what his mother was up to as he was. "I'm going to talk to her tonight about what's she's doing, and hopefully all this matchmaking stuff will stop."

"Okay," she said, not knowing what else to say. For the few moments following, neither said anything, and then she said, "I was just about to eat dinner. I have plenty and you're welcome to join me if you'd like."

He watched her chew on her lip; that same bottom lip that he'd been drawn to yesterday; the same one he was drawn to again today. Evidently, she was nervous, uncertain as to what his response would be. The last time she had invited him to dinner, not only had he turned her down, he had been downright rude. Maybe this was a way to make up for that day.

"I'd love to stay for dinner if you're sure that you have enough," he heard himself say.

He could tell by the expression on her face that she was surprised he had accepted her invitation. "Yes, I have enough. Come on in," she said, taking a step back. He entered and closed the door behind him.

Marcus glanced around thinking that she had a real nice place, neat, tidy. Her color scheme was that of autumn. Everything looked like sunburst, and somehow she was able to find a leather sofa of burnt orange that gave the furnishings such a vibrant effect. The crème-colored accessories toned things down nicely and a huge bookcase filled with books added character to the room, providing a lived-in effect. "Nice place," he said.

"Thanks, and make yourself at home. It won't take me but a second to put the food on the table."

"Need help?"

"No, thanks, I can handle things. But if you want to catch the evening news, the remote is on the table over there."

"All right, thanks."

"I didn't cook Sunday since the singles group went out to eat after church, but I did cook yesterday. I hope you like meat loaf."

"Yeah, I do."

"Good."

"Okay."

"Do you want anything to drink?"

He smiled, knowing she probably didn't have beer in her refrigerator. "What do you have?"

"Umm, iced tea, lemonade or water."

"I'll take a glass of lemonade."

"I'll be back in a minute."

Marcus took a deep breath as he watched Naomi walk off. She was wearing a pair of jeans and a top and he thought she looked damn good in both. Her scent was becoming familiar since he had smelled her yesterday. She was wearing the same fragrance today. He didn't know what it was called but he liked it.

Deciding to think about other things and not how Naomi looked and smelled, he walked across the room and picked the remote off the table and with a quick flick of his wrist, he brought her television to life. He then did as she suggested and took a seat and began watching the evening news.

"Dinner was wonderful, Naomi, thanks for inviting me to stay."

Naomi smiled as she walked Marcus to the door. "I'm glad you did. I enjoyed your company."

During dinner they had talked about a number of things that included movies, music, books. Marcus decided not to mention that the last book he had read was *The Playa's Handbook*. He did mention that he had finally gotten around to reading one of Eric Jerome Dickey's books and had enjoyed it. Her taste in reading was more along the inspirational line of books.

She stepped out on the porch with him. Outside it was pitch dark and except for the quarter moon in the sky, the only light came from the few street lamps that lined the road. It was almost November and he could tell there were freezing cold days headed their way. There was a cool breeze in the air and he saw Naomi shiver, wrap her arms around herself to ward off the chill. "You didn't have to walk me out. It's chilly out here, you might want to go back inside."

"I'm fine," she said, glancing up at him. "Have you thought any more about Sunday?"

He stared at her for a moment then shook his head. "Not really. I probably won't know what I'm going to do until Saturday night." He decided not to tell her that he had pretty much made up his mind not to accept her invitation to church after all. Like his mother, she would know when he didn't show up. "Well, I better get going. Thanks again for dinner."

"You're welcome."

Their gazes met, held for a moment and then Naomi watched as he quickly turned and trotted down the steps to his car.

———

Marcus frowned in irritation when he once again tried to call his mother only to find the line was still busy. Since she had call waiting, that meant she was carrying on more than one conversation, probably with members of her church. Hanging up the phone he decided he would definitely call her tomorrow. He intended to have his say.

He smiled when he thought about dinner tonight with Naomi. He had to admit that he had enjoyed himself. It was nice dining with a woman with no expectations of jumping her bones when the meal was over. When he'd begun going to Fantasyland it seemed as if his body had been starved for sex—since he had gone without it for so long—but now he seemed to have worked it out of his system. Hell, on some nights he and Breathless had done it almost a dozen times, nonstop. They had tried every position known to man and a few they had created on their own. But nothing had prepared him for the request Breathless had made the other night. He had certainly gotten a jolt when she had suggested that they remove their masks. Damn, he had almost freaked out.

Taking off their masks was the last thing that he wanted to do. He liked not knowing who she was and her not knowing him. Since he had pretty much stocked up on enough sex to last a lifetime, he didn't intend to ever go back to Fantasyland.

He was about to strip to take his bath when the doorbell rang. He wondered who would be dropping by this time of night as he walked to the door. It was almost nine o'clock.

"Yes?"

"I have a delivery for Marcus Lowery."

Marcus raised a brow and glanced out the peephole. Sure enough, it was a UPS man. He unlocked the door and opened it. "You're working late tonight, aren't you?" he asked the man as he handed him the box.

"Yes, but you're the last delivery. I just need your signature right here."

After Marcus signed the necessary paper, the guy said, "Have a good night."

Marcus smiled. "You do the same."

Closing the door, Marcus wondered who would be sending him a package. He sure hadn't ordered anything for himself. He checked and there was no return address on the box but it appeared to have been mailed locally.

Going into the kitchen, he got a small knife out the drawer to slide along the taped sides. After pushing aside the bubble wrap he pulled out the item that had been neatly placed inside.

A mask.

Marcus stilled. Perspiration suddenly broke out on his forehead. He knew who had worn this particular mask at Fantasyland and then remembered the last conversation they'd had.

He inhaled deeply and the only thing he could say at that moment was, "Shit."

23

Phillip, Terri and the girls

Phillip leaned back in the chair at his desk. He was on a three-way phone conversation with Sam and Marcus, and he could hear the panic in Marcus's voice.

"Don't start freaking out, Marcus," he said. "Getting that mask delivered to you last night might not mean anything," he said, although he personally didn't believe it for a second. There was a saying that "once you go black you didn't go back" and it seemed that this Breathless character was taking the saying to heart.

"I want to know how she found out where I live. I don't like this shit. I have a good mind to call the police."

"And tell them what?" Sam asked. "You don't have a name or a face, man. She could be any white woman with blond hair that you pass on the streets. It's my guess that she found out where you lived by following you home one night. Once she got your address, it was easy to find out who you are. It's a matter of public record."

"So what am I supposed to do?"

"Nothing," Phillip told him. "All she's done at this point is send you her mask and she might not do anything beyond that. I personally think she's trying to make a statement to let you know that she knows who you are but you don't know who she is. But if she continues to harass you, you might contact your cousin Connor for advice. He's still a policeman, right?"

"Yeah, he's still on the force." A few moments later he said, "I don't like this, man."

"Yeah, but for the time being there's nothing you can do about it. Don't let her get next to you. You said her parents had a lot of money, so she probably has nothing better to do with her time than to play games."

"I don't want to play games. I just want her to get out of my life and leave me alone," Marcus snapped.

Moments later after ending the conversation, Phillip stood and walked over to the window. In a way his situation with Terri was pretty damn similar. He knew who she was but she didn't know him. He wondered how she would feel if she ever found out he was the man who had made love to her that night at Fantasyland? The man she had shared not only her body with but some of her innermost secrets.

He hoped and prayed she didn't end up hating his guts.

"Oh, Daddy, I had so much fun. Didn't you have fun, too, Star?" Chandra McKenna asked her new friend as they each held their respective parent's hand while heading back to the car. Each girl was carrying a stuffed animal that was as big as they were, along with a bag of popcorn.

"Yes, I had lots of fun," Star Davenport said excitedly.

Terri glanced over at Phillip and smiled. The girls had been on their best behavior, and she had to admit that she had gotten caught up in the circus acts as much as the girls. The UniverSoul Circus was made up of veteran circus performers of African descent from around the world, and according to what she'd heard, the circus traveled to over forty-five cities annually. That was a lot of shows to do. What she liked best was the fact that the circus took traditional circus acts and surrounded them with rhythm and blues of the seventies, hip-hop and urban music of the nineties, salsa, gospel and jazz. She had found herself jamming in her seat most of the night. To say she had enjoyed herself was an understatement.

She stood back and watched as Phillip opened the car door for the girls and patiently waited while they found a place for all the stuff he had purchased for them, then carefully strapped them in with their seat belts. This was the first time Star had been out with any man other than her father, and Terri had been worried that her daughter wouldn't interact with Phillip, but she had worried for nothing. It seemed that now that Chandra was Star's new best friend, she could find nothing wrong with Chandra's daddy.

After the girls were taken care of, Phillip then opened the car door for her. "Thanks," she whispered.

He smiled. "You're welcome." That smile sent a shimmer of need straight through her. She stared at him for a moment, tempted to reach out and touch his face with the palm of her hand. Instead she quickly got inside the car and buckled her own seat belt, then watched him walk around the front of the car to get in.

After fastening his own seat belt, he glanced over his shoulder at the girls in the back seat. Neither appeared sleepy and it was after nine since the circus had lasted for two hours. They were talking a mile a minute about what they had seen that night, totally ignoring the two adults in the front seat.

"I bet we have to wrestle them awake for school in the morning," he glanced over and whispered to Terri, grinning.

Chuckling, she nodded. "Yes, but even I have to admit that it will be well worth the hassle. The circus was wonderful and I really appreciate you taking us."

Phillip smiled again. "It was my pleasure."

His words, spoken in a downright sexy tone, sent shivers through her body.

"You're cold?"

She met his gaze. "No, why do you ask?"

"Because you were trembling a second ago. If you want I can turn on the heat."

She shook her head. "No, thanks for the offer, but I'm fine." She leaned back in her seat and watched as he expertly maneuvered his

car out of the parking lot that was jammed with other vehicles trying to leave the circus.

"Do you have to be in court in the morning?"

His deep baritone sent shivers through her. They were shivers
she was aware of this time. Her secret lover also had had a deep
voice. Oh, for Pete's sake! She couldn't believe that she was sitting
here comparing Phillip McKenna to her secret lover, actually looking for similarities. She was really losing it, had definitely gone off
the deep end. "No, there's nothing on the books tomorrow, surprisingly," she said quickly.

"Will you have lunch with me?"

She glanced over at him. He was looking straight ahead, keeping
his eyes on the road, yet she saw his smile and again it warmed her.
At the moment she couldn't think of anything else she'd like better
than to have lunch with him, but tomorrow wasn't a good day.
"Star has an appointment at the dentist tomorrow. Sorry."

"Friday, then?" he asked, meeting her gaze when he brought the
car to a stop at a traffic light.

Swallowing hard, almost finding it difficult to breathe, she nodded. "Yes." Although she did have to make a court appearance on
Friday, she would be finished by noon. "Thanks for asking."

Although he didn't tell her that it was "his pleasure" again, the
words were there in his eyes nonetheless and she saw it. There was
something about him that made her feel safe, secure and special.

Half an hour later, when Phillip parked his car in front of her
house, he felt regret for the night to end. After unfastening his seat
belt, he glanced in the back seat and chuckled. "Forget about waiting to wrestle them in the morning. I think we're going to have a
fight on our hands tonight. They're both out like a light."

Terri grinned as she also glanced over her shoulder. "Yes, I think
you're right."

"Go ahead and open the door and I'll bring her to you," he said.
That way he wouldn't have to leave Chandra alone.

"Okay."

BRENDA JACKSON

Terri quickly pulled the key out of her purse and made her way to the door and opened it up. She stood in the doorway and watched how Phillip gently handled Star, taking her into his arms without waking her.

"Tell me which room is hers and I'll carry her on inside while you stay here and keep an eye on Chandra," he said quietly, so as not to wake Star.

"Her room is down the hall, the first room on the right."

Phillip nodded and walked off with Star still cuddled in his arms. He smiled when he entered her room. No wonder she and Chandra had hit if off, he thought, glancing around after placing Star on the bed and noticing the room's decor. It seems that she was a big Disney fan, too.

On his way from Star's room he passed what he knew to be Terri's room. His gut clenched when he saw the king-size bed and suddenly a vision of two bodies, theirs, in that bed invaded his mind. He quickened his steps to where he knew Terri was still standing in the doorway, waiting for his return.

"Thanks, Phillip. Now all I have to do is put on her pajamas."

He nodded. "I'll be doing the same thing since Chandra is staying with me tonight." He stared at her for several seconds before saying, "I want to thank you and Star for joining us. I'll call you tomorrow to get ideas of where you want to go on Friday."

"All right."

"Good night, Terri." He wanted to pull her into his arms and kiss her but he knew it was too soon. Her sweet feminine scent would follow him to bed tonight and he wondered if he was biting off more than he could chew with the stunning Terri Davenport. All through the evening his body had responded to her nearness.

"Good night, Phillip."

Terri watched as he quickly walked back to his car where his child was still sleeping. And as she closed the door, she couldn't help but look forward to lunch with him on Friday.

230

24

Marcus

Marcus sat in bed with the remote in hand, trying to find something interesting on television but his mind was elsewhere. There had been another delivery to him tonight. This time the box contained a pair of black lacy panties; a pair similar to the last ones he'd taken off Breathless. And he had a strong feeling she wasn't through playing her crazy game.

Tonight was one of those nights that he wished there was someone he could hang out with. He had called Sam earlier but could tell that Sam was sort of preoccupied, like he had a lot on his mind. Phillip had taken the attorney and her daughter to the circus so he couldn't talk to him. And his mother was the last person he wanted to call, although he knew he really should since he still hadn't spoken with her about interfering in his life.

Thinking of his mother's antics made him think about Naomi. He had to admit he had enjoyed having dinner with her yesterday. And he had to also admit something else. There was more to Naomi than her good looks and tight skirts. A part of him felt bad about having judged her so harshly after that incident in his home. She hadn't forced his body to get aroused. It had reacted on its own because he'd been attracted to her. He still was.

He sighed deeply, turning the power off his television and deciding since there was nothing worth watching, he might as well make it an early night. Hell, it wasn't eight o'clock yet. As he lay there, he thought of everything that had happened to him since Dottie's death. He had done some good things like getting involved in that college scholarship in her honor, as well as becoming a member of Grief Relief. But still, there were things he knew he should have done differently, like the way he had decided to reenter the dating scene.

That fiasco with Internet dating should have taught him a hard lesson, but instead he had begun looking for action at Fantasyland and had gotten just what he thought he'd wanted, sex and plenty of it. But what was going on with Breathless had taught him an even harder lesson. He wasn't cut out to be a playa. He was a man who needed to be involved in a solid relationship with a good woman; a woman he could depend on when the going got rough; a woman who could be his friend as well as his lover.

He closed his eyes when he felt himself getting sleepy. Exhaustion was weighing him down and he began slipping into a deep state of unconsciousness. He knew that he was dreaming when he saw flowers and plenty of them. Hell, he didn't do flowers, so he couldn't understand why he was suddenly surrounded by them. They were practically everywhere, all colors and types.

"Marcus . . ."

He heard Dottie softly calling his name and looked around, but all he saw were flowers and a beautiful blue sky. He had never seen a sky that particular shade of blue before and wondered how anything could look so radiant and peaceful.

"Marcus . . ."

He heard her call his name again and sharpened his gaze to see through the flowers and then he saw her and his heart nearly stopped beating.

Dottie.

She was dressed entirely in white, wearing a long, flowing gown, and she looked more beautiful than he had ever seen her before. She was surrounded by flowers; they were everywhere, adorning her head, sides and feet. His heart burst with love, happiness and he made a move to go to her. He wanted to sweep her into his arms, hold her, kiss her, show her how much he missed her, still loved her, but he found that he was rooted in place. He couldn't move. It was as if his feet were cemented to the earth.

His gaze held hers and the smile that she had on her face sent a jolt of emotions through him. She seemed to be so happy when he had been nothing but miserable since that day she had been taken away from him. He knew the one question he had to ask; the same question he had asked over and over again since her death. "Why?"

His voice came out as a whisper, so soft he almost couldn't recognize the sound as being his own. When she didn't answer, he asked again. "Why did you leave me?" He needed to make sure she understood what he was asking.

"I had to go, Marcus," she responded in a voice that was softer than he'd ever known it to get. "It was time."

He felt the lump form in his throat. He felt the tears sting the back of his eyes. "Why do you say that?" he asked feeling somewhat angry. "It wasn't time. We were supposed to last forever, grow old together. We never got around to buying that summer home we wanted on the beach in Virginia. We never started a family. We never went back to school to work on our master's degrees like we had talked about doing so many times. We never—"

"What we did do was love each over very much, Marcus. We shared the kind of love that few people will ever know or understand," she said quietly. "I don't regret the time I spent with you and will always cherish those moments, and I want you to do so as well. But the time has come for you to let go. Don't look back but look ahead. Don't be angry with anyone for me leaving but rejoice. It was time."

"No."

"Yes. Would you have preferred to not have known me? Would you have preferred it if our paths did not cross?"

"Of course not."

"Then thank God for the time that we spent together. They were good years. We did a lot, had planned to do more. But what we didn't do and should have done was to live each day like it was our last and not make plans for a time that wasn't promised."

"But—"

"Please listen, Marcus. I don't have much time but I wanted to see you, to talk to you, to get you to understand that you can't continue to hold anyone responsible and you have to continue to live, rejoice. You are a special man, Marcus, and there is a woman out there who needs you and you'll come to realize that you need her as well."

He blinked. Surely she wasn't referring to Breathless. As if she read his mind, she said, "You've been looking for the wrong things in the wrong places. And you have turned your back on the one person who can help you through everything, and that person is God. You won't find peace again until you accept Him for who He is and give thanks to Him for allowing us the time we did share on earth. Our Father gives and He can take away. It is His right. Think about it. Please think about it."

Marcus couldn't stop the tears that flowed down his cheeks. "It's hard to let go, Dottie."

"I know but you must. And only then will you find peace and joy in living."

Marcus watched as she slowly began fading into the flowers and his breath caught, and a sense of panic struck that she was leaving. "Wait! When will you be back? When will I see you again?"

The smile she gave him touched his soul. It was a beautiful, serene smile, a peaceful smile. It was a smile that reached out to him and reminded him of all the reasons why he had loved her so much. It was also a smile that told him she was happy and that she wanted him to be happy as well.

"We will see each other again when you come to Paradise. It's a beautiful place and you will love it here as much as I do. But until then, do what you know is right. Be willing to open up your heart to receive the blessings of love again. Live for today and not for tomorrow and, most importantly, bring God back into your life. He is the only way. Good-bye, Marcus."

Then she was gone and the only things left were the flowers and the radiant blue sky.

Marcus slowly opened his eyes to the dazzling light that was shining through his bedroom window.

It was morning.

A quick glance at the clock radio beside his bed indicated it was a little past seven. Instantly, his thoughts shifted to the dream he'd had last night, and the stillness of early morning made his dream somewhat of a reality. Dottie had come to him and she had come for a reason.

He slowly sat up in bed and wiped sleep from his face, knowing what he had to do. He had to get away for a while and think and do what Dottie said he needed to do and that was to put the past behind him and move on. He had told himself he had done it before but he had only been fooling himself.

He knew what he had to do and where he had to go: Virginia Beach, a place that was special to him and Dottie. Reaching across the bed he picked up the phone and began dialing. First he needed to call his job to let them know he was taking the rest of the week off. Then he would call his mom to let her know that he was leaving town for a few days.

25

Lance

Lance glanced down at the glass he held in his hand and wondered when he had developed a taste for brandy. He never liked the stuff but lately it seemed to have become his drink of choice.

He walked over to the window and glanced out. It was almost midnight and the city below was quiet. Strains of Chopin floated through the room but he barely heard the sound, so intense were his thoughts, his desires, his obsessions.

He took another sip of his drink then expelled a slow, deep breath. How had something that should have been so elementary, so basic, become so complicated and complex? Where was simplicity when you needed it? He had wanted Asia Fowler and had been determined to get her; a relatively simple task. But what he'd found was not a woman who was weak and needy, but a woman who was ordered, disciplined and strong.

A woman who was complicated.

Asia Fowler was a woman who had beat him at his own game, and for the life of him, he could not figure out how nor could he get her out of his mind.

He was a man schooled in keeping his emotions harnessed. He didn't need women but made damn sure that women needed him. *Use them before they got a chance to use you* had been the motto he had lived by, survived by, and when it came to women, it came down to only the strongest surviving. Two failed marriages and a mother who was anything but had taught him that. Business and pleasure were the same; personal affairs and business affairs became Lance Montgomery's affairs and that was the way it went.

Until Asia Fowler entered the picture.

He glanced down at his drink. Maybe he should change and go out jogging and let the cold night air slap some sense into him. He needed something to kick his ass into gear since the brandy didn't seem to be working.

He looked up when he heard the sound of the doorbell. Carrie had paid him another unannounced visit and had returned to Florida after spending a week with him. Most of her time had been spent at the stores, stocking up on what she'd called the latest fashions. Surprisingly, some of the items she'd purchased had been to cover more of her body than less of it. Go figure when she usually enjoyed pushing the limits of exposure to the max.

Crossing the room he took a glance through the peephole. He smiled, opening the door and wondering what had brought on his brothers' visit. He stood in the doorway and studied the two men standing there. The three of them used to be referred to in the neighborhood as the "Montgomery boys." They had grown up well liked, respectful and determined to get the hell out of Gary when they got older. Logan and Lyle had always planned to take their pops with them when they moved away but the old man wouldn't budge, which meant they had to return every so often to check on Dad.

And, Lance thought, to check up on him as well.

"To what do I owe the honor of this visit?" he asked, stepping aside to let them in.

Of course it was Logan who answered. "Carrie's worried about you."

Lance shook his head. Of the three, it was Logan, standing six four, who was more like Jeremiah Montgomery than either of them in looks, height, build and the need to say what he meant and meant what he said. He didn't sugarcoat anything, which often made Lance wonder how he had become such a successful plastic surgeon. He could just imagine Logan telling a client, "Yes, you do look awful and a new face will work wonders."

Lance glanced over at Lyle who was slightly taller than him at six two. He was the one who made a living repairing people's hearts. When he'd made the decision to become a heart specialist, no one had been surprised. After all, he had been the one who'd spent hours in the high school lab dissecting anything he could get his hands on.

Both men were tall, muscular and, even Lance had to admit, good looking. They were Montgomerys. Nothing less was expected. "Carrie talks too damn much," Lance muttered, closing the door behind his brothers.

"I'll drink to that," Lyle said, taking the glass of brandy out of Lance's hand and downing what was left of it. Lance watched as his brother licked his lips.

"Nice taste," Lyle said, smiling as he handed the empty glass back to him.

"The bottle cost enough, thank you," Lance replied. He glanced over at Logan. "So what did Carrie say to make the two of you join forces to come to Chicago?"

Logan shrugged as he headed for the living room to sit on the sofa. "It was time to check on Pop anyway, and when she claimed you had started drinking and—"

"She claimed I've started drinking? I don't call having a glass a brandy a night excessive."

Lyle joined Logan on the sofa. "For a man who always claimed he hated brandy it is. So we're here to find out just what else you may have developed a taste for that you never liked before. Women perhaps?"

Lance frowned. "I've always like women."

Logan chuckled. "Oh yeah, that's right. You like them but you don't respect them."

Lance crossed his hands over his chest and glared at the two men sitting on his sofa. "If the two of you need a place to stay tonight I suggest you start being nice. First of all, what I think of women and how I treat them is my business."

"It used to be but now there's someone else to consider," Lyle said, going through the candy dish on the table and picking out the assorted mints.

Lance crossed his arms over his chest. "Who?"

"Carrie," Logan said. "She's at that impressionable age. I wouldn't want her to think the way you operate is the way most men do. If she thought that we might never get her married off to someone. And heaven forbid if that were to happen. I need peace and quiet in my old age."

Lance smiled. Carrie was the best thing that ever happened to Logan and all three of them knew it. Being the oldest, Logan always had this "let me boss you around" mentality. It had never worked on him and Lyle but it seemed to work on Carrie, who thought the sun rose and shined on her oldest brother. Now Lance and Lyle were another matter. She saw them as pushovers and basically when it came to her, they were.

"Look, no matter what Carrie thinks, I'm okay."

Lyle studied him like he was analyzing something under a microscope, and Lance could feel Logan studying him, too. "Why do I get the feeling that you're lying? Are you?" Logan asked.

Lance sighed deeply. The one thing he could never pull off when it came to his brothers was the art of pretense. They could see through it every time. Growing up they had been close, so close they once thought they could read each other's minds.

He sighed again, not ready to answer Logan's question. Instead he had one of his own. "Why the interrogation, Logan? Don't you and Lyle have women waiting for you back in Florida and Texas?"

Lyle smiled. "No, I'm a free man at the moment."

Logan grinned. "So am I, but our freedom doesn't have anything to do with that handbook you wrote. By the way, I have issues with that book."

Lance raised his eyes to the ceiling. "You would." Neither of his brothers had ever been married. Both claimed they had nothing against the institution once they found the woman they wanted to spend the rest of their lives with. Finding her was the problem. Lyle was waiting on a woman who could make his heart tremble, and Logan claimed he was waiting on a woman who wouldn't need plastic surgery during their years of marriage.

"Anyway," Logan said, trying to get the conversation back on track. "We're waiting on an answer."

Lance didn't answer. Instead he walked over to the window and looked out. Carrie was right, he wasn't okay. He was a mess. The emotions Asia had made him feel had scared him shitless. There must be a reason for the hell he was going through. There had to be a name for it other than "a pain in the ass kind of feeling" that made him do things he typically didn't do—like get on an airplane and fly across the country just to hear her speak, pick her up at the airport in a limo, give her flowers, prepare dinner for two in his suite, give her pleasure and withhold his own. Then there was that thing with Rachel Cason. After Asia had left, he had had every intention of making love to Rachel, needing the body of another woman to remove any trace of Asia from his thoughts and mind. But he hadn't been able to go through with it and had sent Rachel packing. And to make matters worse, he hadn't touched another woman since that night with Asia.

"We're waiting, Lance."

Lance closed his eyes when the realization of just what he felt for Asia hit him like a ton of bricks. He'd known all along what he was facing and had tried fighting it all the way. Hell, it would take his brothers to make him face those fears and admit what was best left alone.

He opened his eyes and turned to them. They were staring at him intently. Waiting. "No, I'm not okay," he said quietly, needing a drink of brandy, although he knew it wouldn't do any good.

Logan met his gaze. "So, what's the problem?"

Lance knew he couldn't deny it any longer to himself, nor could he deny it to his brothers. "The problem is a woman by the name of Asia Fowler. I've fallen for her. Big time."

26

Sam and Falon

Sam drank his morning coffee while standing at the window that overlooked the park across the street. In the distance he could see a couple walking, holding hands, their heads close as they laughed at a shared joke. Even from where he stood he felt it: their closeness, their connection, their commitment to each other.

And as he continued to watch them he thought about the brief affair he'd had with Tina. There hadn't been any closeness, no connection and definitely no commitment. Only sex and plenty of it.

He turned away from the window and drained the last of the coffee. For the past four days, he had been in one funky mood. He knew that Phillip and Marcus had picked up on it. Hell, even Lance had picked up on it when he'd call yesterday.

He sighed deeply. His life was becoming frustrating as hell and all because of one damn kiss. A kiss he couldn't get out of his system; a kiss from a woman he only wanted friendship with because he wasn't ready to venture into anything else.

He shook his head wondering exactly what he felt for Falon. She was a looker so there was definitely an attraction. But a part of him knew there was more to it than her beauty or else he wouldn't be worrying about things so much. And his mother hadn't helped matters when she had alluded to the idea of him losing Falon to someone else only because Sam wasn't brave enough to face his fears and move on. And what if she did get that job in Paris? Where in the hell would he be then?

He frowned thoughtfully as he looked down at his empty coffee cup. When had Falon begun meaning more to him than the girl down the hall? Then again, he had to admit, she might have meant something all along, he just hadn't been ready to acknowledge it while trying to be a playa and all. Sex and plenty of it had been his, Phillip and Marcus's motto, along with those damn rules from *The Playa's Handbook*. He started to tell Lance yesterday just what he could do with that damn handbook. Instead of giving him pleasure it hadn't done anything but give him grief. Instead of building up his life, he was tearing it down and about to let probably the best thing that ever happened to him slip right through his fingers.

He looked up when he heard a knock at his door. He didn't have to take Falon to the airport until around ten and hadn't seen her since Monday night when he had taken her to the grocery store. He'd deliberately been avoiding her because he had needed to think.

He crossed the room to the door then smiled when he glanced out of his peephole. He quickly opened the door, glad to see her. "Falon, you're early aren't you?" he asked, stepping aside to let her in, then closing the door behind her.

"Yes, but I wanted to bring you these," she said, handing him a container that he knew was filled with brownies since his nose was trained to pick up the scent of chocolate.

"Thanks, and how did your presentation go at that high school?"

She grinned. "I think they liked my brownies more so than they liked me. The guys thought I should be able to sing and wiggle my butt and I had the hardest time convincing them that I'm not related to Beyoncé."

Sam chuckled. "Well, you do look like her. That's the first thing I thought when I saw you."

"Oh, and what's the second thing you thought?" she asked, smiling up at him.

He gave her a smooth grin. "That you can come over and use my phone any time."

Falon shook her head, smiling. "Well, I'm almost through packing and will be ready to go in an hour. And you're sure you don't mind taking me to the airport? I hate for you to have to go into the office late today."

"Hey, I have the time, trust me. Besides, I want to do it."

She met his gaze. "Thanks, and I'd better get back to my packing. I wanted to bring the brownies over just in case you wanted something sweet with your coffee, but it seems like you've had coffee already this morning," she said, glancing at the empty cup he was holding along with the container of brownies.

He chuckled. "Yeah, but there's a thing called a refill."

Falon laughed as she headed for the door to leave. "Yeah, I think you're right."

Falon glanced around when Sam pulled his SUV into Midway Airport's parking lot. "Hey, it's not crowded today at all."

Sam nodded. "I bet you can't say the same thing about O'Hare," he said about Chicago's busy airport. "I'll help you with your luggage."

"Hey, there's no need, I only have this one piece, a carry-on. It's easy to handle and I can get it."

"You're returning on Sunday evening, right?"

She smiled over at him. "Yes, around four that evening and you're sure it won't be a bother for you to pick me up?"

"Yeah, I'm sure."

She nodded and met his gaze. "Well, then, I guess I'd better go," she said, unfastening her seat belt when he brought the truck to a complete stop. "I'll see you on Sunday evening."

"All right."

She was about to open the door to get out when he touched her hand. "Falon?"

She turned to him. "Yes?"

"This is for good luck with your interview." He lowered his head and kissed her lightly on the lips. At least it was supposed to be light, a kiss between friends.

Yeah, right, he thought when he decided to deepen it. And when she didn't protest and parted her lips as well, he slipped his tongue inside her mouth, touching hers, tasting, remembering the sweetness, absorbing the warmth. God, he needed this, had longed for it and couldn't seem to get enough. There was something so intrinsically stimulating, downright arousing, about being inside her mouth tasting her, greedily sapping her up like a starved man.

When a car honked behind them, he slowly pulled away and cleared his throat, licked his lips. "Have a safe trip, Falon," he said quietly.

Falon said nothing but continued to look at him. Sam smiled. Good. She looked as confused as he felt. When the car behind them blew its horn again, he said, "I guess you better get going."

She blinked and then nodded. "Umm, I guess I'd better."

He watched as she walked away from the truck, tugging her carry-on behind her, and the only thing Sam could think about was that he missed her already.

27

Phillip and Terri

Terri gave herself a pep talk as she walked away from her car and headed toward the restaurant where she was meeting Phillip for lunch. It would be the first official date she'd had with a man since Lewis's death and she was downright nervous.

On Wednesday at the circus, Star and Chandra had kept things on a less personal note, but today with only her and Phillip present things would appear a lot more intimate and she wasn't sure how she felt about that. But she was sure that she wanted to see him again and get to know him.

In her job as an attorney she came across a lot of men. Some were men who thought a lot of themselves and their profession; men who expected women to cater to their every whim. During the short time she had been around Phillip she had found him to be unlike most men. He had a warm, loving personality that appeared to be an innate part of his nature. She had noticed the way he handled the girls the other night—like the job of fatherhood was something he saw as an honor and not as a chore.

Then there had been the way he had treated her, solicitous of her every need, asking her time and time again if she needed anything. Then there was the arrangement of flowers he had sent to her yesterday, with a smaller arrangement for Star. The card said they had been sent from both him and Chandra, again thanking them for sharing the evening with them. Star had beamed in delight at the thought of actually getting flowers like her mommy. To say that he had made both of the Davenport ladies' days was an understatement.

She smiled. Star was still talking about "Chandra's daddy" and how nice he was and the flowers he had sent. And as for her, she had to admit she looked forward to getting to know Phillip McKenna better.

When she stepped into the restaurant and glanced around, she immediately saw Phillip sitting at a table. Their eyes met and she suddenly felt shaken by the intensity of his gaze. She'd never had a man look at her like that since that night . . .

She sighed deeply. Why was she doing this to herself; it certainly wasn't fair to Phillip. But she couldn't shake the feeling that so many things about Phillip reminded her of a man she just couldn't forget.

Phillip stood as he watched Terri walk toward him. The impact of seeing her again after Wednesday night almost rendered him speechless. There was something about her that went deeper than it should. Maybe it was because he knew things about her and the life she'd spent with her husband that others didn't know.

Then again, maybe it was because he saw beyond all her outside beauty to the woman she was underneath, a woman even more beautiful on the inside. He knew just how caring she was as a mother and would never forget how she'd handled the biting incident involving Chandra. He had known then that she was special. He hadn't known just how special until weeks later. He suddenly felt stirrings of emotions he hadn't felt in a long time rip through him.

Phillip's eyes softened, warmed, when she reached the table. "Terri, thanks for joining me for lunch," he said, meaning every word.

She smiled. "And thanks for inviting me," she said, sitting down in the chair that he'd pulled out for her. She glanced around. "Nice place."

"Thanks. When you didn't have any suggestions as to where to do lunch, I checked with a couple of guys at the office and they suggested this place. I understand the food here is delicious."

She nodded and smiled. She hadn't wanted to suggest that they eat at any of the places she usually dined for fear of running into some of her colleagues. She had wanted to have lunch with Phillip at a place where she could relax and truly enjoy his company. "And thanks for the flowers. Both Star and I are enjoying them."

He smiled. "You're welcome."

At that moment a waiter came up, and seeing that Phillip was drinking a glass of white wine, Terri decided to order a glass for herself. The waiter also gave them menus to look at before walking away. Terri glanced around. It was a very nice restaurant. She had heard of this place. It wasn't as crowded with the lunch crowd as other places mainly because the items on the menu were pricey, and this was not a place someone would typically have lunch if they were on a tight budget.

They were sitting at a small round table for two that overlooked a beautiful lake. When she glanced over at Phillip, she saw that he was studying the menu but then, as if he'd felt her looking at him, he looked up, met her gaze and smiled.

"So, how did Star's dentist appointment go yesterday?" he asked, breaking into their contented silence.

Terri chuckled as she cringed. "Umm, let's just say it was better than the last time. Star hates going to the dentist."

Phillip nodded. "So does Chandra. There's a strong possibility she'll need braces in a few years and I'm not looking forward to that either."

He paused. "The reason I invited you to lunch wasn't to talk about Star and Chandra," he said softly, holding her gaze.

She lifted a brow. "Oh, it wasn't?" she asked teasingly, as a smile curved her lips.

Phillip's guts clenched and a part of him wanted to lean across the table and kiss that smirk of a smile right off her mouth. "No. The reason I invited you to lunch was because I wanted to see you again. I want to get to know you and I want you to get to know me. I haven't dated a lot since my divorce for a number of reasons and—"

"Are you still in love with your wife?" Terri asked, deciding that she needed to know that right up front. She didn't want to become involved in a relationship where she would be part of a threesome. She would guess that a man who looked like Phillip did a lot of dating and was surprised to hear that he didn't. In her book, there had to be a reason.

Phillip sighed deeply, hoping his next words would help her to understand his relationship with Rhonda. "For Chandra's sake, Rhonda and I have remained friends." He decided not to mention that at one time they had still been lovers, even after their divorce. "She's the mother of my child so I'll always care about her well-being, but as far as me still being in love with her, the answer to that is no. There were things that happened during our marriage that it wasn't strong enough to endure. Getting a divorce was the right thing for us to do. I didn't want to subject Chandra with having to be around two parents who always bickered and argued constantly. When I saw that as a possibility, I knew I had to do something to prevent it from happening. That would not have been a pleasant environment for a child. And kids these days are smart. They can figure out things."

The waiter came back at that moment to bring Terri the glass of wine she'd asked for, as well as to take their order and they both decided to try the grilled salmon. When the waiter walked away, they resumed their conversation.

"What about you, Terri? Have you dated a lot since your husband's death?" Phillip asked the question although he knew she had not. He wondered how truthful she would be with him and how much she would open up and tell him.

She met his gaze. "No. I've been too busy spending time with

248

Star and working to take time off for me. The guys at work see me as one of them, although a few did ask me out after they felt a decent period of mourning had passed. But to be quite honest with you, this is my first official date in almost two years."

Phillip's smile widened. He appreciated her telling him that. "Then I feel special."

Terri returned his smile. "You are. I felt it the first day I met you; that day you came to my house with Chandra. What made me think so was the way you handled your daughter. Lewis loved Chandra very much."

Phillip nodded. "Since this is a *getting to know you better lunch,* let me tell you something about myself," he said softly. "I was born Phillip Eric McKenna in Baltimore, Maryland, thirty-two years ago, to a mother who thought I would be a cramp in her style and a father who thought she got pregnant just to trick him into marriage. So by the age of three I had become part of the legal system, a foster child. I was blessed to have wonderful foster parents so I feel I had a good childhood considering everything . . . at least until the Garrisons were killed in an auto accident just months before my eighteenth birthday."

"Oh, how awful."

Phillip met her gaze. "Yes, it was, for all eight of us. They had brought into their homes eight children who needed them, and even today, although we're spread all over the country, we still stay in touch and consider ourselves family."

"That's wonderful."

He smiled. "Yes, I think it's wonderful, too. I was able to finish high school and I went to Howard to become a pharmacist. I worked for a pharmacy for a few years before deciding to work at a pharmaceutical firm as a chemist. The pay was better and so were the hours. I like what I do and over the ten years I've worked there, I've moved up the ranks and now hold the position of executive manager of my department. I work for a good company and with a wonderful group of people."

Terri nodded. She sat back in her chair. She had begun feeling comfortable while listening to Phillip talk. She not only liked hearing the sound of his voice, but found the information he was sharing with her endearing as well as vital.

"Well," she said, after taking a sip of her wine and noticing he had stopped talking, "my parents were hard-working people who had two children, me and my brother Teddy, who's older than me by four years. He's still single and lives in Texas, where he works as a sales manager for the Dallas Cowboys. I went to law school at Florida State University because I was determined to get away from Indiana's cold weather for a while. I returned to Gary to be near my parents since my brother was dead set on living in Texas. I thought at least one of us should remain close by them as they got up in years." She chuckled. "Although some days I'm convinced they have more energy than I do."

She took another sip of her wine before continuing. "I'm thirty years old, and moving from the twenties to the thirties wasn't as bad as I thought," she said smiling. "As you know I'm an attorney and most of my cases involve delinquents. I work closely with the Youth Services Department and enjoy doing that. My husband and I met when I tried my first case. I was working for the DA's office and he was one of the officers connected to a case I'd been assigned to. I had to interview him a couple of times to prepare for trial. We began dating, and less than a year later we were married."

She took a sip of her wine, deciding now was not the time to tell him that's when her hell had begun. "Lewis and I were married a year then I got pregnant with Star."

He met her gaze. "Sounds like you had a wonderful marriage."

"I think that I did. Lewis was a good man and a wonderful father to Star."

Phillip nodded. He knew the man may have been a wonderful father, but in his book he'd been a selfish husband by not allowing his wife to experience everything that she could in the bedroom without fear of him thinking badly of her.

The waiter came with their food. "Everything looks good,"

Terri said, moving her wineglass out of the way so the plate could be placed in front of her.

"Do you have to go back to work after lunch?" Phillip found himself asking when the waiter walked off again.

Terri glanced up and met his gaze. "No, why?"

"Would you like to do a movie?"

She blinked, surprised. "Today?"

He chuckled. "Yes. Most people are working and kids are in school, so we'll probably have the entire place to ourselves. And the timing would be perfect. The movie will be over in time for you to pick Star up from school."

Terri nodded. "My parents pick Star up from school every day for me. They claim it gives them something to do and it certainly helps me out with my schedule at the firm. Once in a while I might get stuck in court later than I had expected."

"But you still manage to balance your time as a mother and career woman."

She smiled. "Yes and that's important to me. Star will always come before any job. I take my role as a mother seriously."

Phillip leaned back in his chair, appreciating the fact that she did. He wished Rhonda thought that way. "So how does the movie thing sound?"

Terri smiled. "Mmm, it sounds great and I'd love to go to the movies with you."

28

The Gang

Marcus glanced over at his friends, who were waiting patiently to hear what he had to say. He had come straight to Sam's place from the airport since it was closest, and had called Phillip en route on his cell phone and asked that he meet him there.

He sighed deeply after taking another sip of beer then said, "I saw Dottie." Upon seeing the look on their faces, like they thought he had completely lost his mind, he thought he had better explain.

"She came to me in a dream Wednesday night. We had a long talk and she basically told me that I needed to get my ass in gear. Although she didn't use those words the message was the same."

He took another sip. "Our conversation seemed so real. That's the reason I went to Virginia Beach, to think and to get myself together."

Marcus stood and walked over to Sam's window and looked out. "Over the past two days, I've come to the realization that getting plenty of sex isn't about nothing. I need stability with a woman. I need a connection, commitment. I need all the things I had with Dottie. That's the kind of guy I am and I think that's the kind of guy the two of you are, too. It took *The Playa's Handbook* to make us realize that."

When Sam and Phillip said nothing but continued to look at him, he continued, "I know the two of you are seeing women who you think are special, but you're not sure you want to take the relationship beyond the bedroom, if it ever gets there. But take it from a guy who knows that life is short. Tomorrow isn't promised. If you think you've met someone you want to share your life with, then don't let what happened in the past cloud your judgment or make you afraid to take a chance again."

He took another sip of beer then chuckled. "Hell, we weren't nothing but playa wannabes. We wanted to play the game but we weren't ready for everything that came our way."

Sam finally broke his silence and said, "I've been doing a lot of thinking myself and have decided I want more with Falon. And when she gets back from New York tomorrow, I'm going to let her know. If she gets that job in Paris, that will be okay, too. I'll get my passport in order and learn how to conduct a long-distance romance. But the main thing is letting her know that I want to share a meaningful relationship with her."

Phillip took a sip of his beer and thought about Terri and how he had enjoyed their date yesterday. And the movie had been really special. He sighed deeply. His problem with Terri went a lot deeper than Sam's with Falon. Terri had invited him to dinner on Sunday after telling him since there was no school Monday, Star would be staying at her grandparents for the weekend. That meant they would be alone. He couldn't continue to deceive her; he had to tell her the truth—that he was the man that night at Fantasyland. He had decided to take his chances and come clean on Sunday, and he wasn't sure what the outcome of that would be. She might decide never to see him again. But he had to be honest with her. A relationship founded on lies and deceit wasn't good and he wanted a relationship with her.

"And I want more with Terri, too," he spoke up and said, "although I'm not sure she's ready for more. But I agree with what you said, Marcus. We aren't the playa types. We're used to love and commitment and a part of us can't deviate although we might have tried. It takes time to build a solid relationship with someone and we need to be willing to take the time if the woman is worth it."

He then glanced over at Marcus. "What about you? Is there a woman you have in mind? Someone you're interested in?"

Marcus smiled when he thought of Naomi. "Yeah, Naomi Monroe. She's the woman I told you about who attends my mom's church. I had dinner at her place Tuesday night and I really enjoyed her company. She's someone I'd like to start seeing on a serious note."

He sighed deeply. "Something Dottie said in the dream really made me think."

Sam met his gaze. "What?"

"She said I've been looking for the wrong things in all the wrong places and that I should be willing to open my heart to receive the blessings of love again, and that's what I want."

Marcus studied the expressions on Sam and Phillip's faces and a part of him knew that's what they wanted as well.

29

Marcus and Naomi

The next day Marcus walked in the doors of the Ebenezer Baptist Church and glanced over at his mother, sitting in the deaconess corner. When she saw him, a huge smile touched her lips and even from the distance separating them, he could see her eyes began filling with tears. He blinked, feeling misty-eyed himself. He knew this was where he needed to be today.

"Welcome to our Family and Friends Day," an usher whispered to him. Is there a family member or friend you'd like to sit with?"

He smiled at the woman. "Yes, I'm here as a guest of Essie Lowery and Naomi Monroe." He doubted that they would sit him in the deaconess corner with his mother, but to make sure they didn't, he said, "I'd like to sit with Ms. Monroe if I could."

The woman smiled. "All right. I'll take you over to join her."

The usher escorted him down the aisle and he saw the surprised look on Naomi's face when she saw him. She smiled and made room for him to sit beside her. "Thanks for coming, Marcus," she whispered and proceeded to share her Bible with him. Everyone stood when the minister began reading the scripture.

Marcus inhaled deeply. He had no idea what the minister would be preaching about, but he had a feeling it was a message he needed to hear.

"Marcus, I'm glad you came to church today," Essie Lowery said cheerfully, as she took a tray of macaroni and cheese out of the oven.

"Thanks, Mama, and I really enjoyed the service." And he had. The minister had spoken about God's love and how He loved us in spite of everything that we did.

"And I hope you didn't mind me inviting Naomi for dinner."

Marcus shook his head. He never did have that conversation with his mother about trying to play matchmaker, but now he didn't see the point in doing so. He wanted to start seeing Naomi, and if his mother wanted to take credit for it then he would let her do that. Naomi had accepted his mother's invitation to dinner and said she would be coming by after going home to change her clothes.

"What made you decide to come, Marcus?"

He glanced up and met his mother's curious gaze. "I haven't liked the way my life's been going lately and I guess Dottie hasn't liked it either. She came to me in a dream and made me see that I needed to get my act together, and that getting back in God's graces was one of the first things that I needed to do. I had to get away this week to think about things and I came to the realization that she was right."

His mother nodded. "Dottie was a special girl, Marcus, and you were blessed that she was a part of your life."

"Yes," he said, remembering everything Dottie had told him. "I was truly blessed." Deciding to change the subject, he asked, "Do you need help with anything?"

"Not in here but you can set up the table out in the yard. It's too gorgeous a day to eat inside. I think it would be nice for us to gather outside under those trees."

Marcus nodded. "Okay, I'll be back."

Moments later he was busy outside getting the table set up when he had the strangest feeling that he was being watched. He glanced around and frowned when he saw that a car had slowed down, almost to a complete stop, in front of his mother's house. It was a nice ride, a Mercedes sports car and it stuck out like a sore thumb in this neighborhood. The hairs on his arms suddenly stood up when he noticed a white woman with blond hair behind the wheel.

Breathless! For some reason he knew it had to be her.

"Marcus, you haven't finished yet?"

He turned at the sound of his mother's voice and watched as she came down the steps carrying a tablecloth under her arm. He quickly glanced back toward the street but the car was gone.

Marcus refused to let Breathless's appearance put a damper on his day. He had enjoyed the church service, he had enjoyed the food his mother prepared for dinner, and at the moment he was enjoying Naomi's company.

For the past couple of hours they had laughed and joked about a lot of things, and he was surprised to discover that she was a huge football fan and that they had the same favorite team, the Chicago Bears.

"It's too nice a day for you young people to waste," he heard his mother say while clearing the table. "Why don't the two of you go somewhere and enjoy what's left of the day."

Marcus smiled as he looked over at Naomi, knowing what his mother was trying to do, and from the smile on her face he knew that Naomi knew as well. "And do you have someplace in mind, Mama?" he asked innocently, inwardly smiling at her.

She shrugged her shoulders. "There's always something showing at the movies, but I heard on television that there's an art festival going on over in Chicago this weekend. I'm not into that sort of thing but I would think most young people would be."

Marcus grinned. He wasn't into art himself but he wouldn't mind taking the drive into Chicago. He glanced over at Naomi. "What about it? Do you want to go?"

She smiled. "Yes, I'd love to."

Not to be bothered with two cars, Marcus followed Naomi home from his mother's house and waited while she went inside for a jacket. He kept glancing through the rearview mirror, making sure he hadn't been followed. He couldn't believe the woman was actually stalking him and was doing so in broad daylight like she didn't care if she was seen. A car like the one she was driving drew attention.

Speaking of attention, his thoughts were suddenly pulled away from Breathless and to Naomi when she walked out of her house. She had kept on the same blouse but was now wearing a pair of jeans instead of a long skirt. He'd thought she had looked good in her skirt but she looked real good in jeans.

"Thanks for waiting," she said, opening his car door and sliding into the seat next to him. "I decided to change into jeans to be more comfortable."

He nodded. He also was wearing jeans. After church he had gone home to change clothes before going to his mother's for dinner. "That's fine." He then pulled out of her driveway. "And I meant to tell you the other day that the perfume you're wearing smells nice."

Naomi glanced over at him. "Thanks, Marcus." She watched as he plugged Alicia Keys into the CD player and thought that his taste in music mirrored hers. His invitation, although offered with a little help from Ms. Essie, couldn't have come at a better time. She had been dying to be alone with him again. All she had thought about most of the week was the dinner they'd shared at her place Tuesday night.

Naomi leaned back against the seat as he smoothly pulled his car onto the interstate and headed toward Chicago and knew she was right where she wanted to be. She was finally going on a date with Marcus Lowery.

Navy Pier, Naomi thought, was the best place to be if you wanted to enjoy the beauty of the lakefront. With over fifty acres of parks, gardens, shops, restaurants, and not to mention a one hundred and fifty foot Ferris wheel, it was here on a section of the east end that the art festival was being held.

Naomi thought she hadn't seen so many beautiful paintings by so many gifted artists on display before. The weather wasn't so bad for October; the temperature was in the fifties. A warm sensation flowed through her. From the time she and Marcus began walking around the pier, he had taken her hand in his. This was the first time he had ever initiated any type of physical contact with her.

"Hungry?" Marcus asked when they passed a booth where a woman was selling cotton candy.

Naomi glanced up at him and smiled. "Are you kidding? I can't think of eating anything else after Ms. Essie's dinner."

Marcus chuckled. "Well, I can," he said, as he pulled his wallet out of his back pocket. "I'm still a growing boy." After Marcus got his treat, they continued to walk hand in hand taking in all the sights and exhibits.

"Are you game for a ride on the Ferris wheel?" he asked her awhile later.

Naomi lifted a brow. "Hey, call me the Ferris queen. When it comes to Ferris wheels I can hang tough."

Marcus chuckled. "Spoken like a true Bears fan. Come on, let's go for a ride."

30

Sam and Falon

Sam glanced down at his watch. Falon's plane was due to arrive any moment. He wondered how she did in New York and if she got the job that would take her to Paris for a year.

He sighed deeply, not wanting to think about that. But what he did want to think about was the decisions he had made regarding her. He had to admit that Marcus's speech yesterday had helped. Sam had been forced to admit that he wanted more than just friendship with Falon. He was ready to get into a relationship that was going somewhere. He was no longer afraid of taking risks.

His thoughts were interrupted when the voice on the intercom announced the arrival of Falon's flight. He leaned against a brick planter, ready to see her again. These had seemed like the longest two days of his life.

Moments later he strained his eyes when he saw people hurrying down the terminal, but he didn't see Falon. He continued to search the crowd and finally, he saw her. She was dressed in a snug pair of faded jeans and a pullover sweater. Her hair flowed around her shoulders and the two things that suddenly stood out in his mind were that he was glad to see her and that she looked so damn good.

At that moment something inside of him seemed to break. The hard cast he had placed around his heart had finally found a crack, a big one. All he knew was that he could barely stand there and watch her. He wanted to go meet her and hold her and kiss her.

So he began walking toward her.

He knew he was about to take the biggest risk of his life, one that involved his heart, since he didn't know how she felt about him. There was a chance that all she still wanted from their relationship was friendship. There was also a chance that his decision to take action might be too late, but he didn't care. She was a woman he wanted to be involved with, not for a short while but for a very long time.

He noted the exact moment she saw him. He saw the way her face lit up, the way her mouth tilted into a smile and when they came to a stop in front of each other, he looked down into the honey brown eyes that had kept him awake the past few nights.

"Hi, Sam."

"Hi, Falon."

Before either could utter another word, he leaned down, slanted his mouth over hers and captured her lips in his. Her response was quick, instantaneous. Instead of pushing him away, she grasped the side of his head, locking their mouths in place while she pressed her hips solidly against his. At the moment neither cared that they were standing in the middle of the airport with their mouths locked while people either walked around them or stared. For the first time in his life, Sam felt out of control and he didn't give a damn.

Finally for breathing purposes, and only for breathing purposes, he reluctantly pulled his mouth away. Her lips were wet and seeing them that way filled him with a hunger to taste them again. But now was not the time and this was no longer the place. They needed privacy, first to talk and then to kiss some more.

"Wow, and I'm glad to see you, too," Falon said teasingly, as a smile touched those same wet lips.

He said nothing but drew her closer into his arms, needing to hold her a minute longer.

"That was some kiss," she said softly against his shirt. "Reminds me of the kiss you gave me Friday when you dropped me off. Would you like to tell me what's going on?" she asked lightly.

He leaned back and met her gaze. Although her words sounded lighthearted, he knew they were serious. "It's a long story," he said, holding her gaze.

She pulled back a little. "But I'd love to hear it anyway, especially since we've made spectacles of ourselves in a way that's unusual for two people who're nothing more than friends."

Sam nodded. What she'd said made perfect sense and he knew he owed her an explanation. "Come on let's go. We can talk on the way."

They began moving toward the exit doors with Sam's hand on the small of her back. Touching her there felt protective and possessive, and at the moment, Sam was feeling satisfied with both.

They hadn't gone far when Sam pulled his SUV into the parking lot of a convenience store. They'd barely spoken since leaving the airport.

When Falon lifted a brow, he said, "I thought we should talk now instead of waiting until we got back to the apartment." He watched as she drew in a deep breath, gazed over at him and slowly nodded. "Okay."

He turned to face her, needing to look into her eyes while saying what he had to say. As with a mind of its own, his hand lifted and his finger traced a path across her bottom lip. "I tried being nothing more than your friend, Falon, because I had convinced myself that's all I could be. What you wanted from a man was a lot more than I could give and maybe a few weeks ago that was true."

She continued to hold his stare. "But not now?"

"No, but not now. Over the past couple of weeks, I've come to realize a very important thing."

"What?"

"That a person can't always change their makeup. Your personality is who you are and it's what shaped you into what you are.

After Kim's betrayal, I convinced myself that being in a loving and committed relationship was no longer for me, that when it came to women I wanted something short term instead of long term and, no matter what, the focus would be all about me."

He inhaled deeply then said, "Now I find I want something totally different."

Falon angled her head. "And what do you want now?"

He held her gaze. "You. And not just in a physical way. There are so many things I admire about you; things I find endearing. I admire the fact that you're true to your convictions and won't let any man try to sell you short. You know what you want and you refuse to accept second best; you refuse to let anyone box you into a corner. I admire that you didn't let what happened with your ex-boyfriend turn you against wanting to love someone again. A part of me always knew that if I were to become interested in someone on a serious basis again, you would be the type of woman I'd want to become involved with."

He sighed deeply. "With the possibility of you moving to Paris, things may be too late for us but I wanted you to know how I felt."

"Let me make sure I understand this correctly," Falon said quietly. "Are you saying that you want us to start seeing each other, become involved in a serious relationship?"

"Yes, I want an exclusive relationship with you and I mean totally exclusive, but the question of the hour is whether or not you want that as much as I do."

Falon reached out and put a hand on his arm. She smiled softly. "Yes, that's what I want. And I didn't get the job."

"You didn't?"

"No. It seems that the guy who was their first choice decided to take the job after all, so they flew all of us to New York for nothing. However, it wasn't a wasted trip since I had fun taking in the sights."

Sam nodded, and thinking ahead, already including her in his future, he said, "I've only been to New York once but would love to see it again. Perhaps we can go there together later this summer."

Falon smiled. "I think that would be nice."

Sam thought it would be better than nice and thought kissing her again would certainly make his day. Pleasure and heat flowed through him and he leaned forward to capture her mouth. The scent of her, combined with the sweet taste of her mouth, aroused him. But he wanted more from her than sex. He wanted a solid relationship that was going somewhere.

He wanted her in his life, and he knew by the time the kiss was over she would be totally convinced of that as well.

31

Phillip and Terri

"Dinner was wonderful, Terri, and I appreciate you inviting me."

Terri smiled over at Phillip as he help her load the items into the dishwasher. They were always thanking each other for something. Deciding to borrow one of his lines, she said softly, "It was my pleasure."

Recognizing it for what it was, Phillip laughed. He really liked this woman. He had seen her three times this week. Some would say their relationship was moving fast but he was glad it was moving at all. He no longer had a problem with the thought of becoming seriously involved with someone again.

In fact, with Terri he was looking forward to it.

But first, he knew that he had to be completely honest and tell her about that night at Fantasyland.

When she loaded the last dish he reached out and took her hand. "Can we talk for a few minutes?"

She stared at him before saying, "Okay, let's sit in the living room where we'll be comfortable."

They sat together on the sofa with an appropriate distance between them. He wasn't sure where to begin so he decided to start at the beginning. "A few months ago, me and a couple of close friends decided that we were doing a lousy job getting back into the dating scene so we purchased this book called *The Playa's Handbook*."

She chuckled. "A guy at work bought a copy of that book, too. Out of curiosity I checked it out but never got past the first page. Those rules were so outrageous."

Phillip smiled. "Yeah, I know. But since neither Sam, Marcus or I were ready for a serious involvement we decided to play by the rules—the playa's rules that is."

She nodded. "Oh, I see."

Not yet she didn't but pretty soon she would, Phillip thought. "One night Marcus and I went to this place, an exclusive club, invitation only, very high-class, ritzy. A place where people went to indulge in their fantasies, no matter what they were."

He watched the expression on Terri's face change. He saw the smile drain from her features. "Their fantasies?" she asked in a soft, low, cautious voice.

"Yes, in fact the name of the place is Fantasyland."

She quickly stood. "Look, it's not necessary for you to tell me what you did months ago, I—"

"I think you've been there, too, Terri."

She blinked, stared at him then sat back down. "What did you say?" she asked, slowly. "I— I'm not sure I know what you mean."

Phillip looked at her as he swallowed a lump clogging his throat. His greatest fear was her thinking he had deceived her, used her by knowing something that no one else was supposed to know.

"Terri, please listen to me. Will you do that?" When she nodded, he released a deep breath then continued.

"I went there because I hadn't slept with a woman in months and needed a quick sexual fix. I was paired with this woman who had an unusual fantasy, and before the night was over I think I actually fell for her. And that was even before I recognized who she was. Although we were wearing masks, there was a mark on her body that I recognized. A tattoo on her shoulder; that of a star."

Terri stood and walked over to the window that faced the backyard. He could see the slump of her shoulders and the nervous way she was rubbing her hands together. "Going there had to have been hard for you," he said softly, and wanted more than anything to cross the room and pull her into his arms. But how they proceeded after this would have to be her decision.

"But a part of me," he continued, "will always admire you for making that decision, and nothing could stop me from fulfilling your fantasy that night."

Terri slowly turned around and when she met his gaze, the tears in her eyes nearly tore him apart. He quickly crossed the room and pulled her into his arms.

"I'm sorry but I wanted you to know, Terri. From the first time we met, I wanted to get to know you better but felt your resistance. That night at Fantasyland made me understand why."

Terri stared up at Phillip. How many times had she sensed something unusual in what she was feeling for him? Had compared him to her secret lover? And now she knew why. He *was* her secret lover.

"You were different than any man I've ever known, Phillip. You took the time to listen and you didn't rush me or push me into anything and you let me be me. I felt an affinity to you and I felt I could trust you even before we became intimate."

He didn't say anything for the longest time, then he said, "I guess the big question now is where do we go from here? Just so you'll know, I haven't seen another woman since that night. You are the only woman I want."

Terri held his gaze. What she saw shining in the dark depths took her breath away. No man had looked at her like that since that night at Fantasyland, and she doubted any man would look at her this way again. Phillip McKenna had done more than fulfill her fantasy that night, he had given her a new lease on life, and the thought that her secret lover was here with her now sent sensations all through her body.

They were sensations she wanted to act on. They had already done things out of order so to start doing things in order now wouldn't make much sense. Working on that basis, she leaned toward him and on tiptoe she touched her mouth to his.

That was all the encouragement Phillip needed. He groaned and pulled her closer, entering her mouth with his tongue then locking in tight, and just like that night at Fantasyland, it tasted sweet and hot as hell. He slid his tongue along hers, mating, absorbing her taste into his own. He pulled her even closer as he deepened the kiss, thinking he could kiss her for the rest of the day, the week, the month, the year and never tire of doing so. He reluctantly pulled back when breathing became necessary.

"Umm, I think I have a new fantasy now, Phillip," she whispered, looking at him.

"What?"

"My fantasy is to relive that night," she said softly.

Her words made his body temperature jump up a few degrees. "I don't think that's possible but we can sure as hell try."

He swept her into his arms and carried her into the bedroom he knew was hers and placed her in the middle of the bed. He stood back and began unbuckling his belt to remove his pants. He remembered the last time and how rock-hard he'd gotten and the difficulty she had in pulling his zipper down. He doubted he had the patience to let her try tonight.

"Need help?"

He glanced over at her, saw the smile that curved the corners of her lips and remembered how she had brazenly unleashed her sexuality that night and done things with him that she had never done with another man. She had let herself go and set free all her hidden desire and he had enjoyed every single minute of it.

"No, I don't need help but a striptease show from you would be nice."

Terri smiled as she lifted up on the bed on her knees and removed her blouse. He stopped what he was doing, spellbound, watching as she removed her bra. She was pure temptation.

She leaned back on the bed to remove her Capri pants leaving her lower body clad in a pair of sexy black panties.

"You want me to continue?" she asked, still locked in his gaze.

"Most definitely."

He sucked in a deep breath when she slowly pulled her panties down her hips and legs, leaving nothing covered. The instant he saw her totally naked, a sharp reminder of the impact of their lovemaking that night bore down on him, and he quickly removed his clothes.

He did remember that he needed to take care of protection and took a condom packet from his pant's pocket. "Do you want to do the honor again?"

"Yes." She scrambled to the edge of the bed and took him into her hands. Phillip could barely keep still with her hands touching him.

She glanced up at him as she skimmed her thumb over the soft, velvety tip. "There's something else I wanted to do that night but didn't get the chance."

Before he knew what she was doing, she dipped her head, opened her mouth and took him in. *Oh, shit.*

Phillip gasped as sensations jolted him. When he felt himself losing control, he gently pushed her back in the bed and joined her there, moving his body over hers, needing to get inside of her. Fire, hot and intense, was flooding his veins and he needed to be intimately connected to her when the explosion hit.

His hand grabbed her hips and the long, thickness of his erection found its mark and pressed against her wet flesh. Then he remembered what he hadn't done. The condom! He met her gaze, locked into it.

"I'm on the pill to regulate my periods," she said, reading his mind. "You're the only person I've made love to since Lewis. I had a physical recently and I'm safe."

He nodded. "My recent physical said I'm safe, too."

She smiled. "Good."

Phillip slowly eased inside of her, wanting to cherish every moment of doing so. The moment the tip of his arousal met her warmth, his body jerked. Her inner flesh was pulsing, he felt it. He also felt it clenching him, trying to pull everything out of him, determined to pull him deep into her hot depths.

He thrust forward and heard the sharp intake of her breath. He felt her stomach tighten beneath his and felt the hard tips of her breasts press into his chest. She tilted her hips to take him deeper and he instinctively groaned and thrust again. Then again, and again. Over and over.

When he felt her body explode, actually come apart beneath him, he threw his head back and poured into her. His body felt electrified, totally attached to hers. He swallowed hard at the impact of what he was feeling, experiencing. It was an orgasm stronger than any he'd ever had in his life. And he knew she was meant for him. There were no ifs, ands or buts about it. He had fallen in love with her.

Just months ago he'd been absorbed in a book with rules to keep a man from falling for a woman, yet here he was a man in love. This was absolutely crazy, downright mad. But another word that quickly came to his mind was incredible.

"Phillip!"

He felt her body jerk when she climaxed again and he followed. He hoped her pills were potent enough to withstand a double dose of Phillip McKenna. And if not, and she became pregnant then he, she and the girls would live together as one big happy family.

He blinked. Was he actually thinking about getting married again? He smiled. Hell, yeah, he was and definitely to this woman. She had touched a part of him he thought was closed off forever. He leaned down and captured her mouth in his. With her he had found love again.

32

Marcus and Naomi

Naomi smiled at Marcus as they stood underneath her porch light. "Thanks for taking me to the arts festival. I had a wonderful time."

He returned her smile. "So did I. I understand the Harlem Globe Trotters will be in town this week. How would you like to go with me to see them?"

Naomi blinked, not believing he was asking her out on another date. Dropping her eyes she bowed her head slightly, silently praising God, giving Him thanks for the way things were turning out. She lifted her head and met Marcus's gaze. "I'd love to go. It's been years since I've seen them perform."

"Good. I'll call you this week and let you know the day and time." He chuckled. "It just occurred to me that I don't have your phone number, although I guess I can get it from my mother."

"Oh," she said laughing with him. "If you got a few minutes, I can write it down for you."

"Sure."

Marcus stepped aside as she unlocked the door and then followed her inside, closing it behind him. He leaned against the closed door and watched as she crossed the room to a table to where a piece of paper and pen lay and began writing, trying not to notice how her jeans were seductively shaping her behind.

He smiled when she finished, folded up the paper and began

walking back over to him. "I also included my cell number and how you can reach me at work."

He took the paper from her and put it in his pocket. "Okay, thanks."

They stood in silence for several moments before he said, "I'd better go. I know tomorrow is your off day but for me work is at eight."

Naomi's heart skipped a beat when he still didn't move, and the way he was looking at her was turning her insides to mush. He had beautiful dark eyes and the intensity of his gaze was reaching out to her, touching her in places she hadn't been touched in years.

Marcus watched Naomi nibble her lower lip, a lip he'd been obsessed with tasting ever since last week. He cleared his throat, knowing that he wasn't dealing with an ordinary woman. He was dealing with a Christian woman, although he knew that Christians had wants and needs like anybody else. They weren't perfect. That day she had come to his home and touched him in an inappropriate manner had proved that. But still, he was trying to get back into God's good graces, and he didn't want to get thrown out of them again by tempting one of His saints.

He watched her nibble her bottom lip again and thought he couldn't take it any more. "Can I ask you a question, Naomi?" he asked in as calm a voice as he could manage.

"Yes, you can ask me anything, Marcus."

He nodded. "May I kiss you?"

Her gaze locked with his and she nodded. "Yes, if you want to."

He grinned. "Yeah. I want to."

He slowly leaned forward, first deciding to nibble on her bottom lip the way she had been nibbling on it earlier. Then when he had gotten his fill doing that, he began nibbling from each corner of her mouth to the hollow of her ear before tracing a path down her neck.

He heard how her breathing had picked up and liked the sound of it. He then moved back upward to her mouth and when his lips touched her, he hungrily slanted his mouth over hers.

Naomi was suddenly bombarded with sensations she had never felt before. Pleasure and heat erupted inside of her, and when his tongue took hold of hers and began doing all kinds of delicious things to it, she thought she would certainly pass out. The feel of his mouth on hers, the way his tongue was taking control and the masculine scent of him was driving her insane, to a point of no return, and she couldn't do anything but hang on and enjoy.

Sensations were ripping through her nerve endings and jolts of gratification had her enthralled, and she couldn't help but release a moan from deep in her throat.

She felt a deep sense of loss when she felt him pulling back and heard him chuckle when he brought her body close to his. "I've wanted to do that since last week."

She looked up at him, surprised. "You have?"

He laughed. "Probably longer than that if I was to be honest with myself, but I've been dealing with a lot of issues over the past year."

She nodded. "And now?"

He sighed deeply. He was no longer dealing with issues concerning Dottie but now was dealing with the likes of a woman he only knew as Breathless. But Naomi didn't need to know that. Breathless was his concern and he would handle her as he saw fit. "And now I want to move on with my life, let go. I loved my wife very much and she will always have a place in my heart, Naomi."

"That's understandable, Marcus, and I would expect no less."

"But that doesn't mean I can't love again. I realize that now. I know Dottie would want that for me."

Naomi nodded again. "Yes, I'm sure that she would. The few times that I met your wife, I found her to be a very nice person; a real lady."

He smiled. "She was but then so are you."

She lowered her head. "A real lady wouldn't have come into your home that day to speak God's word then let the devil use her the way he did."

He reached out and lifted her chin up. "Hey, we've put that

273

behind us remember. Besides, I wanted you that day, too. I can admit it now. We all get physical urges every once in a while."

She smiled. "Don't I know it. I've been celibate over four years."

Her words gave him pause. He stared at her then decided to make sure he had heard her right. "You've been celibate for four years?"

"Yes. I promised myself that I wouldn't have sex again until a good Christian man came into my life."

He chuckled. "Well, I guess that means I better buy me a couple of new suits because I plan to start attending church more regularly." He moved his finger from her chin to caress her cheek when he saw she got the meaning behind his words.

"But I don't want you to think that will be my only reason for going to church," he decided to add. "I know that I have to get my life back on track to receive all the blessings that I believe that God has in store for me." *And I do believe you are one of them, Naomi Monroe,* he wanted to say, suddenly seeing her through different eyes.

At that moment Dottie's words came back to him. *"You are a special man, Marcus, and there is a woman out there who needs you and you will come to realize that you need her as well. And one day you will also realize that you can love her as much as you loved me."*

"Marcus, are you okay?" Naomi asked him, lifting a brow. "For some reason you're looking at me kind of funny."

He smiled and pulled her closer into his arms. "Yes, only because I suddenly see you in a whole new light; a truly special light."

And then he leaned down and covered his mouth with hers once more.

33

Marcus

"Good morning, Mr. Lowery, and welcome back. There's a delivery waiting for you on your desk. They tried to make it Friday but you were out, so they returned today."

Marcus raised a brow at his secretary. "Who did?"

"The florist."

Marcus frowned as he walked into his office, closing the door behind him. A huge arrangement of flowers was sitting on his desk. He immediately crossed the room and pulled off the card that read:

> *Roses are red, violets are blue;*
> *I can't wait until the next time I do you.*
> *Breathless*

"Damn," Marcus muttered under his breath. He picked up the phone and began dialing. He intended to put an end to this nonsense once and for all. His cousin Connor picked up on the third ring. "Hello."

"Connor, I need to see you about something real important, man. Can we meet someplace for lunch?" And just in case he was being followed, Marcus added, "And don't bring your patrol car."

He sighed after hanging up the phone. He moved to the window, dismissing the flowers from his mind. His thoughts automatically went to Naomi. After kissing her a second time last night, he had left while he'd had the mind to do so. Then after going home and taking a shower, he had called her and they had talked past midnight.

He turned around when the phone on his desk rang. He crossed the room to pick it up. "Yes, Mary?"

"There's a call for you but the person refuses to give her name."

Marcus raised a brow. "Okay, I'll take it."

As soon as the connection was made a low, sexy voice came on the line and said, "I want you again, High Intensity."

Anger took over Marcus. "I don't know how you got my name and address but what you're doing is harassment and I—"

"I've sent you another present. It will be delivered there today. You're going to like it."

"Look, I don't want another package from you. I want you to leave me alone and if you don't I'm going to the authorities. There's a law—"

He heard the solid click in his ear. "Damn." The woman refused to hear anything he had said.

At that moment his phone rang and he wondered if it was her calling him back. He picked it up. "Yes, Mary?"

"Security just called, Mr. Lowery. A package has been left for you downstairs."

Marcus frowned. "A personal package?"

"Yes, sir."

"Does it indicate who it is from?"

"No, sir. Nathan said there's not a return address but it appears to have been sent locally."

Marcus sighed deeply. "Tell Nathan to trash it, and Mary, these flowers that were delivered to me this morning, have a courier take them to one of the local nursing homes."

"Yes, sir."

He knew his secretary was curious as heck as to what was going on, but at the moment he couldn't worry about that. He had more important business to take care of.

"Let me get this straight. Some white woman is stalking you?"

Marcus raised his eyes to the ceiling. Leave it to Connor to make it seem like what was happening was so unbelievable. "Yes."

"And you don't know her name?"

"No."

"And you don't know how she looks?"

"She has blond hair."

Connor lifted a curious brow. "Is she a real blond?"

Marcus's thoughts shifted back to the time he had seen her completely naked. "Yes, she's a real one."

"Damn. I've always wanted to do a real blond. One time I thought I was doing a blond and discovered she was actually a brunette. Boy, was I disappointed. I hear blond women give the best blows."

Marcus shook his head, deciding not to tell his cousin he'd had no complaints about the ones he'd gotten from Breathless. "Look, Connor, I need some advice here. I met her at a secret masquerade party so I don't know how she looks. We got together a few times after that, always in secret. One night she evidently followed me home and has been harassing me ever since. I need to know what to do."

Connor raised a brow and leaned back in his chair. "A secret masquerade party? I think you better start from the beginning and tell me everything."

Marcus sighed deeply. He was hoping that he wouldn't have to go there with Connor but evidently he would have to. He'd forgotten his cousin was a person who had to have all the facts. That was one of the things that irritated him while they were growing up. "Okay, it's a little deeper than that. I actually met her at this place called Fantasyland."

Connor eased forward a little. "Nice place."

Marcus stared at his cousin. "You've been there?"

Connor's lips curved into that sly smile that was known to get him into trouble. "Yeah, several times. What I do on my off time is my business. Besides, there's nothing illegal about the place."

"I didn't say there was."

Satisfied that was understood, Connor took a sip of his drink. "So what's this woman's fantasy?"

"To do a black man."

Connor laughed. "And evidently she hasn't gotten enough yet. Umm, what I need to do is to find out who she is and then I'll take her off your hands."

Marcus frowned. "I'm serious, Connor."

Connor smiled. "So am I. Like I said, I heard blonds give the best blows."

Marcus shook his head. From the time Connor had started noticing girls he'd always had this playa mentality. Now, at the age of thirty, it seemed his cousin hadn't outgrown that state of mind. In fact, it sounded like he was worse than ever. "Are you or are you not going to tell me what I should do?"

"You stay out of this and let me handle things from here."

Marcus frowned. "And how will you handle things?"

Connor gave him that sly smile again. "You're better off not knowing all the details." He stood. "Hey cuz, you should have called me sooner."

Marcus sighed. "I didn't want to get the police involved."

Connor smiled. "And you haven't. This is strictly a family matter and I will handle it as such." He took his keys out of his pocket. "By the way, what kind of car does she drives?"

"A brand-new black Mercedes sports car."

Connor's smile widened. "Sounds like she has money."

"Her family does but I understand she's supposed to have access to her own trust fund when she turned twenty-seven, which was last week."

"This sounds better already. Oh, by the way, this is my last week on the force."

Marcus raised a brow. Connor had been a police officer for at least ten years. "Why?"

"A couple of us are tired of getting shot at, misused and abused, and have decided to go into business together."

"Doing what?"

"We're opening a security firm in Portage. We figured if we're going to put our lives on the line, we might as well make a profit doing so. The business should be ready to open in another month. I'm surprised Aunt Essie hasn't mentioned it."

Marcus decided not to say that his mother had been too busy playing matchmaker to think of Connor's career change. "Is that what you want to do?"

"Yes. I've been on the force long enough and want to do something different. Besides, being my own boss will give me more free time to take care of all the women. You don't know how much nooky I've had to pass up because I wasn't off-duty. The women will be happy that I have more time to tighten them up."

Marcus shook his head again. Connor could be an arrogant ass when he wanted to be, which was usually most of the time. "And you're sure you'll be able to handle things with Breathless?"

Connor frowned. "Who?"

Marcus chuckled. "I forgot to tell you that at Fantasyland her name was Breathless."

"Oh." Connor grinned. "Breathless . . . hey, I like that, and yeah, I'll be able to handle things. Once I've had a long talk with her and let her know what can happen if she continues to harass you, then that should take care of things. Usually a lot of legal mumbo jumbo works every time."

Marcus sighed. "Man, I hope so."

Connor placed a hand on his shoulder. "Don't worry about it. You won't be bothered by her again. Trust me."

Connor Hargrove smiled as he watched the blond-haired woman leave the store at the mall and walk to her car. Damn she was good looking. It was a shame that Marcus had never seen her face or he would have thought twice about dropping her. Well, his cousin's loss would definitely be his gain and to know that she was a real blond . . .

His smile widened when he thought about everything he had found out about her. Discovering her identity had been easy. A fellow officer who patrolled the area where Marcus lived had gotten her tag number when she had cruised Marcus's neighborhood again last night. A quick phone call to the precinct had given him all the information he had wanted to know.

She was Courtney Hampton; twenty-seven; graduate of the University of Illinois with a degree in social work. She was connected to the Hampton family, one of Gary's families of old money and prominence. For centuries the Hamptons owned a huge manufacturing company that employed hundreds. Miss Hampton had no arrest record or prior convictions; not even a traffic violation.

But as Connor slid on his aviator glasses, he saw that she did have a body that was just calling his name. And since she had gotten a taste of black and couldn't seem to go back, he would gladly see how he could be of service to her. He usually didn't do leftovers, but when leftovers looked this good and delicious, he might as well indulge himself. And when it came to sex, he believed in equal opportunity. Any female of legal age, no matter the race, creed or color, was game.

He followed her, knowing she was probably headed back to Marcus's neighborhood. Moments later, he watched as she circled the block a few times. It was obvious that she was trying to determine if he was home. What she didn't know was that Marcus had taken some woman into Chicago to see the Harlem Globetrotters.

So, feeling bolder than hell and aroused as he wannabe, Connor pulled his SUV right in front of the Mercedes sports car, effectively blocking her in on the cul-de-sac. He cut off his engine and got out and walked over to her car.

"Who are you?" she asked, staring at him through the car window she had lowered halfway.

He smiled, thinking she looked better up close and smelled

good. "I should be asking you that, and what are you doing hanging around Marcus's house?"

She lifted a haughty brow and glared at him. "What's it's to you?"

"I'm wondering why you're wasting your time with him. He's not interested in you."

She frowned. "He told you that?"

"Yeah, and he also said he told you to stop harassing him and if you continued he would take matters further."

She laughed. "He doesn't even know me."

Connor smiled. "But I do, Courtney."

He watched the smile vanish from her face and then she glared. "So, you know my name, big deal."

"Yes, it is a big deal, sweetheart. I happen to know a lot about you." His smile widened. "Including your fantasy."

She narrowed her gaze at him. "So, what of it?"

"Nothing. I'm just wondering why you'll settle for hamburger when you can have steak."

She lifted a brow. "Meaning?"

A smile curved the corner of Connor's lips. "Whatever Marcus can do, I can do better."

He watched Courtney lick her lips; she had taken the bait. She looked him up and down, taking in what she saw; a well-built male body in a pair of jeans and a T-shirt. He could tell that she was interested and was definitely sizing up the possibilities. Then she said, "You're pretty sure of yourself, aren't you?"

He grinned, feeling cocky as usual. "I have no reason not to be. I've never had any complaints and most come back for seconds. Are you interested?" He knew that was a dumb question because from the look in her eyes she was definitely interested. He recognized that look. She was pretty damn horny. It seemed like this would be his lucky night.

"Maybe," she finally said.

He straightened from leaning against her car and met her gaze.

"Don't play games with me, Courtney. You're interested all right. I smell your scent and it's potent as hell. Your panties are probably wet already. If you want what I got then follow me." Not waiting for a response he walked back to his car.

"Hey, where are you going?"

He smiled at her over his shoulder. "A place where you can get what you want, as many times as you want it." He didn't intend on telling her anything else as he got into his truck and pulled off.

A quick glance in his rearview mirror indicated she was right on his tail; pretty much like he planned to be on hers in a little while. Marcus would kill him if he knew what his plans were for this woman. Hell, he had promised his cousin he would handle things and he would. Marcus didn't have to know how he had accomplished the task.

He drove the few miles out of Gary into Portage, to the area where construction was underway on the building for the security business. After parking the truck, he got out and waited for her to follow. Without saying anything, she walked beside him toward the dark, empty building.

She finally broke the silence and asked, "What's inside this place?"

"Nothing now, but there's a bed in one of the storage rooms. I often spend the night here to keep the thieves from running off with my tools."

She glanced up at him. "Oh? What sort of work do you do?"

He smiled. "I'm a handyman," he lied.

"Sounds interesting."

He chuckled. "It is." He opened the door for her to go inside and he followed. He shook his head. For all she knew he could be a rapist, or worse a serial killer; but she had meekly followed him, showing him how desperate she was for a sexual fix.

He locked the door behind them. She then followed him to the back of the building where a bed was located. It wasn't much but it would serve a good purpose tonight. Usually he or one of the other two owners would spend the night to keep an eye on things.

He saw Courtney smile when she saw the bed. She turned to face him. "Now what?"

He chuckled. "Now get naked, get on the bed and spread'm."

Connor leaned back against the wall as he watched Courtney slowly waking up. He smiled. What he'd heard was true. Blonds, true blonds, gave the best blows. And it seemed that when it came to sex this woman had an insatiable appetite. She had begged him to keep going and going and she had kept coming and coming . . . but then so had he. He had experienced more orgasms than he cared to count.

She turned and slowly opened her eyes, looked over at him and smiled. "I don't think I'll ever be able to walk again."

He shrugged. "Hey, you got what you asked for."

She slowly flipped on her back and smiled. "Yes, I did, didn't I? And you were right, you're the best."

He chuckled. "Only because I'm more experienced. I've been finding my way between women's legs for years. After a while you get pretty damn good at it, but you can always learn something new."

He walked across the room to the bed. "Before you go, I need to show you something."

She lifted a brow. "What?"

"This," he said, showing her a video camera. "And I want you to leave here with a warning."

He leaned closer to her, to make sure she could hear his every word. "I don't take the stalking of people that I care about very well, so leave Marcus alone. I've collected enough photos of you to make your family bury their heads in shame. What would they think of all those things you and I did last night? And I wouldn't hesitate to send copies of these pictures to your parents, the newspapers, even to the tabloids if I have to. If I see your car someplace where I think it shouldn't be, or if I hear about Marcus getting another package from you, then that will piss me off. Do we understand each other?"

She glared at him. "Yes."

"Good, now you're free to leave."

Courtney couldn't help but laugh. "Hey, I kind of like you. Got a name?"

He gave her his best glare as he began putting on a pair of the black gloves he kept around the place. "Yeah, some people call me OJ."

He inwardly laughed as he watched the smile vanish from her face. She evidently remembered what OJ was known for other than football. She quickly scrambled off the bed and began putting her clothes on, practically falling all over herself in her haste to get dressed. When she had finished and was ready to leave, he walked her to the door. "And remember what I said. Stop being a damn nuisance. Leave Marcus alone."

He watched her run across the parking lot to get to her car, and then she drove off with her feet pressed to the pedal. Chuckling, he tossed the gloves aside and went to the bathroom, feeling the need for a shower. Afterward, he intended to finish reading a pretty interesting book he'd purchased last week called *The Playa's Handbook*.

34

Sam and Falon

Sam checked his watch when he heard the knock at his door. He smiled. Falon was right on time.

He glanced around the room. He had wanted to make this night special for her, for them. It had been a full week since he had told her he wanted an exclusive relationship, and tonight he wanted them to celebrate. Crossing the room he walked to the door and opened it.

He smiled seeing her standing there in his doorway, remembering the first time he had opened this door to find her there. "Falon."

She smiled. "Hi, Sam."

He stepped aside to let her enter and then closed the door behind her. He watched her glance around, seeing the table set for two, the candles, the bottle of champagne that was sitting in ice and the flowers he intended to give her later.

She turned to him and the smile that tilted her lips made his stomach quiver. "You didn't have to do all of this."

"Yes, I did. You are special to me."

"And you are special to me."

He crossed the room to her and stared at her, wondering why he had wasted so much time in not loving her from the beginning. "It was a week ago today that we decided to become a couple and I wanted to celebrate."

"I like the idea of that," she said, sliding her hands up his chest to his shoulders. "But first I want a kiss."

He smiled. "I intend to give the lady what she wants." He leaned down and covered his mouth with hers, needing her heat, wanting to ignite her hunger. He immediately deepened the kiss, no longer caring that emotions he had held at bay for months were being stripped away.

When he finally dragged his mouth away and gazed into her honey brown eyes, raw sensuality tore at him and he took a step back. There was something he needed to do and if he kept kissing her he would completely lose the thought.

"The flowers are yours," he said. "And so is this." He reached out and captured her hand, and opening it up, he placed something in the palm of it. She glanced down and looked back at him. "A key?"

He smiled. "Yes, a key to this apartment. I want you to have it and I want you to know you are free to come over any time regardless if I'm here or not." He doubted that she knew the magnitude of him giving her that key, essentially breaking the number one rule in *The Playa's Handbook*. But as far as he was concerned, the rules didn't apply to him anymore. He no longer had a playa card. What he had was the woman he wanted and loved more than life itself.

Yes, he loved her and he intended to spend the rest of his life proving how much.

He closed the key in her hand and brought her hand up to his lips and kissed her knuckles then pulled her into his arms and kissed her again. The next time it was her who pulled back and gazed up at him. "This key . . . I can use it anytime I want?"

He smiled and leaned down and began nibbling at the corner of her mouth. "Yes."

She nodded, liking the feel of what he was doing to her lips. "Umm, and what if it's in the middle of the night and I want to see you?"

"You know where I live," he whispered between nibbles. "You're welcome anytime, just come on over." He placed a hand on the curve on her backside, pressing her closer, wanting her to feel what messing around with her mouth was doing to him.

"And what if I don't want to sleep on your sofa when I get here?"

Sam's heart hammered in his chest and he lifted his mouth from hers and stared into her eyes. For a solid week they had indulged in some heavy-duty kissing and fondling sessions but had not made love. He hadn't wanted to rush her. He had given her full rein of setting the pace between them. He knew he loved her but wanted her to feel comfortable with how their relationship escalated.

"And where would you want to sleep?" he asked, drawing in a shuddering breath at the thought of one possibility.

She held his gaze and said, "Your bed."

He nodded and just to make sure he understood her clearly, he asked, "And where will I sleep?"

She smiled wickedly, seductively. "In the bed with me. But I don't think we would get much sleep."

He arched an innocent brow. "And what would we be doing?" He suddenly felt the glide of her hand across his stomach, and then it came to rest at the waist of his jeans. "Oh, I can think of a number of things. You want me to show you one?"

His entire body began to ache. "Yes, by all means."

She quickly, efficiently unsnapped his jeans, and he inhaled a sharp breath when she slid her palm inside and grabbed hold of him. And he didn't feel assaulted, not the least little bit. What he felt was heat flare through his veins and most of it settled right at the tip of his shaft; that very part she began touching, caressing, making him rock harder than before.

Too close to losing it, he pulled her hand from inside his jeans and swooped her up into his arms. "I think I have a good idea where you're headed."

She laughed and wrapped her arms around his neck. "I was hoping you would."

He took her into his bedroom and placed her on the bed and stood back and watched her. She stretched like a cat and didn't seem to mind that her skirt was up around her waist and he could see a lot, including her panties. He wasn't ready for the intensity of fire that suddenly blazed through him. Burning him. Scorching him.

"Are you sure you don't want to eat first?" he asked, as sensation after sensation tore through him as he watched as she continued to stretch out on his bed, as if finding the most comfortable spot.

"I'm positive. Now come make love to me."

Sam hit the bed and pulled her into his arms, kissing her like tomorrow wasn't promised to either of them and he intended to prove to her now, today, just what she meant to him. He quickly removed her clothing, then his own, and she lay back against his comforter and watched him put on a condom. When he was finished, she opened her arms to him, welcoming him.

Sam's heart began to race and he knew love drove him. This was not sex-making but lovemaking at its finest and he wanted her to know that. He drew her closer into his arms. "I love you, Falon. I didn't think I would ever be able to say that to another woman again, but I'm saying it to you with all my heart."

He saw the tears that came into her eyes. "Oh, Sam, I love you, too, and I didn't think I would be saying that to another man, either. But in my heart I know I was made to love you."

He knew she was made for him, too. With all the love in his heart, he knew he had to show her just how much he loved her, and using his hands, mouth and tongue, he set about to drive her crazy with desire. Soon he had her moaning, groaning and writhing beneath him.

It was then, and only then that he moved his body over hers, and capturing her mouth in his, he slid into her, her warmth, heat and fire. It was as if as soon as they connected, hot swirling sensations grabbed hold of them tightly. He began thrusting in and out, branding her, stamping his possession. The thighs on his muscles flexed as he pumped into her at a rhythm that only the two of them recognized. They were in sync and shuddered and groaned in tune with the sensuous tempo.

"Sam!"

She became swept up in a huge tidal wave of sexual pleasure and he followed her, throwing his head back as an orgasm struck him with the force of a mighty rushing wind. His thighs continued to flex, pump and when she wrapped her legs around him and dug mercilessly into his back, he growled out her name at the same time she screamed his.

And then they were tumbling over the edge, together, and Sam knew what it felt like to finally find the person who was truly your other half.

Your soul mate.

35

Lance

"Welcome to the party, Dr. Montgomery."

"Thanks for inviting me, Mrs. Patterson."

Lance glanced around. The place was crowded and most of the people there were connected to the world of publishing since John Patterson owned one of the largest PR firms in the country. But Lance was there for one purpose and one purpose only. To let the woman he loved know how he felt. He knew Asia was here somewhere. Carl had finagled the information from her agent Melissa James. Once he had been able to get a flight, he caught it and arrived in New York merely hours ago with one intention in mind.

He had to see Asia to tell her that he loved her.

He had thought of calling her but had decided after the way they had parted, he needed to see her, talk to her and explain everything. No longer was he having a hard time dealing with his feelings for her. Confessing it to his brothers was one thing, now confessing to her was another. He had hurt her and would beg for her forgiveness if he had to. Whatever it took he would do it.

He frantically searched the crowd and then he saw her. He frowned. She was standing talking to a group of people and Sean Crews was by her side, with his hand on her back. A part of Lance wanted to cross the room and snatch the man away from her but he decided not to. She may have come with Crews but he was determined that she leave with him tonight.

He continued to hang back and watch her. She was more beautiful than ever, it seemed she glowed, and his heart clenched at the pain he had seen in her eyes the last time they had been together. He had a lot of explaining to do and hoped and prayed that she would listen and then find it in her heart to forgive him.

He saw the host, John Patterson, whisper something to his wife and she smiled, then John spoke up, getting everyone's attention. "Ladies and gentlemen, I think this is a good time for all of us to share in Asia Fowler's happiness tonight. I've just been told that recently, just this morning in fact, she became engaged and will be marrying Dr. Sean Crews in June."

Lance stopped breathing as he watched everyone crowd around the couple, giving their best wishes and congratulations. He felt as if a knife was sliding through his heart when Sean pulled Asia into his arms and kissed her.

Lance tore his gaze away, not believing what he was seeing and hearing. He couldn't have lost her, not now when he knew how much he loved her. Rage tore through him. Dammit he wouldn't lose her when he knew that she didn't love Crews!

Hope propelled him forward. He needed to talk to her. He'd make her admit that she wasn't in love with Sean Crews. She loved *him*. Why else would she let him touch her?

Something made Asia look in his direction and he saw the surprise in her eyes. He also saw the hurt and pain there. She narrowed her gaze and suddenly he felt his hope wavering.

Sean Crews glanced up and saw him and stiffened. He whispered something to her and she nodded. A few more steps and Lance stood in front of them.

Everyone had moved on, leaving the couple alone and it was Sean who spoke up. "Dr. Montgomery, good seeing you again," he said, offering Lance his hand. The smile on the man's face didn't quite reach his eyes. "I hope you heard our good news. Asia and I are getting married in June."

The handshake Lance exchanged with the man was brief. His gaze left Crews and went to Asia then returned to Crews to tell him that he would marry Asia over his dead body, but then he decided not to make a scene. Instead he turned back to Asia and said, "May I speak with you privately for a minute?"

He watched as she shook her head. "No," she whispered. "You said all that you needed to say, Lance, and I was hoping that I would never see you again." She turned to Sean, but not before he saw the tears that sprang into her eyes. "Please take me home."

"Certainly, sweetheart." He glared at Lance. "Excuse us, Dr. Montgomery, but my fiancée isn't feeling well and we're leaving."

Ignoring Crews, Lance reached out and touched Asia's arm. "Asia, please wait, I—"

She drew back as if his touch revolted her. "Don't touch me, Lance," she whispered. "You won't ever get the chance to touch me again." And then she walked away with Crews's arm protectively around her as they made their way to the Pattersons to let them know they were leaving.

Lance watched her go, knowing how it felt for someone to actually hate his guts. He had screwed up and the way it looked, beyond repair. His heart felt torn, ripped by his own hands. He turned and headed for the door feeling defeated, broken down.

He had lost the woman that he loved.

READERS' GUIDE QUESTIONS

1. Do you think it is okay for men to be "playas" as long as they are up front with women about their intentions?

2. Considering Sam, Phillip and Marcus's histories, do you understand why they would not want to jump into serious relationships without first playing around?

3. Considering Lance's history with women, do you think his attitude toward women and his decision to write a book like *The Playa's Handbook* is understandable?

4. Should Phillip have let Terri know that he recognized her that night at Fantasyland before they slept together?

5. What did you think of Courtney (Breathless)? Do you think Marcus brought his problems with her on himself? What do you think of Connor's treatment of her?

6. Do you think women are "playas," just like men?

7. Do you think Sam, Marcus and Phillip were right when they decided they weren't cut out to be "playas"?

8. Do you think Asia is marrying Sean for the right reasons?

9. Do you think Lance deserves another chance with Asia?

10. What was your favorite part of the book? Your least favorite?